Please feel free to send me an ema
filters these emails. Good news is :

Danielle Ogier - danielle_ogier@a

CU00820842

Sign up for my blog for updates and freebies!
danielle-ogier.awesomeauthors.org

About the Publisher

BLVNP Incorporated, A Nevada Corporation, 340 S. Lemon #6200, Walnut CA 91789, info@blvnp.com / legal@blvnp.com

DISCLAIMER

Praise for Broken Wings

One of the best and first vampire books I have ever read, great story amazing characters, I was very pleased of it end. This book is and always will be one of my favorite books.
—Marwa Osman

Broken Wings will have you on the edge of your seat wondering why the mysterious Shadow acts the way he acts? Or whether or not Violet will realize that maybe... just maybe Shadow isn't the monster she believes him to be?
—Alexis Norton

Broken Wings provides a whole new view on the supernatural world, and turns the much loved sub-genre of vampires on its head. It deals with important issues with relatable characters and an enrapturing plot, leaving you wanting more. Love it!
—Erandi Kuruppuarachchi

Broken Wings is a story unlike others I've ever read! It is a beautiful story that isn't anything short of amazing!
—Megi

This book is amazing! I couldn't stop reading it once I started!
—Paige

Broken Wings taught me how to fly even without wings.
—Emily Ann Roberts

Broken Wings

By: Danielle Ogier

BLVNP

ISBN: 978-1-68030-919-5
© DanielleOgier 2017

Table of contents

For my grandad, who always believed and encouraged me to chase my dreams.

FREE DOWNLOAD

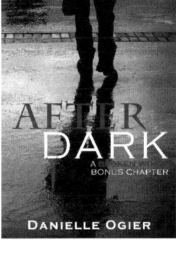

Get these freebies and MORE when you sign up for the author's mailing list!

danielle-ogier.awesomeauthors.org

Prologue

"Where is Mum going?" I asked my dad as I walked into the kitchen.

"What do you mean, honey?" he asked me, confusion written all over his face.

"She's got her suitcase out..." I trailed off, not quite sure why she had not told him she was packing.

He did not answer me though his eyes did widen upon hearing my words. He stood up from his spot on the couch, running past me, straight up the stairs, and disappearing from sight. His behaviour was odd, and I was curious as to what was going on, but I shrugged it off. If it were important, they would have told me.

Debating what to do with my day, it was not long until I heard shouting coming from upstairs. I sighed, shaking my head as I walked into the living room and sat down on the sofa. Although I loved my parents, the arguing was beginning to get on my nerves. It was becoming a daily thing. I was not even sure what they had left to argue about, and yet every day, they still surprised me by finding something else.

"I'm sorry!" I suddenly heard my mum scream, making me jump and almost drop my phone that was in my hand. Glancing at the ceiling, I knew it could be a while until they both calm down though I did wonder why she had her suitcase.

I was about to call my best friend, Rose, when I heard footsteps storming down the stairs. Craning my neck to look, I almost gasped at their appearance. Something was definitely wrong; that, I was certain of. My mum was red in the face, tears streaming down her cheeks as she gripped tightly onto her suitcases. She had two—two of the biggest ones we owned— and was looking anywhere but at my dad. He looked even worse. He looked as though he was about to tear his hair out, wiping his panic-struck eyes as he begged with my mum not to leave.

"What's going on?" I asked carefully, shakily standing up as his words processed in my mind. She was leaving? Leaving where?

"Darling... I want you to know that I love you so much," she spoke through her sobs, turning to look at me. Although she did not explain, I understood. She was leaving for good. The shock hit my body like a ton of bricks, and my legs almost gave way underneath me. My mum was leaving. She was leaving me.

"Why?" I asked, feeling the tears build up in my eyes.

"I'm not happy anymore."

"B-but..." I stuttered, not quite sure what I could say. I just knew that I could not let her leave us because I loved her.

My dad loved her. Why would she give that up? I couldn't understand.

"I will always love you both, just remember that." She spoke as she walked over and pulled me into a soft hug that lasted only a few seconds before she quickly planted a kiss on my dad's lips.

Then, without looking back at us, she opened the front door and exited the house, shutting the door behind her. Just like that. Just like that... and my mum was gone.

I turned to my dad. "Dad."

His head snapped to me, and I saw how upset he was, so I ran into his arms, hugging him as tight as I could, not quite understanding how mum could just walk out on us like that. It was how easy she made it look that both shocked and confused me. How long had she been planning this? How could she leave her husband and her fifteen-year-old daughter? I couldn't understand it. It didn't make sense.

"It's okay, darling. We'll be okay. We don't need her." He whimpered through his sobs. I wasn't sure who he was trying to convince more, himself or me.

He lied.

Nothing was ever okay again.

Chapter One

Shivering from the cold night air, I walked through the streets of Scarborough. I was on my way home from Rose's house. She had just broken up with her boyfriend of three years because he cheated on her. I could not imagine the pain she must be going through. It was bound to be hard on her, and I felt awful knowing I could not help. I did not believe relationships would work out in the long run because I had been betrayed by everyone I know. It was because of that that I was at a complete loss on how to help her. I tried to take her mind off it, but every little thing seemed to remind her of him though I guess it was to be expected. I tried to tell her that he did not deserve her and that she could have anyone because let's face it, she could. She had a supermodel figure; curves in all the right places, bright blue eyes that always seemed to shine constantly, and wavy, mid-length blonde hair. She was the epitome of beauty. Apparently, this was not what she wanted to hear, but I did see a smile on her face.

Turning the last corner, I was relieved when I saw my home at the end of the street because I would soon be out of the cold weather. That soon changed when I thought about what would be waiting for me there. I sighed, feeling an overwhelming sadness threatening to take over. I truly wished that I could afford to move out, to get away from my alcoholic father.

He never treated me the same after mum left. Gone were the days where he would take us down to the beach so we could have an ice-cream when the weather was hot. After she left, he hit an all-time low, drinking every night, taking his anger out on me. It had been four years since she left, and he had not gotten better; if anything, he had gotten worse. I think he expected her to come back one day, and as more time went by, the more he realised that was not going to happen. As a result of that, he took it out on me. Obviously, because why not? I was a living, breathing reminder of the life he once had.

What I had suffered throughout the years had a profound effect on me. I believed every harsh words that he threw at me in a blaze of anger. I believed that I was the reason my mother was not happy. I believed I was the reason for everything going wrong, and why shouldn't I believe it? My own father seemed to think it was true, so there must be some truth to it, right? I was not sure anymore. I was not sure of anything these days. I had been betrayed so much by the people who I loved most, and because of that, I closed myself off. I found it harder to trust people, to open up to them. I did not go out with the group of friends I once had, and I started lying about my bruises so no one would ever find out what went on behind closed doors. I became isolated. The only person I would see is my best friend who I needed to keep me sane.

I didn't mind not having a lot of friends anymore. At first, it bothered me, but then, as time went by, I realised it was the better option. I distanced myself from them before they could do it first because they would. Eventually, they would have stopped bothering with me. So being alone was the better option; it meant I would not be hurt by anybody else. Being alone meant that I would not have to suffer the heartache when someone else leaves because, in the end, they all leave. That's just what people do.

No one knows about the abuse. Not even Rose, and she was my best friend. I knew if anyone found out, then the consequences would not be good. He had told me often enough. He would scream in my face that he had nothing else to live for so if anyone else knew, he would have no problem making sure they would not go and tell the police. I felt like telling him that he did have something to live for, that he had a daughter he was supposed to love and protect no matter what, but I knew it would only make things worse. In his eyes, I was no longer his daughter. I was merely his punching bag.

Punching bag or not, he had to keep up the pretense that everything was normal. He paid for my phone bill each month and bought me clothes when I needed them, but I knew if he did not have to, he would not bother. He hated me now. Knowing that hurt more than the abuse I sometimes endured because he was still my dad. I just wanted him to go back to the way he used to be when he actually loved me.

Reaching my house, I hesitated outside the front door, fearing what would take place once I was inside. I had to take a few deep breaths before I could gather the strength to open the front door, walking into my so-called home.

"WHERE THE HELL HAVE YOU BEEN?" I heard him yell the second I had shut the door behind me. I froze in fear, still standing by the door, as my eyes landed on my father who was already drunk. Clutching a bottle of vodka in one hand and a cigarette in another, he glared harshly at me—so hard, I actually flinched. The fact he was drunk already made me nervous. I did not know what to expect.

"Answer me, you bitch!" he yelled, putting his cigarette in the ashtray on the table beside him. Then, without warning, he stormed over and grabbed hold of my hair, making me cry out in pain.

The second he threw me onto the ground, kicking my legs out from under me, I knew that I was going to get it tonight. I could feel it.

"I w-was with R-rose," I stuttered, shaking in fear by this point.

"You should have been back to make my dinner an hour ago." He glared, kicking me straight in the stomach. Gasping in pain, I clutched my stomach hoping that it would dull the pain, but it did not work. It never did. I was in a never ending pain as he continued to kick me everywhere he could. Tears fell freely from my eyes as I bit my lip. I did not want to give him the satisfaction of hearing me cry out.

Someone, please save me, I begged silently. I did not know how more I could take. I could not stand it any longer.

"Stupid, stupid cow! You are the reason your mother left! She hated you so much, she left me! It's all your fault!" He continued to yell as I lay there on the floor, taking everything he gave me. I could not fight back because I knew there would be no point; it would only increase his anger and I would undoubtedly lose. I just wasn't strong enough to fight back.

I shut my eyes as I thought of my mother. She was beautiful; she really was. She had long, flowing black hair and bright blue eyes. The only thing I had inherited from her was her eyes. I had gotten my hair colour from my dad; a lifeless brown. She always seemed so happy, always smiling and doing whatever she could to make sure my dad and I were happy. Lovable Leanne, that was what people called her. She was loved by everyone. Every man lusted after her, and every woman wanted to be her. So it was hard on dad and me when she just left, claiming she was not happy anymore, because in our eyes, she had no reason to be unhappy. She had everything she could possibly want and more.

"Get out of this house and don't ever come back!" my dad suddenly screamed at me. My eyes flew open, meeting his green ones that were shining in anger as he glared down at me. "I don't want you here anymore! Get out, get out, GET OUT!"

"W-where am I supposed to g-go?" I whimpered, clutching my stomach, as he walked over to the sofa and sat down—almost as if nothing had ever happened, almost as if he had not just beaten his daughter black and blue.

I should have been relieved and happy that he was kicking me out. Finally, I would be free of the abuse. Although there was a slight happiness knowing I would be out of here, I was also terrified because I had nowhere to go. I could not go to Rose because she did not know, and I could not put her in that position. I did not have enough money to last a week in a hotel, so I was screwed either way. I just did not have anywhere to go. There were my grandparents, but I could not risk them getting hurt. They were my mother's parents so I could not be too sure that he would not hurt them too.

He probably knew that I would be stuck. He was probably expecting me to beg to stay in this house with him because then, at least, I would have some place to live. He was manipulative, extremely so. I could not put anything past him.

He did not reply to my question, so on shaky legs, I struggled to my feet, leaning against the wall for support. My whole body was aching, an excruciating pain flooding through my body in waves that were almost overwhelming, but I knew that I could not stay here anymore. I had to get out. I did not care what his motives were for telling me to get out. For once, I was going to listen to him and get the hell out of the house. I had to. If I did not, I was going to die. One way or another, I would die in this house.

"Fine. I'll leave," I said, walking slowly to the stairs and heading up them as slow as I possibly could without causing too much pain.

Once in my room, I shut the door and grabbed the suitcase that was in the corner of my room. I unzipped it and left it open on my bed. Knowing that he could come charging up here any second to hurt me even more, I opened my wardrobe and began taking all my clothes from the hangers, flinging them on the bed. I did not have the time to fold them carefully, so once I had as many clothes as I need, I shoved them all into the suitcase. Shoes, socks, bras, underwear... all went into the suitcase and were squashed down as much as they could. Thankfully, it was quite a large suitcase, so everything fit well enough.

Glancing around the room, I then grabbed a few personal items: the few bits of jewellery my mother had bought me, books, writing pads, laptop, and charger. I grabbed my phone charger and shoved it into a side pocket. I grabbed everything I could think would fit in the suitcase.

When I was satisfied I had everything, I glanced around the room one final time, knowing it would be the last time I would see it.

Taking a deep breath, I exited my bedroom and headed back downstairs, still wary of the pain. I was racking my brain for something to say to my father, anything at all to let him know just how much he had ruined not only my life but his as well. To be honest, I did not even know where to start, but I did not want to leave without saying something. I would surely regret it if I did not say something.

Leaving the house keys on the table when I reached the end of the stairs, I bit my lip. He was not looking at me as the TV had his full attention, so I took the chance to say something. I was relying on the fact he was drunk because if he had not been, he might have chased me down the street. With the state he was currently in, he was in no position to be chasing anybody. He was only more likely to trip over his own feet than anything else. Then again, I doubted he would risk chasing me just in case someone happened to see.

"You know," I started, taking another deep breath as I continued to say whatever came to my mind. "You aren't the only one who lost someone you love. You may have lost your wife, but the day she walked out on us, I lost both my parents. You take your anger out on me because you think I'm to blame, and maybe I am, but no amount of pain you put me under will bring her back. She isn't going to come back because she'd have done it by now, but you still had me! You could have looked after me like you were supposed to and we would have gotten through it together, but no. You left me more alone than I've ever been before. I just hope you're happy with yourself."

I shocked even myself with the things I had said. I had not planned on saying all of that though I was glad that I did. I needed to say it, and he needed to hear it. At least now he would be alone, something he really does deserve. Him being alone meant he could not hurt anybody else the way he had hurt me after all.

I could feel the intensity of his gaze on my back as I turned to face the door, but I did not look at him. I had said what I needed to say, and that was it. There was nothing else left to say.

So, with that thought in mind, I opened the front door and stepped out into the night, dragging my suitcase along with me.

Alone.

Terrified.

Free.

Chapter Two

Once I was outside, I stood in silence for a couple of minutes, trying to figure out where the closest hotel was. With the amount of pain a simple step caused me, I knew it would have to be extremely close but also far enough away that my dad would not think to look if he decided to search for me. I was not entirely sure that would not happen.

In the end, I recalled that there was a hotel about a ten-minute walk from my home—old home, I should say. I was not sure how much it would cost me to stay there, but I could only hope they would take pity on me and let me stay, just until the morning.

Nodding to myself, I decided to head to the hotel anyway, knowing I had no other option. It was either that or risk collapsing here, and I was not so sure what my dad would do if he found me unconscious on his doorstep.

The further I walked down the street, the more relieved I felt. I was finally out of that house. I was finally free of the torment and abuse I had endured for so long. I did not ever expect to get out of it; not alive, at least. The thought had seemed impossible to me and yet, here I was, walking down a darkened street to head to a hotel. I could hardly believe my luck.

Walking as fast as I could in my state, I suddenly tripped over a rock I had not noticed until the last second. I fell to the ground as my suitcase somehow remained standing. Hissing in pain, I gritted my teeth together. My breathing was becoming uneven as the pain I was already in tripled.

"Stupid rock," I mumbled under my breath.

That was when I heard it.

A laugh.

I froze in fear, momentarily forgetting the pain as I wondered who it was. As far as I was aware, there was no one but me around, so to say I was scared was an understatement. Assuming it was my dad coming for me, I struggled to my feet, crying out as the pain in my ribs flared up. There was a strong possibility that they were broken by now. It was getting harder and harder to breathe properly.

Grabbing my suitcase, I hurried along the street. The fear within me did not diminish as I turned a corner, walking a bit faster than before. It was difficult, but I knew I had to push myself. I did not feel safe, and I knew I would not feel safe until I reached my destination.

Seeing multiple houses with lights on made me feel a little safer at the thought I could knock on their doors if I needed to, but that feeling soon changed when I suddenly felt as though I was being watched though I heard no one. Shivers ran up my spine, and the hairs on the back of my neck stood on end as I glanced around nervously, hoping I would not see my dad. I did not. In fact, I could not see anyone.

It could only have been around twenty minutes since I left the house, but it felt like an eternity seeing as I knew there was someone following me—someone I just could not see. I was on edge more than ever, and I had to bite my lip to stop from crying. Hadn't I endured enough tonight? Why couldn't things go right just once?

I was not sure whether I was just being paranoid and the laugh had just been a figment of my imagination, but I did not care. Whether or not there truly was someone following me, I did not want to slow down and risk finding out.

I would definitely need a lot of painkillers once I reached the hotel, though—if it was even open. I was not sure what time it closed, but considering it was pitch black outside, I knew I had to hurry if I was going to make it.

Just get to the hotel, I told myself. *I'll be safe there.*

"Hello there," a deep voice spoke suddenly.

Spinning around, I squinted in the darkness, once again trying to find the source of the voice though I still could not see one. All I could see were houses and cars. No people. Just me.

So who spoke?

I did not fancy sticking around to find out, so I set off walking again, thinking about that voice. I was pretty sure by now that it was, in fact, my dad coming to take me back though I was determined to not let that happen. There was no way, no way in hell that I was going back there. To say I was scared was the understatement of the century. I was terrified, confused, and in pain. I needed to get to safety. Now.

"Slow down!" the same voice called out again. I almost burst into tears then, but I managed to keep them contained. I had to get out of here. I just had to.

I sped up my pace. The pain in my legs was making it difficult to walk properly, so I was pretty much limping as I tried to get away. There was no chance I would be able to run, not without falling over again, and that was something I could not afford.

Being almost one hundred percent sure that it was my dad following me terrified me because that meant he wanted me back home. That meant more beatings, more pain, more terror. It meant more sleepless nights, more crawling up the stairs because I could not stand, more hiding from him whenever I could. So when I heard scuffling coming from behind me, I hoped that he had tripped over his own feet and had fallen like I had because it gave me the chance to get away.

"Stop!" The voice seemed different from the first voice I had heard. That confused me because that meant...

"Oh, god," I whispered to myself as the realisation hit me like a slap in the face. There was more than one man. Which meant it was not my dad coming after me because nobody knew about the abuse. That meant that someone else was after me, someone who wanted me for something else. I gulped, speeding up until I was jogging. Biting my lip hard enough to draw blood, I no longer cared about the pain for I had to get out of there and to the hotel. I no longer knew who was behind me, and it had me wondering who it was and what they wanted with me.

Was it a rapist? A murderer? I was not sure.

"You won't get away from me."

My breathing was becoming laboured, and I soon heard footsteps approaching me, coming closer and closer with each step. It would not be long until they caught up with me. I had a few minutes at the most. I told myself that I was not going to go down without a fight, but in my condition, I would do more damage to myself than my attacker.

With only a few minutes until I finally reached my destination, I then did something you only saw in horror movies.

I tripped. Again.

Cursing my clumsiness, I braced myself for the impact of the concrete, but it never came. That was when I became aware of an arm wrapped securely around my waist, preventing me from face planting the floor. Not checking to see what the person looked like, I quickly elbowed him in the ribs. He instantly let go of me, groaning in pain. I took that as my chance to escape.

"Will you just stop? I can heal you! I just want to help!" It was the second person I had heard, but it was not that that made me momentarily stop in my tracks to take a look at the man. It was his words that made me stop. 'I can heal you'... What does that even mean? If he were a doctor, which I was presuming he was, he would not use that word. That specific word made my brain hurt just trying to figure out what he meant by that.

Maybe I was just imagining things. Maybe the tidal wave of emotions was causing me to lose my mind and hear things. Maybe I had suffered one too many blows to the head that all rational thoughts had escaped me.

"Come here," he said, straightening up and gesturing me over to him. I remained where I was, not believing that he just wanted to help me, not when he had been following me. I was not sure what to do, but I knew that nothing good would happen if I went over to him.

For a moment or two, I wished that it was not so dark outside so I could actually see what the man looked like. It was too dark to make out his features. I quickly snapped out of my thoughts because all I knew was this guy did not have anything good in his mind. He could have plans to kill me, and I was just standing and staring like an idiot, wanting to see what he looked like.

I was definitely going insane.

I had only managed a couple of steps backwards. In the blink of an eye, the man was directly in front of me, centimetres from my face. I gasped in shock, taking another step backwards, but he grabbed hold of me, winding his arms around my waist.

This is what I get for being such an idiot, I thought to myself as I struggled to get out of the man's grip. Letting go of my suitcase, I thrashed around, but the harsh movements only caused me more pain, which only resulted in me whimpering. He did not look fazed, though, not in the slightest. In fact, I was sure he had a smirk on his face.

Words seemed to have failed me; I was unable to form even a simple sentence. It was like they had gotten stuck in my throat, and I could not get them out. The man looked at me, raising one hand, so it rested against the side of my head.

I was terrified, whimpering not just in pain but out of fear. I really did have the world's worst luck.

"Let me go!" I finally found my voice, the desperation clear. Why I even bothered, I had no idea because it was obvious he was not going to listen. He did not even say anything.

The last thing I remember before I fell unconscious was the sharp pain in the side of my head as it connected with the wall beside us.

Chapter Three

Feeling the warmth of the sun shining on me caused a smile to form on my face. It made a nice change from being cold all the time.

The few seconds after I wake up were often the moments where I found a sense of peace. In those few seconds, everything was as it should be because all the bad things in my life did not come to mind. It was like everything was okay for once.

Fluttering open my eyes and blinking a few times as the sunlight hit my eyes, I took a look at my surroundings.

I immediately gasped. I was not in a place I recognised, and that was when everything I wished to forget came rushing to my mind: everything with my dad and then that man... Thinking back to the minutes before I fell unconscious, I gasped again. I was suddenly aware of a sharp pain on the side of my head and winced as I gently touched the area were the throbbing sensation was coming from.

Who was that man? I panicked, glancing around the second time. He must be deranged. There was no other explanation as to why he assumed he could 'heal' me. What did that even mean? Why had me brought me here?

Where even was here?

Oh, god, I had been kidnapped. Could my life get any worse? I needed to escape before he came back, and since he was not in the bedroom with me, I knew that he could return at any second.

I jumped straight out of bed, not giving a single thought to the injuries I had sustained.

Clutching at my stomach, I waited for the pain that would undoubtedly flare up, but it did not come. There was no pain at all, and that just did not make sense. I should be in an unbelievable amount of pain, not just from my head being smashed against a wall but the rest of my body, too. How could there be no pain whatsoever?

I pulled my top up to look at my skin and instantly grimaced. The cuts and bruises were still there; the pain was not. I did not understand it. That sort of pain does not just disappear overnight, I knew that for a fact.

Pulling my top back down, I looked around the bedroom I had been placed in. It was a room fit for somebody who was extremely rich, leading me to wonder what on earth they could possibly want with me as I had nothing to give them. The bed was a four-poster bed. Black lace material was spread around the sides of the bed, along with a black duvet cover, and it made the room look too dark. It needed some colour. It was definitely clear that the person who had decorated the room had only two favourite colours, red and black. The walls were blood red with intricate black patterns decorating it. All in all, it was a room that only made me more uncomfortable because as nice as it was, it only made it more obvious that I was not where I was supposed to be.

Across from the bed were the windows, but I glanced at the white door instead, a bright contrast against the otherwise gloomy room, wondering if the man was even here at all. I had to make sure I would not be caught escaping. I shuddered to think of what would happen if I was.

I headed over to the wardrobe, knowing that if the man were lurking around, facing him with some sort of weapon would be better than nothing. He would have to come and check on me eventually, and I wanted to be armed when that happened.

The wardrobe told me that the room I was in belonged to a woman, making me panic at the thought of another person wishing to harm me. The clothes were not gothic looking like the rest of the room, however. They were the type of clothes you would see in any clothing store. Apart from the dresses that looked as though they would be suitable for a ball of some sort, that was it. There was nothing else other than shoes.

In other words, nothing that I could use.

As I remembered that I had had a suitcase with me when I was knocked unconscious, I searched the room for it, knowing I could at least hit the man or woman with my laptop if the opportunity arrived. I could not spot it anywhere though.

Maybe I could jump out the window, I thought to myself, rushing over and peering out of it. I could have groaned in frustration when I saw that I was too high up. There was no way I would be able to survive a fall from the height. I would surely die.

That left the door as my only means of escaping this place. I was not feeling confident that I could actually pull off an escape, though. I did not even know where I was or how many people were here. There could be four people in the house for all I knew.

I turned back to the window, hoping that I would recognise a building that would give me some indication of how far away I was from Rose's house. She was the only person I could go to now. Yet when I looked back out the window at the buildings, I noticed something that both shocked and terrified me.

I was in London.

I began to panic, even more, terrified that I would never get out of this alive. Why he had brought me here, I had no idea, but it cannot be good. He probably brought me here to kill me!

I did not plan on sticking around to find out.

Looking frantically around the room for somewhere to hide, the only places where either under the bed or inside the wardrobe. As those were the first places the man would check (it was a typical horror movie thing), I did not know what to do.

There was only one way I could leave this room, and that was by going out the door. I would have done it already if I knew how many people there were. If there were more than one, I would be caught. If I were caught, I would be killed for attempting to get away.

Before I could even figure out what to do, I heard a voice speak.

"Planning an escape?"

I jumped in fright, taking a step back automatically. I looked at my kidnapper.

My jaw dropped as I took in his appearance. From his jet-black hair to his grey eyes, he was extremely good looking. The colour of his eyes was surprising, though, since I had never seen such a colour before, and I briefly wondered if he was wearing contact lenses.

It did not surprise me, however, to see that he was dressed from head to toe in black. With just one glance, I could see it suited him well. I guessed that he was in his twenties because he did not look that old. That only made me wonder what a guy like him could want with a girl like me.

"Why am I in London?" I backed away from him, wanting to put as much space between us as I possibly could. "Why did you kidnap me?"

"I didn't kidnap you," he replied with a smirk on his lips.

"I'm in London against my will. I'm pretty sure that's kidnapping," I said before I could stop to think about what I was doing.

"I'd watch my mouth if I were you," he spoke, leaning against the doorframe. "You say I kidnapped you, so how can you be certain I'm not planning on killing you?"

My breathing hitched, terrified. "Take me home!"

"You don't have one," he said, looking more amused by the second, seeming to enjoy seeing me so scared.

"H-how do you know that?" I stuttered, my eyes widening. It did not really hit me until then that I did not have a home anymore, that I was technically homeless. So even if he did, by some miracle, agree to take me back, I had nowhere to go.

My life is gradually getting worse by the second, and I cannot do a thing about it.

"I saw you leave."

"You followed me from my house?" I exclaimed. "What do you even want with me? I don't have much money so please, just let me go!"

"And have you running to the police?" He raised his eyebrows. "I don't think so. No, you'll be staying here when I can keep an eye on you. You should be thanking me, anyway."

"Thank you for what?"

"Because if it wasn't for me intervening last night, you would have been raped or murdered. It could have gone either way really," he stated as though it was nothing. He did not seem bothered in the slightest.

"What?" I gaped at him in shock.

"There was another man last night, following you. It was obvious what he was going to do when he started following you, so I killed him."

I tensed up upon hearing that. He had killed someone. The other man that had been following me was now dead. The man in front of me was not just a kidnapper but a murderer as well.

Shit.

"You look scared," he commented, still leaning against the door with his arms folded across his chest.

"I've been kidnapped by a murderer," I spoke, deadpan. How was I ever supposed to get away when he had no problem ending someone's life?

"If I wanted you dead, you'd already be dead. I won't kill you, not unless you piss me off or I get bored. I'm going to keep you around for a bit because you might prove to be useful."

Well, wasn't that reassuring, I thought sarcastically. If he got bored, I was dead. If I pissed him off, I was dead. Was there even a chance of me getting out of here alive at all or was that just wishful thinking?

"I want to go home," I said in a shaky voice.

"What home? You don't have one." He reminded me again, smirking still.

"I don't care." I shook my head, feeling the tears building up in my eyes. "Just take me back! You can't just keep me here against my will like this!"

Two words, that was all I got in response before he left me alone with my thoughts.

"Watch me."

***

I was kept locked up in the bedroom for the rest of the day, with no means of escape—unless I wanted to risk jumping out the window. He had locked the bedroom door, and I actually wished I had taken my chances earlier because it must have been unlocked then… seeing as I had not heard him entering the room.

The fact I would probably die if I jumped from the window seemed a whole lot more enticing that waiting around for a murderer to come and end my life.

I remained in the room, though, curled up in the corner of the room, hoping and praying I would be able to get out of this somehow. I had no idea where any of my belongings were, and as he had taken my phone from me, I could not call for help.

I could not do anything but sit and wait, and that was torture in itself becauseq even the slightest noise from outside made me jump.

So, as to how I fell asleep, I still have no idea.

***

I was rudely woken the next morning by someone shaking me roughly. Not wanting to get up, I groaned, slapping the hand away that I presumed belonged to Rose. When I opened my eyes to see those grey eyes staring back at me, I knew I had not been dreaming. That alone was enough to assure me that it had not all been a dream, a result of being knocked unconscious. It was enough to assure me that I had actually been kidnapped by a murderer.

I immediately got to my feet, widening my eyes as I stumbled away from him, fear taking over. "Get away from me!"

"Relax, I'm not going to hurt you." He rolled his eyes as he straightened up. "Not yet, anyway. Get dressed and come downstairs. Seeing as you will be staying here for a while, it is probably best to give you a tour."

Honestly, I was not even sure what to make of that because as far as I was aware, no kidnapper offered to take their hostage on a tour. In fact, the whole 'keeping them locked up' thing seemed to be the norm, so what this man was playing, I had no idea, and I did not like it. I did not like it one bit.

Before I could even figure out what to say, though, he was gone. He was obviously the type of person that demanded rather than asked, the kind that was not used to being polite. Then again, he had kidnapped me and was probably planning to kill me, so being polite was a pretty pointless thing to do.

I could not help but wonder, though. If he was going to kill me, why not just get it over with? Why delay the inevitable? If he got bored, I was dead. If I annoyed him, I was dead. Hell, he probably did not even need a reason to kill me, he would just do it. So why hadn't he?

And what if I never saw Rose again? We had been friends for seven years, and she had always managed to help me through the darkest times of my life. She may not have known about the abuse, but just having her in my life was a huge help to me.

Now that I was alone, things were different. I did not have Rose to help me, to give me advice. I only had myself, and that was not a good thing because it brought the thoughts back, thoughts I desperately tried to push to the back of my mind.

I felt weak. I felt afraid. I felt anxious. I knew that if I did or said the wrong thing, it would result in my death, and I honestly was more afraid of him than I was of my dad. That was saying a lot considering how terrified I had become of my dad.

Still, if there was a slight chance he meant what he said when he claimed he was not going to hurt me, I'd better not do anything to risk him changing his mind.

I did not bother changing, though; I did not feel comfortable rifling through the wardrobe or wearing someone else's clothes. There was not actually anything wrong with the clothes I was already wearing: a pair of black skinny jeans, a white top, and a black zip-up jacket. I saw no reason to change. I was even wearing my converse, the comfiest pair of shoes I owned.

I stared at my reflection in the mirror on the wardrobe door, checking for any blood or dirt stains. I had gone through quite a few tops lately because my cuts would often open up and seep through the material, so it was just better to make sure.

I did notice that my hair needed to be brushed and that my eyes, my once bright blue eyes, were now a dull, lifeless blue. It was like the light had been sucked straight out of them. I glanced away then, not wanting to look at my reflection a second longer.

"HURRY UP!" the man suddenly yelled, causing me to jump in fright. I expected him to come bursting through the door in a rage, but he did not; not that it relaxed me because it only put me more on edge than I was, to begin with.

Running out of the room, I made sure to take note of my surroundings just in case I had an opportunity to escape. I noticed that I was on the top floor. As I was running down the stairs, I assumed that there must be around four bedrooms. That meant that there could be four people living here, four people that could be exactly like the man that had brought me here.

I only had a tiny shred of hope left in me that I would be able to get away.

Passing each door, I then raced down the second flight of stairs, gripping on the bannister to prevent me from falling down the stairs.

Once at the bottom, my eyes immediately locked on the front door that was just ahead of me. I knew that I could make it to the door because no matter what room the man was in, he would have to chase after me. If he were faster than me though, which was a strong possibility, he would soon catch up. Yet if I did run, I would be outside, surrounded by people. I could easily call for help.

Decision made, I cast a quick look around for any sign of the man—or anyone else that was maybe inside. When I did not spot anyone, I pushed myself forward and ran as fast as I possibly could to get to the front door.

I made it in seconds, gripping my hands tightly onto the door handle. Relief flooded my entire body when I twisted the handle, only for it to turn.

It was unlocked.

My relief was short-lived, however, because the second I had flung open the door, I felt a presence behind me, and I froze in fear.

"Don't even think about it." The tone of his voice told me he was not pleased, and that frightened me all the more. I had assumed I would have at least been able to make it to the street before he caught up with me.

"Shut the door and turn around," he demanded, fanning his hot breath on my neck that only made me more aware of how close he was to me. I was quick to do as he said, knowing I had probably just made things a whole lot worse for myself.

Well done, Violet, I berated myself silently, *you couldn't have moved a little faster, could you?*

"I'm s-sorry." I trembled.

"You can't escape from me. I will always find you." The way he said that had me more than a little creeped out, and I gulped nervously. "But I won't kill you even though I should for that little indiscretion, but if you ever try to escape again, I will torture you in ways you have never even heard of."

I gasped.

"Understood?" He leaned closer, staring straight into my eyes.

I nodded weakly, seeming to be incapable of speech all of a sudden. He truly was terrifying but knowing he had murdered someone already did not fill me with much hope that it was an empty threat.

"Good. Now, considering you aren't going to be leaving London any time soon, I thought it best to have you familiarise yourself with the area. I will be by your side, though, and there are some… rules. You will not walk away from me, you will not tell anybody how you got here because if you do, I will not only kill you, but I will kill the person you told as well. I'm sure you don't want someone else's blood on your hands, do you?"

The look on his face told me how serious he was, so I immediately shook my head. As much as I wanted to try to make contact with someone to tell them what was going on, I could not risk it.

"Good," he said.

"Who are you?" I whispered, still shaking my head. "What do you want with me?"

"My name is Shadow," he told me, choosing not to answer my second question.

"What kind of name is Shadow?" I blurted out before I could stop myself. In my defence, it was the first time I had ever met someone with such a strange name, one that you would give a pet, not a person.

Shadow seemed to take offence to my words because he glared harshly and then, a low, rumbling noise sounded from him. I was taken aback by that noise because it sounded like… well, it sounded like he was growling at me. Whatever it was, it sent unpleasant shivers down my spine.

"I'm sorry!" I quickly apologised, feeling my heart beating rapidly in my chest as I realised I had just annoyed him; the one thing I was trying not to do. "I didn't mean it like that!"

"Shadow is the name I was given," he stated, glowering at me.

"I'm sorry," I repeated, my hands shaking. "I really didn't mean to offend you."

"Do it again, and I will end your miserable life." He practically spat the words at me, pushing me out of the way so he could get to the front door. "Now come on. You've pissed me off enough for one day, so do not do it again."

I merely nodded in response, too afraid to open my mouth and risk saying anything else that would offend him. It was obvious he had severe anger problems, and that was not just because of his psychotic, murderous tendencies either.

But knowing how evil he was still would not stop me from attempting to escape. He had no intention of ever letting me go; he had said as much. To know that I would be stuck here with him until he killed me was not very comforting. I would rather try to get away than stay with him, just waiting around for the day he would decide to kill me. Now I knew his name and what he looked like, he was never going to let me leave.

So for now, I would have to act like I had not been kidnapped by the most attractive, most dangerous man I had ever had the misfortune to meet.

Chapter Four

Walking around London with the man that kidnapped me could have given me a million and one chances to get away from him. I could have told him that I needed to go to the toilet and tell someone what was going on. I could have run away from him screaming, rushing over to the two policemen that we had walked past.

I did not.

I was too afraid—too afraid of what would happen if Shadow somehow managed to convince them that I was making it up for whatever reason because then, I truly would be a dead girl walking. He would undoubtedly kill me, and I had no reason to believe otherwise. So I remained quiet, hoping that if I did, he may take pity on me and let me go. Or maybe that was just wishful thinking.

Walking around, I noticed Shadow seemed a whole lot more happy and cheerful than he had been back at his home, and as much as I knew, that was because he had to keep up appearances. I was glad he was not walking around with a permanent scowl on his face; he was terrifying.

He had shown me around the tourist attractions such as Buckingham Palace, Big Ben, and the London Eye. Though he would not speak as we reached each one, I was glad he was showing me around. It meant more time outside where I was safe. However, with each tourist attraction he took me to, it only led me to believe he had bipolar disorder. Angry one minute and fine the next... it was confusing trying to keep up.

What kidnapper even shows their victim around the place they live, anyway? It was like he thought he was doing a good deed by showing me around, but what for? What twisted game was he playing?

Currently walking around Covent Garden, I asked the question that I had been wanting to ask ever since we left the house.

"Why are you doing all this? Showing me around and being... nice?"

"Being my usual self would attract attention, too much attention, in fact." He looked amused by his own words, but I did not call him out on it; it was nothing worth knowing.

"Are you ever going to let me go?"

"That's for me to know," he stated. His tone changed, signalling that that would be the end of the conversation.

I did not drop it, though. I wanted to know. I needed to know.

"Why did you even take me?" I asked as annoyance spread through me. "I have literally nothing to offer you, and you have nothing to gain by taking me. I have little money if that's what you're after, and you know I don't have a home, so if you're trying to get ransom money, you're shit out of luck there too, considering my dad wouldn't care. So don't you see? You've nothing to gain from this. So please, I'm begging you, just let me go!"

Unwanted tears filled my eyes, and I blinked them back; I did not want him to see me cry. I hated crying in front of people. It made me feel weak.

Shadow frowned upon hearing my words, mulling them over in his mind, perhaps. I was not sure what part he was dwelling on the most, and I did not want to ask him in fear that it would lead to questions I just did not want to answer. Not now, not ever.

Thankfully, he did not ask me about what I had said though he did tell me that I was not going anywhere and that he had his reasons for taking me. What those reasons were, however, he would not reveal to me. Whatever they were, they had better be important.

"Are you going to kill me?" I asked, hesitantly. I was not sure why I wanted to know because knowing was only going to make me feel even worse, but a part of me had resigned myself to the fact I probably would die. In fact, I had never expected to make it up to this point in my life. I had always assumed my dad would one day go too far and end my life, so dying really was a thought I had come to accept. That did not mean I did not want to delay the inevitable if I could, though.

"If I was going to kill you, would I really heal you?" he asked, forming a pointed look on his face as he glanced at me.

"Heal me? What are you—"

I cut myself off and furrowed my eyebrows as the realisation came to me. Amidst everything that had happened, I had completely forgotten that I was not in any pain anymore. I was not sure how it was even possible to forget something like that when I had been so used to having to take careful steps in order not to cause further injury, and yet that is exactly what happened. I forgot about the fact I was no longer in any physical pain.

"How did you do that?"

"That isn't important," he replied, shaking his head.

"Of course it is! How did you stop it hurting when the bruises are still there?" I asked, causing him to halt suddenly, turning to look at me.

"Bruises?" he asked sharply, furrowing his brows. "What bruises?"

I was not the only one confused now.

"I healed the pain in your head from when I smashed your head against the brick wall," he told me slowly. "Sorry about that, by the way. You just weren't listening to me."

"You told me you could help me before you did that," I stated.

"Yes because you fell. I thought you'd hurt yourself. I healed your legs too as you were limping."

"I'm so confused," I admitted.

"As am I, so it's time you explained what you meant by bruises." He was staring into my eyes with such intensity that it made me flinch and avert my gaze. I had really dropped myself in it now. If Shadow would not going to kill me, then my dad surely would.

He took me to the nearest Starbucks, expecting answers—ones I could not give him. I was not sure I could even get out of it, but I knew I had to try. I could not let him know. He would use it to his advantage. That, I was sure of.

One thing that did not make sense to me was the reality that he did not know I was covered in bruises. How could he not? There was no denying he had taken the pain away, so how could he not have found out about the bruises covering my body? How the hell did he even heal me, anyway?

Sitting down while he went to order, I thought hard about my situation. The thought of escape was becoming so much more appealing. I could leave right now while he was in the queue, and he would not know until it was too late. I could get away from him. The more I thought about it, the more appealing it became, but I remained where I was out of fear that he would find me. He knew London better than I did after all. I was not entirely sure how much chance I had.

Besides, as long as I did not get on his bad side, I could keep myself alive a little longer—perhaps. That was better than being sent back to my dad because he would definitely kill me without hesitation.

I sighed, glancing at the table, as my hair fell, covering my face. I just wanted to have a way I could go back home without the trouble that would come from it. I only had Rose to rely on, and I could not even get in touch with her. It was taking its toll on me, and I was not sure how I was going to cope.

"Here." Shadow's voice made me jump, not expecting him that quickly. He set down two cups on the table, passing one to me before taking a sip of his.

"What is it?" I asked him, eyeing the cup warily.

"Hot chocolate."

I nodded, taking the cup and holding it in my hands.

"What bruises?" he soon asked, making me sigh in response.

"It doesn't matter. Just forget it. How did you heal me? That's not possible, and yet I feel no pain. I don't get it," I said, lowering my voice so nobody could hear what I was saying.

"Why were you kicked out?" he asked instead.

"Because my dad hates me," I replied, shrugging as though it was nothing when it actually hurt more than I let on. Not that anyone could expect any differently. He is still my dad.

"You said he doesn't care, and now he hates you. What happened?" he asked.

"None of your business." I snapped, not wanting to go into the details.

"I'm making it my business," he said, glaring at me.

"Why is it so important to you?" I asked him, trying not to let his harsh glare faze me. "I mean, you kidnapped me for fuck's sake! You don't need to know anything!"

"I'd be careful how you speak to me if I were you," he said, still glaring.

"Or what? You'll kill me? Go ahead. I don't care anymore!" I said, standing up quickly, and without waiting for a response, I ran outside. I was not sure what I was doing anymore, but the fact that I really did not care if he killed me had hit me hard. I had been so scared of saying the wrong thing that would result in my untimely death. Now, though, I truly did not care. I was not sure when the sudden change had occurred within me, but now, if Shadow were to decide to kill me, I would not try to fight back. I would welcome it.

There was definitely something wrong with me.

I was aware that Shadow was chasing me, quickly managing to catch up and grabbing the back of my shirt to pull me to him. I almost fell over at how fast I had stumbled backwards, but I was prevented from doing so, falling into Shadow instead.

"What did I tell you before we left?" he said, practically growling in my ear.

"You said you'd kill me if I left your side."

"Exactly."

"So do it. I don't care," I said sadly, shaking my head. "I really don't."

"Why?"

"Because you'd be doing me a favour!" My voice raised, finally admitting the truth. Was it really so bad that I wanted the pain to end?

Shadow tensed at my words, and I knew he was trying to think of something to say in response. He did not say anything, though. Not to me, anyway. Instead, he spun around, still keeping a tight grip on my wrist. I was pulled in front of him, slamming my back against his chest.

"I'm giving you ten seconds to get the fuck away from here, or I will kill you." Shadow glared, staring straight at two men only a few steps away from us. Both were glancing in our direction though their eyes had widened considerably.

"Dude, how the hell did you hear us?" one of them spoke.

Glancing back and forth between the two, I quickly deduced that they were brothers; they looked too much alike. Both had dark hair and the same face shape. I could not tell what eye colour they had though I guessed they were probably the same too. They could even be twins with how much they looked like one another, apart from the fact the one on the left was slightly taller and muscular than the smaller one.

"I happen to have excellent hearing, but that is beside the point. Either you leave right now, or I kill you. It's that simple," Shadow stated.

Shadow was definitely deranged to threaten to murder someone in broad daylight. It made me wonder just how many people he had killed. What if he was a serial killer? I did not believe for a second that he had only killed one man.

Hearing that he was intent on killing them—I doubted he believed in empty threats—sent a wave of terror through my body. I was terrified that he truly was going to kill them. It did not matter that we were in a crowded place because for all I knew, he could find out where they live. I knew nothing about Shadow after all.

I had to warn them, somehow. But how? Saying anything would only put myself in more danger. Maybe I had a death wish, but that did not mean I wanted to be tortured beforehand. *Think, Violet, think! You have to do something!*

"Why would we apologise? We're only talking."

Apologise for what? I asked myself with a frown on my face.

"The fact that I am standing here is exactly why you should apologise. Now, do you really want me to come over there and slit your throats, or will you apologise to the lady?"

I quickly raised my hand and made the motion of slitting my throat, hoping that they would get the message that messing with him was not a good idea. They did not seem to understand.

"You want us to apologise for something she didn't even hear?" the taller man asked, frowning. "Are you dating or some shit? It sure didn't look that way when she was running away from you, dude."

"I said, apologise," Shadow spoke through gritted teeth. "Now."

"I ain't apologising for speaking the truth," he replied, holding his hands up in mock surrender.

Shadow, moving me to one side, took a step forward with a determined expression on his face. I made the motion of slitting my throat again, and this time, they seemed to understand that something was not right because they were quick to run away.

They did not even apologise for whatever it was that they had said though I did not care. I was just glad that they were safe.

"Let's go," Shadow spoke harshly, turning back to face me.

"Where?"

"Back to my home."

Great, I thought sarcastically, just great.

Chapter Five

Once back at his home, I became tense. Being alone with him was not exactly in my best interest considering he was already angry. I had no idea what he had in mind now, but I had been hoping we would be out for longer. I felt safer in public because he could not do anything. Now we were alone, and the possibilities were endless.

I followed Shadow into the living room and sat on the edge of the sofa awkwardly. I chose that spot deliberately because it was the closest to the door. I did not take my eyes off him, watching in fear as he paced back and forth with his fists still clenched and his jaw tight. He showed no sign of calming down any time soon, and that only worried me more.

When he suddenly spun to face me—glaring so harshly, I flinched—I instantly jumped up. The way he was looking at me told me that I needed to get the hell away from him or I would end up dead. He took a step towards me, and that was all the reason I needed to run from the room. I had already seen Shadow lock the front door and pocket the key so I could not escape outside, but the house was pretty large, and I was hoping I would be able to find somewhere to hide.

I ran into the kitchen first, grabbing the first knife I saw. It was only a small one, but at least it was not a butter knife. It would still do some damage if I had to use it to protect myself though I was hoping it would not come to that. Not that I would actually have a choice. If he tried to attack me, I was going to defend myself. It was different to when I had been living with my dad because I had nowhere to go then and he was still family. Shadow was just a stranger to me, someone that may or may not be planning to torture me. I was not going to let that happen if I could do something about it.

He stalked into the room just as I was about to leave, causing me to take a few steps back. The determination on his face was obvious; it told me all I needed to know. He had something planned for me, and judging from the slight smirk on his face, it was not going to be good.

"Stay away from me!" I demanded, pointing the knife in his direction, not taking my eyes off him for a second.

"Put that thing down before you hurt yourself." He snapped, rolling his eyes.

"Get back!" I said as he took another step towards me, leaving only a small distance between us now. Even though I had a weapon firmly in my grasp, I did not feel safe at all. I knew that Shadow was intent on hurting me to some extent, and I was determined not to let that happen.

"You know, you may not have been here long, but you've been a real pain in my arse ever since I brought you here. I should have just killed you that night rather than bringing you here, thinking it was the best place for you. Don't worry, though. I'll rectify that soon enough," he spoke, his eyes glittering dangerously in the light.

Fear dominating my body, I gulped and almost dropped the knife I held.

"You think you can beat me?" he asked with a smirk on his face. "You think you have what it takes to kill me?"

"Get back!" I repeated, dodging out of the way because he was so close that he could have grabbed me if he had taken the opportunity. I felt like I was a scared little mouse and he was the big, bad wolf. He was the predator, and I was the prey.

"I would like to see you try," he spoke in amusement.

Considering he had had multiple opportunities to kill me ever since he had brought me here, I knew he liked taunting me. He probably got off on taunting his victims, and I briefly wondered just how many victims there were. I quickly pushed the thought away; now was not the time to be thinking things like that when Shadow obviously wanted me to be the next victim.

I was not going to let that happen.

Before I could even so much as blink, he had lunged towards me, reaching for me. Just as his hand wrapped around my arm, I snapped out of my momentary shock at how fast he had moved and swung the knife towards him. At the exact same moment, he moved forward, even closer to me.

Hearing the gasp that followed seconds after told me that I had hit my mark. I glanced down, and my eyes widened as I saw the knife was now lodged in his stomach. The sight of it instantly made me feel sick. I had not intended on stabbing him.

Taking advantage of the fact he was currently in no fit state to chase after me, I rushed from the kitchen. It was only when I reached the stairs that I realised I still could not get out of the house. It was locked, and I did not fancy going back to the kitchen to get the keys from him.

So I then did the one thing I always complained about when watching horror films.

I ran up the stairs.

When I had reached the bedroom I had been staying in, I started freaking out. I was up here waiting for someone to die from a stab wound I inflicted on them. I was now a murderer. I was no better than Shadow himself even though I had just been protecting myself. I had not intended to stab him. I just wanted him to back away. I just wanted him to leave me alone.

What if his friends came back? Hell, I did not even know if the guy had any friends, but since I was staying in a female's room, he must know somebody. What if she came back and saw him bleeding out on the kitchen floor? What if she was just as psychotic as him and came after me? I doubt I had it in me to hurt another person the same way.

Sinking to the floor, shock coursing throughout my body, I curled up into a ball. My mind would not stop repeating what had happened. It was an endless loop, making me even more horrified each time... I had just killed someone.

I was not equipped to handle something like this. I could not even bring myself to move, too shocked, too scared to do anything. Rocking back and forth, I ducked my head, resting my forehead on my knees. With the way my arms were wrapped around my legs, bringing them tight to my chest, it was like I was trying to hold myself together, but it was not working very well.

I was not sure how much time had passed by because all I could focus on was everything that happened. I knew I should be trying to escape in case one of his friends came back, but I could not. It was like I was stuck firmly to the spot, unable to move, and my breathing started coming out in short pants, and tears fell from my eyes as my chest felt tight all of a sudden.

And then the bedroom door crashed open with such force, it flew off the hinges and fell to the floor.

The second my eyes landed on the figure in the doorway, catching the blood on his shirt, I nearly screamed. He did not give me the chance to because he was suddenly in front of me, mere centimetres from my face.

Yanking me to my feet, he gripped my arms tightly with a fire in his eyes that had my heart racing.

"You stupid, pathetic bitch!" He spat the words in my face, causing another tear to stream down my face. Not only did his words make me realise that I was going to die, but it was also a reminder of my dad who had frequently said the same thing in a fit of anger.

I suppose that was what I get for not trying to escape after I stab someone, I thought to myself bitterly, too stunned that he seemed okay to even try to get away.

"Ever since that fucking night I saved you, I've been resisting temptation, trying to control myself, but you've pushed me too far this time."

"W-what are you g-going to do?" I stuttered, fearfully.

"What I have wanted to do since the second I saw you." Shadow smirked, burying his head in the crook of my neck.

Pain.

An unbearable amount of pain filled me, and I screamed loudly in protest. Shadow placed a hand over my mouth to drown out the noise.

The pain was excruciating. Every nerve in my body felt as though it had been set on fire, and there was nothing I could do to extinguish the flames. What was happening to me, I was not sure. It was as though I could no longer distinguish what was going on or where I was. All that I remembered was Shadow burying his neck in the crook of my neck and then, pain.

That was all I could focus on. Soon realising that struggling only made the pain even worse, I stilled, hoping that whatever was happening to me would stop.

It did.

The pain was replaced by a stinging sensation, and I started feeling lightheaded. My eyes struggled to stay open, and my body swayed unsteadily. If it were not for Shadow holding me up, I would have surely fallen straight to the ground.

What he had done to me, I had no idea. I could not even begin attempting to figure it out because I was drifting in and out of consciousness.

The last thing I saw before I gave in to it was Shadow's smirking face and the blood trickling down from his mouth.

I did not even have a chance to process that before I was consumed by the darkness.

***

When I came to, I heard voices. I kept my eyes closed, not wanting them to know I had survived whatever Shadow had done to me because he would probably only do it again. Whatever he had done, I was convinced he had been trying to kill me.

So why was I not dead? I asked myself.

"Who is she?" the first voice, a female's voice, asked. "Why is she here?"

"I brought her here from Scarborough." That was definitely Shadow. I recognised his voice. "She's no one."

"You brought her here... as in, you kidnapped her? Shadow, what the hell were you thinking?" Her voice raised. "Her family is going to be searching for her if they aren't already! You promised you wouldn't do this again. You promised me!"

"She has no family," Shadow snapped.

I heard footsteps approaching me, so I concentrated on keeping my breathing even; I did not want them finding out I was awake.

"I saved her from being raped or even murdered. So don't start with me, Leah. I have not hurt her."

"Oh, so that's wasn't you I saw taking a chunk out of her neck," the female, Leah, retorted sarcastically.

That was when I decided to wake up. Her comment struck a chord in me, and it was taking everything in me not to just jump up and try escape.

My eyes flickered, and I opened them hesitantly, aware that whatever he had done to me was something he had definitely done before. My previous concerns about him being potentially being a serial killer had been confirmed; I had to get out before I became another victim of his.

"You're awake!" The female was the first to notice me, staring at me with a small smile.

I did not respond to her; I was too busy taking in her appearance. I had to get away and go straight to the police about this, so I knew I would need to remember everything I could about her.

She had long flowing black hair that reached halfway down her back, and her eyes were brown. I took notice of both her lip piercing as well as the one in her nose because those details would be important later.

She was tall though not much taller than me, wearing black jeans and a purple top that showed off her shapely figure.

Another good-looking person, I mused silently to myself. It was a shame they were both psychopaths. She must be just as bad as him if she knew all about what he did and did not stop him.

I turned my head, wanting to judge the distance between me and the door, but I felt a sharp pain in my neck that made me hiss. I clamped my hand on the spot the pain was coming from, widening my eyes when I realised it was wet. It did not take a genius to figure out it was blood—my blood.

Bringing my hand back to look at it, my suspicions were confirmed. Seeing the blood on my hand only made me panic, and I jumped off the bed I had been placed on.

"What did you do to me?!" I asked, gaping at Shadow as I clutched at my neck again. Remembering that he had blood on his face before I had collapsed, I saw that he was clean now, even having changed out of the shirt he had been stabbed in.

"Nothing," he replied too quickly, and my eyes narrowed at him.

"Then why am I bleeding?"

He shrugged. "You fell."

"Do you honestly expect me to believe that?" I asked, genuinely confused as to why he did not just tell the truth. If he was planning on killing me, why not just be honest? "I know you did something to me, I just… I just don't know what you did."

"Tell her, Shadow," Leah spoke up, crossing her arms over her chest and staring at him in annoyance.

"Because that's likely to go down well." Shadow rolled his eyes, not even glancing at Leah as he spoke because he was too busy watching me.

"She'll figure it out, eventually. People don't forget something like that."

While they continued arguing amongst themselves, I was thinking back to what had happened, to what had caused me to collapse. Leah was right in saying that people don't forget something like that because I could not forget.

There was only one conclusion I could reach upon putting all the pieces together. The strength he had to cause the door to fly off its hinges, the speed in which he came over to me, the pain coming from my neck of all places and—the most important piece of the puzzle— the blood that had been around his mouth.

Either my predicament had become so much more dangerous for me, or I was going insane. I sincerely hoped it was the latter because that I could deal with.

Gently probing the area of my neck where the pain was coming from, I quickly figured out that I was not going insane at all, that this had just rapidly turned into something from a nightmare.

I felt weak all over, and my breathing came out in short gasps that only succeeded in attracting the attention of the two people that were still arguing.

"Is she usually that pale?" Leah asked Shadow, a look of concern flashing over her face. That had me confused, but I did not dwell on it; my thoughts were all over the place.

This could not be happening. I shook my head. This could not be real. It had to be a dream, one I would wake up from at any moment. There was no way I could be standing in front of something from a horror story, something I read about in books. There was just no way.

Yet the more I thought it over, the more I knew it was true.

Shadow was a murderer, that much was true, but he was not human. He was not a human at all. He was something so much worse. He was a monster. A creature that killed with no remorse, something that had no problems in taking a human life.

Vampire.

"She knows," Leah stated, both her and Shadow watching me as I ran my finger gently over the two small wounds in my neck— fang marks.

"Monster." My hands were shaking. "No, no… this isn't possible. You can't be… but you are. Oh, God. I think I'm going to faint."

Of all things that could happen to me, I had to be kidnapped by a vampire. Of all the unfortunate things that could happen to me after escaping my dad, I just had to go and be kidnapped by a creature that should not even exist.

One thing I was sure of; life was never going to be the same again. I had been kidnapped by a creature I had no hope of getting away from. My chances of escape are now non-existent. Vampires, the ones I had seen in films anyway, had abilities. They were faster and stronger than the average human, something Shadow had already proved to be true.

I was not going to make it out of this alive, and yet I knew I had to try.

Running out of the room before they could comprehend what was going on, I pushed my legs to go as fast as possible. I may not be able to outrun a vampire, but it did not mean I was stupid enough to stand around and wait until he decides to bite me again.

I ran down the stairs, straight over to the front door, and reached for the handle. Gripping it tightly, I turned it, letting out a breath of relief when it actually opened; he had not bothered to lock it after Leah's arrival.

Exiting the house, wishing, hoping, and praying with all my might that the vampire inside the house would not follow me, I did not stop running.

How stupid was I to ever think escaping him would be a possibility?

Chapter Six

After my initial escape, there was a split second where I could not believe that it had been so easy. To escape someone who was set on killing me was hard enough, but to escape a vampire that was set on killing me was something I thought to be an impossibility. Yet here I was, running through the streets of London with no destination in mind. I just needed to get as far away from Shadow as I could possibly get before the shock wore off and he chases after me. I doubted I had long.

Not knowing whether vampires had tracking abilities or not, I went to a Starbucks—an entirely different one from the one we had been in earlier. Luck must have been on my side for I had forgotten about the money I had stuffed into my pockets on the day I was kicked out of the only home I had ever known. Buying myself a drink, I went to sit at the back of the cafe where there was one empty table. If Shadow were to come and find me, he would not spot me at the back, not if I slouched down enough. I was just as safe in here as I was anywhere else, but for now, I had to come up with a plan, and I could not concentrate on doing that if I was running around getting lost in London.

Thinking about what I was going to do next had me wondering what happened to my belongings, though. With no phone—assuming Shadow had broken my Samsung—I could not call Rose for help. That was not particularly worrying, though, apart from the fact I loved my phone because I had memorised her number. All I had to do was get to a phone or ask to borrow one. I knew the latter was too risky, though. Nobody would let me wander away with their phone to have a conversation in private. I could not risk them hearing me telling Rose I had been kidnapped because they would tell me to call the police, and that was something I definitely could not do. Shadow would kill them.

He had been right in me not wanting anyone's blood on my hands because I would never get over the guilt I had undoubtedly felt.

Finding out that vampires existed was difficult enough to process without making things worse by getting the police involved. Like they stood a chance against a vampire, anyway.

The fact Shadow is a vampire was not only shocking but worrying too since I had no idea how many others were out there. If there was one, that meant there were more, and I had no idea how many were friends of his. It was difficult accepting that they were real even though the proof was the blood on my neck. I had to pull up the hood of my jacket to hide the bite mark, but I had nothing to clean up the blood with. Cleanliness was not exactly high up on my list of priorities right now after all.

Where vampires were concerned, I only knew what I had seen from the books I had read and the films I had watched. To put it lightly: nothing that I could actually believe in. Dark romance novels were all well and good, but they did not exactly tell me what a vampire is like because they all differed, one book from the next. Some had red eyes, others did not. Some had 'extra' abilities, others did not. Some sparkled for god's sake, so I knew I could not rely solely on fiction.

The only thing I did know about Shadow, however, was that he did have an ability. He really could heal people. He was not just a crazy person trying to lure me into a trap; he had truly meant he could heal me.

Not that it made what he had done afterwards any better but still, it came as a comfort to know I was not just going crazy and imagining him using that particular word.

As it had only been a couple of days since that night, I knew that Rose would be wondering where I was. We rarely went a day without speaking to each other, so to not have heard anything from me must be worrying her by now.

It felt like weeks had passed since I had been taken captive rather than a couple of days at the most—unless my sense of time had been royally messed up because of that blow to the head I had sustained. Having my head smashed against a brick wall could have done all sorts of damage really, and I had no idea just what Shadow's healing capabilities were. What were the limits? I had no idea.

While I sat pondering all of this, causing myself to be driven into almost insanity, I had drunk the contents of the plastic cup I held.

Leaving it on the table, I then got up and left. I had to get to a payphone to call Rose. If I could tell her, she would be able to help, somehow. I knew I could not rely on the police now for obvious reasons. Nobody would win a battle against a vampire, and I was not willing to risk someone's life to get away from him.

Upon reaching the nearest payphone, I froze as my eyes landed on a familiar figure not far from me. She was talking to an old couple, and although they were not in earshot, I knew instantly that she was asking if they had seen me.

Please don't see me, I thought desperately, *please don't see me.*

She did not.

But the old couple did.

The old woman, a small, plump woman with grey hair, looked straight in my direction and had her eyes widening when she saw my panic-stricken expression. Her husband, who was the complete opposite of her as he was tall and thin and had dark hair, had not seen me yet. For that, I was glad because if they both spotted me, so would Leah, and she would take me back to Shadow. I shook my head as I made eye contact with the woman. It was my way of begging her not to tell her that I was here. Even though I could plainly see Leah's face, she would not be able to see me unless she turned her head slightly to the left, so I hoped that the woman would understand.

A couple of minutes later with me frozen to the spot, Leah walked off in the opposite direction while the old couple headed straight over to me.

"That girl is looking for you," the woman spoke up, looking worried as she glanced over her shoulder as if to make sure Leah had not returned.

"I know." I sighed, pushing my hair out of my face as I took a deep breath.

"I told her I thought I saw you about fifteen minutes from here, getting out of a taxi. That should buy you some time," she spoke reassuringly, smiling softly as she looked at me. She appeared to be a kind enough lady since she was happy enough to help me in my time of need.

"Thank you!" I replied. "Thank you so much!"

"Are you okay, dear? Are you in any trouble?" the man, her husband, asked me. Placing a hat on his balding head, he looked around before his eyes rested on me once more.

"I'm fine. I just need to get home," I told them, not wanting to go into too much detail. If they were hurt because of me, I would not be able to live with myself.

"Where do you live? We can help you with directions if you're lost," the woman said. "I'm Jane, by the way, and this is my husband, William."

"I'm Violet. It's nice to meet you," I replied, shaking their hands.

"Violet, what a beautiful name!" Jane said, smiling once more. Smiling seemed to be something she did a lot, I noticed.

"So what was that all about? That girl, Leah she said her name is, claims you ran away from home," William said, concerned.

As they both seemed to be lovely people who were genuinely concerned, I told them as little as possible but making it seem like I was giving them a fair amount of information.

"I don't have a home anymore. My dad and I don't get along, I have no mother, and Leah isn't the type of person I care to be around. I got away from her and her boyfriend, but I just don't know where to go now." I admitted.

"Do you not have a friend you can go to?" Jane asked, looking more and more worried by the second.

"No," I shook my head. "I only have one friend, but she doesn't live here, and I can't afford to go to hers."

"We can help you if you let us," William said, taking out his wallet from his back pocket before I could even protest. "We can't have you wandering around on your own like this."

"No, don't worry! I'm not taking money from you. I just need directions to the cheapest hotel so I can call my friend to pick me up tomorrow."

"I wouldn't feel safe just leaving you here on your own," Jane stated with a shake of her head. "What's this trouble you've gotten yourself in? What is wrong with the people who are looking for you? That poor girl seemed to be concerned for your safety."

Or just worried that I would go to the police and tell them her boyfriend is a murderer, I thought; not that they needed to know that, of course.

"They do drugs." I blurted out, hoping they would believe me. It was the first thing that came to mind so I hoped it would work.

By the way, their eyes widened. It was clear they believed me. At least that would keep them safe; I did not want this sweet old couple to be hurt. They were just trying to help me after all.

In the end, they recommended a hotel, and because of my lack of knowledge about London, they had taken me to the hotel themselves. They told me they would not feel right just leaving me to find it on my own, but I was grateful. When it came to directions, I was more likely to get lost.

On the way to the hotel, I had spotted a bookshop, and in the window was a vampire book. It caused me to pause momentarily, resulting in the couple asking if I was okay. I had to shake my head and act like seeing the book had not affected me at all because they would not understand if I had told them the truth. The truth was not even making sense to me.

I decided to buy a book on vampires when I was no longer in London. All I wanted to do was get to the hotel and contact Rose, knowing I could count on her to come and get me despite the long drive. I would not feel relaxed until I knew arrangements were in place.

Upon reaching the hotel, I paused outside the entrance and thanked the couple for bringing me to safety. After a few words of encouragement from them, they left, and I headed inside.

Thankfully, the hotel had a room vacancy that was within budget, but I would only be able to stay a couple of nights at most with the amount of money I had. That was not a problem, though, considering I was going to get Rose to come and get me as soon as she could, which hopefully would be tomorrow.

Once in the safety of the hotel room, I sat down on the bed and reached for the phone that was on the nightstand. Then, I dialled Rose's number.

I did not have to wait long for her to answer.

"Hello?" Rose spoke through the phone, and I let out a breath of relief at hearing her voice, feeling a sense of comfort I desperately needed.

"Rose, it's me, Violet!" I replied, smiling to myself.

"Violet! Where are you?! I've been texting you like crazy, and you've not replied! I even went to your house, but your dad said you'd moved out!" Rose rambled on, not even giving me the chance to respond. "You didn't even mention that you were moving out, so where the fuck are you? You could have texted me, Vi!

"I'm in London, and oh God... Rose, you won't believe what I have been through the past few days! I've been kidnapped, but don't worry, I managed to escape, but you have to come and get me! I'm begging you to come and get me!" Tears welled up in my eyes as my emotions became too much. All the fear and anxiety was overwhelming me.

Rose was silent for a second or two, no doubt processing what I had said to her. When she spoke, it was clear she was freaking out.

"Oh my God, oh my God, oh my God, Vi! What? You need to get out of there now!" she exclaimed loudly.

"That's why you need to come and get me! I'm scared if I stick around here any longer, he'll find and kill me. I managed to escape, but he knows London better than I do, and I can't afford to stay in a hotel for another few days. Please, Rose, please come and get me! Please! I'm begging you!" A tear streamed down my face as I pleaded with her. The reality was too hard to bare. Not only had I been kidnapped by something I thought to be a work of fiction, but I had barely escaped with my life, and now I'm hiding away in a hotel with not enough money to last.

Reality was a fucking nightmare.

"Oh, God. Don't cry, Violet. I'll call the police, and they'll get you!"

"No, no police!" I protested quickly. "If he sees his picture in the newspaper, he won't hesitate to find me and kill me. I just need to get out of London, please!"

"Okay, that makes sense. Oh god, oh god. Right, erm... Here's what we'll do! I will borrow my dad's car tomorrow, and I'll set off around 8 AM. Do you have your phone?"

"No. He's taken it."

"Oh, God. How am I meant to tell you when I arrive?" she asked, sheer panic in her voice.

"I'll stay in the hotel all day, then you can just go in and ask for me," I stated, wiping away my tears though they were quickly replaced.

"Okay, okay, good," she said, taking a deep breath. "Are you okay, though? Really? I mean, he hasn't hurt you? Oh god. What if he's planning your murder like in the horror films?"

"Not helping, Rose!"

"Oh, sorry. I'm just freaking out..." she spoke sheepishly into the phone.

"So am I."

Rose and I must have been on the phone for about fifteen minutes before she was satisfied I was safe. It was not like I was planning on leaving the hotel because that would be stupid. I was safe in the hotel room, so that was where I was going to stay until the time came to leave.

I had given her all the information she would need to get here, and after promising me she would be here around 1 PM, I hung up.

All I could do now was wait anxiously, fearing every footstep that sounded close to the hotel room I occupied.

Chapter Seven

I was awake far too early the next morning, earlier than I usually woke up to, but the chance of sleeping proved to be impossible since I was too on edge. So I spent three or so hours in the hotel, skipping breakfast entirely as there was no way I would be able to keep anything down. I laid on the bed, letting time pass by and just hoping, praying, that Rose would turn up soon.

So when the clock struck 3 PM, and there was no sign of Rose, I began to get agitated. *Where is she?* I wondered to myself as I headed down to the lobby in the hopes that she would just be pulling up. If she set off as early as she said she would, she should have been here by now.

She was nowhere to be seen.

Using the phone at the reception desk, I tried to ring her, but nothing came of it; she didn't pick up. I tried calling three times but to no avail. I started to get worried. What if she had an accident on her way here? There was no doubt in my mind that she had been speeding as much as she could to get to me as soon as possible. She would do anything for her friends, including risking being pulled over.

Another hour went by of me just sitting in the lobby, watching out for any signs of my friend. Then I spotted two people walking in, people I had not been expecting to see again.

Jane and William came over to me when they saw me sitting in the corner by the elevators. They were both smiling as they came to a stop in front of me, and I could not resist smiling back at them.

"We wanted to see you off," William told me as they sat down. "What time is your friend coming to pick you up?"

"She should have been here by now," I admitted, anxiously.

"Have you tried to call her?"

"She's not answering. I'm beginning to get worried. What if something has happened to her?" I asked though the question was purely rhetorical. I was glad when they decided to answer me.

"I don't think any harm will have come to her," Jane said, nodding to herself. "The traffic is horrendous in London. I assume she's stuck in it and will be here as fast as she can."

"I hope so." I nodded, her words putting me at ease.

"Is there anything you need before you go? We'll be more than happy to help you," Jane asked.

I shook my head. "No, don't worry. You've helped me enough by bringing me here. All I want now is to go home."

They both frowned once I had stopped speaking. At first, I thought they were offended by my words—though I was confused as to why they would be. Then, when William spoke, all my fears once again came to the surface.

"You were taken, weren't you?" he asked but did not pause to let me answer him. "I suspected as much, but now, I'm almost certain of it! Who is it that did this? We should inform the police!"

"No!" I burst out, shaking my head vehemently. "That's not necessary, honestly. I don't think they will come after me once I'm back home. I'm sure of it."

"But if you were taken against your will, who's to say they won't do it to anyone else?" William exclaimed, eyes wide with concern. "You can't possibly want that to happen."

"Of course, I don't," I said, not knowing what else to say because he was right. The police should be involved in this to make sure that everyone is safe from him, but how could I get the police involved when Shadow would just kill them? He is a vampire so he would have no problem killing anybody that I got involved in this. It was his nature, after all, though I did wonder whether he ever felt guilty for taking so many lives. Just because he is a vampire did not necessarily mean he did not hate the fact he had to drain people to survive.

I nearly laughed at the thought. He had shown little remorse for anything, and it was understood that the only emotion he was capable of was anger. How could I put anyone in danger of crossing paths with him? It would not go down well.

"Don't upset the poor girl, Will." Jane frowned at her husband before turning to me. "We will wait with you, just until your friend arrives."

She seemed determined to make sure I was safe, and while I appreciated their willingness to help me—such a thing was rare these days—I refused to put them in any more unnecessary danger. If Shadow had all his friends out looking for me and one of them reported back to him, I could not be too sure he would not kill the old couple just to prove a point. Not knowing how many friends he even had was not doing much to help ease my anxiety. I had no idea how many were out there.

Every time someone walked past the three of us, I was worried that they would turn out to be a friend of Shadow. I tried to figure out who was a vampire and who was not, but I had no idea what to look for, and I knew that unless they walked around flashing their fangs, I had no hope in hell of figuring it out.

Shadow had seemed to be a perfectly ordinary man until he proved otherwise. A crazy person, sure, but just a man. If it had not been for the fact he preferred his meals to have a pulse, I still would have assumed he was just delusional, deranged, and demented—any word that could describe a crazy person, and that was what I would have used to describe him. Now I knew the truth, I had no idea what to believe.

Recalling the books I had seen yesterday, I knew I needed to get my hands on a copy. Books had never failed me before, and since I was an avid reader, I knew that if there was any hope of me understanding anything about vampires aside from the basics, it could be found in a book. Folklore would shed some light. I would have to do my research.

Apart from that, I would also have to tell Rose about my dad because she would want to know why I could not go back to him. It probably would not take much persuasion to get her parents to agree to let me stay with them. They treated me as one of their own.

"Are you okay, dear? You've gone a little pale," Jane spoke, interrupting my thoughts as she then took my hand in hers.

"I'm as okay as anyone can be in this situation." I sighed, glancing at the floor.

"Excuse me, miss?" a voice spoke, interrupting our conversation. The three of us glanced to the source to see that an average sized male with cropped blonde hair was standing with his arms behind his back, staring straight at me. Dressed in a uniform, it was obvious he was an employee at the hotel and from the name tag attached to his shirt, I saw that his name was Ric.

"Yes?" I asked, wondering what he could want.

"There is a young lady asking for you at the reception," he told me, causing me to smile. Rose had finally arrived!

Standing up, eager to leave, the old couple seemed to have the same thought for they both pulled me into a quick hug. I thanked them both for helping me though they both shrugged it off, claiming it was what anyone would do.

As they left, I followed Ric to the reception desk, looking around for Rose. I was so happy, so relieved to finally be going home, to be safe from the clutches of a vampire... that I barely had time to process the fact that it was not Rose that stood waiting for me but Leah.

I immediately tried to back away, but she was in front of me in an instant with a smile on her face.

"I'm so sorry," she said, before gripping my arm to make sure I could not escape.

"No, please. Let me go," I begged her. It was no use; she was not listening. How the hell had she managed to find me so quickly? There were tons of hotels in London. How the hell had she known to come to this particular one?

"I'm sorry." She apologised again before turning to Ric. "What room was she in?"

"207."

"Off we go then. Thanks for the help, Ric!" Leah said, taking me to the elevator and linking her arm through mine so that any onlooker would think we were friends. I knew better; it was to prevent me from making a run for it.

The second we were inside my hotel room, Leah pushed me towards the bed and told me to sit. I did as she said, perching on the end of the bed.

I watched in silence as she whipped out her phone, calling who I knew was Shadow. He was the one looking for me, after all, so it made sense. The conversation did not last long though, only a couple of minutes. All she needed to do was tell him where she was.

I knew that the second Shadow arrived, I would probably be killed. I had done nothing but anger him further in my attempts to get away, and I had actually succeeded. I had done the one thing guaranteed to land me a place in the morgue. My body began to tremble as images flashed through my mind, much to Leah's amusement.

"You act like he's going to kill you." She grinned, leaning against the wall opposite the bed and folding her arms across her chest.

"I'm not stupid. I know that's what he's going to do." I rubbed my hands up and down my arms and managed to stop shaking. *I just have to come to terms with it*, I told myself. It was not like I had much of a choice. *It's just like when I was living with my dad*, I tried to fool myself into thinking. Yes, it was no different.

"You clearly are stupid if you believe that. He isn't going to kill you despite the fact he's probably already threatened to. He thought he was helping by bringing you here. Even if he did change his mind, I wouldn't let him kill you."

"Why?"

"Because despite what you think, he isn't a monster."

"What else would you call a vampire?" I asked her without thinking.

She quickly straightened up, and in a split second, her eyes had changed from their usual colour to a deep red. As she took a step towards me, I saw the fangs.

Another vampire.

Just my luck.

"Get away from me!" I said, scooting further up the bed in fear.

"Oh, calm down. I'm not going to hurt you." She rolled her eyes, calming down as her eyes went back to normal and her fangs disappeared. "Not all vampires are soulless monsters, you know. Shadow saved you and has kept you alive, so you really should consider yourself lucky because he'd usually have killed you by now."

"He could have just let me go," I told her.

"And where would you have gone with little money?" She shot back with raised eyebrows.

Well, she had me there, but that was not the point.

"I'm so confused," I whispered under my breath. Leah heard my words and grinned at me.

"Don't be. Once you forget what you've seen in films, you'll soon realise that we're not as bad as we're portrayed to be."

"So you don't sleep in coffins?" I could not help but ask.

She shuddered. "Ew, no. I prefer a king size bed, thanks."

Although I was absolutely terrified for my life, her response made me smile. In comparison to Shadow, she was not that bad.

The fact I even thought that proved just how insane this whole thing was making me.

"Shadow's here," she suddenly stated, leaning against the wall again, but just before I could question as to how she could possibly know that, the door opened, and in walked the source of my problems.

He did not even spare a glance at Leah because his gaze remained fixated on me as he shut the door behind him, his customary smirk in place. Walking over to the bed, I leaned to one side, trying to put some distance between us even though it was pointless.

I found myself wishing that the old couple had called the police. At least I would have been away from Shadow.

He pulled me to my feet, gripping my arms with his hands as he spoke. "Did you honestly think we wouldn't find you? It was obvious you'd go to a hotel; it was just a matter of finding the cheapest one though we did have Ric helping. I know you've already met him."

So the man that had led me to Leah was one of their friends. Great. Just great. How many vampires were living here?

"What are you going to do with her?" Leah asked him, coming to stand beside him and placing her hand on his shoulder. "You're not going to kill her, Shadow."

"I haven't decided yet," was all he said in response, leading me out of the room with Leah trailing silently behind us.

As we left, I realised he had not said he was not going to kill me, and that only doubled my fear.

Chapter Eight

Walking to my certain death, I tried not to upset the two of them any further than I already had. However, I could not just pretend like it was not scaring me that I was being led to the house that I knew I would die in.

It was strange, when I thought about it, how much I had wanted to die in the hands of my dad but now that I was here in London, kidnapped by vampires, I wanted nothing more than to live. I wanted to get away, go back home, and try to move on from it. I knew I definitely did no want to die, not anymore. It was strange to think how quickly my mind had changed on that fact.

Then again, if I were to die, I would rather do it on my own terms and in my own way rather than being tortured and having the blood sucked out of me—literally. Whatever Shadow's methods of torture were, I knew it was not going to be pretty. I would be in a lot of pain, much more than I had ever been in living with my dad. I would not be able to handle it.

Once at Shadow's home, I was taken to the bedroom I had woken up in the day after I was taken. Before Leah left me alone with

Shadow, she shot me an encouraging smile that only confused me. If it was meant to be reassuring, it did not work.

It was not until Shadow closed the door that I noticed it had been replaced. I knew instantly that it was to make sure I could not escape again.

"Now," he started speaking, releasing his grip on me, so I immediately stepped back. "What do I do with you?"

"Let me go?" I suggested meekly.

"That's never going to happen."

"You can't keep me here." I shook my head. "I'll never stop trying to escape."

"Try all you want, but you'll never succeed a second time."

"I don't understand. If you're going to kill me, then why don't you just do it?!

He shrugged, giving no indication that he was going to answer my question. I was not particularly sure he knew what to do himself, and I had almost convinced myself that he was just winging the whole thing... until he said three words that made me breathe in deeply.

"You will die."

He left the room without so much as another word, locking it behind him.

This is what my life had come to—being trapped in a bedroom with nothing but my thoughts for company and no means of escaping again.

***

Sighing, I sat down on the window ledge and stared out the window, resting my head against it. I could not believe I was now trapped with another male that only wanted to hurt me. I really did have the world's worst luck.

I soon started contemplating everything that had gone wrong in my life, and I could pinpoint it down to one event—just one event, and from there, everything started rapidly going downhill. Everything started to go wrong when my mother left, and I could not help but put some of the blame on her. If she had not left, my dad would not have changed so much. If she had not left, I would not have been abused and then made homeless. If my dad had not kicked me out, I would not have been kidnapped by a vampire and held captive. It was a chain of events that led me to this situation, and it all led back to her leaving.

Of course, I only had my dad to blame for the way he changed. It was not my mother's fault he turned into a selfish ass. It was hard to believe I once had a happy life.

For a moment, I thought about my mother. I had so many questions I wanted to ask her if I saw her again. I did feel a little sadness to know that she did not care about me enough to stick around, and I did feel angry that she had left without bothering to explain herself. She could have gone off to have another baby for all I knew, for she had always wanted another. I did not even know if her and my dad were still legally married or not because I had been so concerned about getting through the days living with him. I had little time worrying about anything else.

I knew I could not ever forgive her for leaving, though, and I doubted anyone would ever make me change my mind about that. To me, I had lost both my parents the day she walked out on me.

***

I was definitely losing it. The reason for that conclusion being that over the hours I was left alone with my thoughts, the fear started to dissipate. Not being as scared of the fact I was locked away with no idea on when or *if* I was ever going to get away was just crazy.

I was now more curious than anything else. That was probably dangerous, but I could not help it. When I was fifteen, I had been fascinated by vampires, and now that I was in the same house as one, I found myself wanting to know about them. It was not like I was scared of vampires in general, it was more of what they could do. As Shadow had so *eloquently* put it—note the sarcasm—he would torture me in any manner he thought necessary, in ways I had never heard of. I shuddered, thinking of what things he had in mind because I had seen a lot of horror movies. I knew a thing or two about torturing someone. So while I may not fear death anymore, I did fear the ways that I would be put to my death. The thing that scared me about Shadow was simple.

He drank people's blood because he had to.

He tortured and killed people because he wanted to.

There was a significant difference between the two. Perhaps, that was why I was more curious than fearful now. If he wanted to torture me, surely he would have done it the instant he had brought me back here rather than take me around London. That was not the typical behaviour of someone who did not want any witnesses. By taking me around London and threatening those men, he had two witnesses that could swear they saw us together. If I was murdered, they would be able to tell the police that they saw me with Shadow.

It was a comforting thought that my death wouldn't go unsolved. Plus, if Rose helped out—which I knew she would—she would be able to tell them that I had been kidnapped and that I had explicitly told her so.

Thinking of Rose suddenly caused a wave of panic to brew up within me. Where was she? Had she arrived at the hotel yet? What was she doing? If she had gotten there and found I was nowhere to be seen, she would be freaking out. I knew she would not hesitate to call the police either. Then my mind started straying towards much darker thoughts.

What if...

No. I shook my head. That was not possible.

Was it? I was not sure, but I knew I had to find out.

Jumping from the window ledge, I ran over to the door and started hammering on it, screaming at the top of my lungs to let me out of the room. It probably would have been a lot easier to convince him if I had pretended I needed the toilet or something, but in the midst of my panic, the rational side of my brain was nowhere to be seen.

Yelling proved to work well enough, though, because it was only a matter of seconds before the door was unlocked and opened. Seeing Shadow standing there with an unreadable expression on his face, I knew I had probably annoyed him, but at that moment, I did not care.

"Where's Rose?" I asked, getting straight to the point.

His facial expression betrayed nothing.

"Where's Rose?" I asked again. "She should have been at that hotel hours before you found me. You've done something to her, haven't you? I swear, if you've hur—"

"Relax." He cut me off, rolling his eyes. "I don't know where your friend is. How could I?"

"You have my phone," I stated, not impressed by his blatant lying.

"It's password protected." He was looking amused now, more so by the fact he had to remind me my own phone had a password. He could not actually get into it.

"Oh." I suddenly felt embarrassed, and a blush formed on my cheeks.

"Speaking of which, I didn't think you would be happy if I smashed it, but if you don't shut the damn thing up, I will break it," he said, pulling out my phone from his pocket and handing it over to me.

I glanced down at it, relieved to see that it had not been broken like I suspected it would be. Why he had kept it for me, I had no idea, but I did not dwell on it because I noticed I had over twenty messages and fourteen missed calls. All of them were from Rose, so I quickly pressed the call button, holding my phone to my ear and staring at Shadow. I half expected him to rip it from my hands, but he did not.

"You're in enough trouble," he said instead. "Don't make things worse."

When Rose picked up, she did not even give me the chance to say anything because she was already yelling down the phone at me.

"WHERE THE HELL ARE YOU?! I've been at the hotel for half an hour, and you're nowhere to be seen! I asked at reception, and they told me you checked out, you fucking idiot! Where are you?"

It didn't surprise me that 'I' had checked out because Shadow probably had his friend, Ric, make it look that way.

Wanting to put her fears at rest, I started to speak, fully aware that Shadow was listening to every word. I knew I had to be careful with my words.

"Relax, Rose, I'm safe! The man that kidnapped me came to the hotel, so I had to leave. I was wandering around trying to come up with a plan when I saw my grandparents. On my mother's side, Rose! I haven't seen them in years, so they took me in, and I'll be staying with them for a while! Isn't that great?" The lie spilled from my lips effortlessly, surprising myself with how fast it had come to mind, but as long as she believed it, that was all that mattered.

"So you're safe? You got away?" she asked though I could hear the scepticism in her voice.

"Yeah, I'm safe." I lied again.

"So why the phone calls and messages asking where I was?" She did not believe me. That much was clear, and I cast a glance at Shadow, who was watching me carefully, waiting to see what I would say. As he made no indication to what I should say in response, I said the first thing that came to mind.

"I thought something had happened. You were late picking me up, and you're never late, so I got worried, and when you didn't answer your phone, I just panicked because you're glued to the thing."

"Well, that makes sense, I guess. My alarm didn't go off, so I didn't wake up until around ten, and I don't answer my phone when I'm driving. But swear to me right now. Are you really safe? Do I need to come kick some guys ass for kidnapping my best friend?" she asks, seriously.

I laughed. "No, you don't need to kick anyone's ass."

"Good because I just had my nails done, and that would seriously do some damage." She teased.

"Hey!" I said, a plan coming to mind. It was the only plan I could come up with that might actually work. "Are you still in London?"

"Obviously."

"Where are you? I'll meet you, and we can walk around for a bit."

It was evident by the glare on Shadow's face that he was not happy about my plan, but as I was on the phone, there was not much he could do. When he reached out to grab my phone, I quickly stepped back and held my free hand up. I felt more at ease knowing that Shadow could not possibly hurt me for saying I'll meet up with Rose. He could not, not when I was on the phone. As far as she was aware, I had gotten away and was safe.

If only she knew.

***

Shadow had been extremely adamant that I don't leave the house after the phone call. Knowing Rose, I explained that there was no possible way she would leave London without seeing me face to face to make sure I was okay, and even Shadow could not deny I had a point. Not when she knew I had been kidnapped. It would only make her more suspicious and go to the police.

That was how I ended up sitting in a cafe with Rose as Shadow and Leah sat at another table. Them coming along was the only possible way I could see Rose. They were too afraid of what I would say to her if we were alone. I understood that, but if they actually did just let me go, I would not have had to tell her anything other than I could go with her.

Clearly, that was not going to happen, and I just did not understand why. If they only just let be free, I could just pretend it never happened. Nobody would ever believe me if I told them the truth, so it was not like they had a valid reason to be worried about me saying something.

"So what happened? You just got kidnapped from your bed?" Rose asked, lowering her voice to a whisper so no one could hear our conversation, apart from the two vampires in the corner—not that she knew that, of course.

"I wasn't at home when I was taken." I shook my head. "I was on my way to a hotel when it happened."

She frowned. "Why were you going to a hotel?"

"My dad kicked me out."

"Why?"

As much as I did not want to tell her when there were two vampires listening in, I knew she would not drop it until she knew. I had planned on telling her anyway, and it was probably better that I just get it out of the way.

"You know when my mum left?" I started, mentally preparing how I was going to say this.

"How could I forget that day?" She smiled sympathetically. "It may have been four years ago, but I still remember you, me, and your dad watching shitty movies and eating our body weight in ice cream."

"Yeah..." I trailed off uncomfortably, remembering the day clearly. After I had called Rose and told her what happened, she had turned up with a bag filled with DVDs and tubs of ice cream. It was the last day my dad acted like a caring, family man.

"What about it, Vi?" Rose asked in confusion.

"Well, ever since she left, things haven't been the same." I took a deep breath. "My dad started drinking a lot more, and when he got angry—which was pretty much all the time—he needed an outlet, I guess. I suppose he figured I was a better punching bag than any actual punching bag. That went on for years before he finally had enough of that and kicked me out."

Tears blurred my vision, threatening to spill over, and I quickly wiped my eyes to prevent that from happening; I refused to cry in a public place.

Rose gaped at me in horror, seeming at a loss for words. That in itself was a miracle because she always knew what to say, but this time, her mouth opened and closed as though all words had failed her.

Her eyes welled up with tears too as she finally managed to speak with widened eyes. "Are you seriously telling me that he abused you for four fucking years? All because your mum left? Shit, Vi... Why did you never tell me?"

"I was scared," I admitted, smiling sadly. "I didn't want to risk him hurting you. It was just better that I keep quiet, but I did want to tell you. There were so many times I almost did, but I couldn't risk it."

"Oh, my god. I'm so sorry. I should have known. I should have realised! You did get all depressed, but I just thought you were missing her. I didn't ever think he was hurting you! How bad was it? I mean, what…. I mean… I don't even know what I mean."

"It got to the point I didn't think I'd make it out alive, and I kinda accepted that. I was struggling to get through an hour, never mind a day, so the thought of death was actually comforting because it meant I wouldn't be in pain anymore."

"In a sick, twisted sort of way, being brought here was the best thing to happen to you then, wasn't it?" she asked sadly, wiping her eyes. "You got away from the man that brought you here, and you're staying with your grandparents. It sort of worked out, didn't it?"

"Yeah..." I had never thought of it like that before. Sure, it had crossed my mind that being here meant I was away from my dad, but I did not ever think that what had happened was a good thing. Then again, she would think that considering she believed I had gotten away.

"You still need to tell the police, though... or your grandparents!"

"No, you can't! I mean it, Rose, you can't! Promise me you won't. Promise me," I pleaded with her to listen, to promise that she would not tell anyone. The consequences would not be good.

It did take a while to convince her to keep quiet about it, but eventually, she seemed to realise what would happen if I did tell the police.

When she had calmed down enough to talk rationally, she then started to question me about it, and this time, I did not hold back. It was a relief to finally get it all off my chest.

"You said he kicked you out, but do you think he would have stopped?" she asked warily, almost like she was afraid of the answer. I could not blame her.

I shook my head. "I had a choice that night, Rose. Either I leave and finally get away from him, or I stay where he would kill me."

"You seem certain he would." She observed.

"With the things he did… I wouldn't put it past him."

"How could he do that to you? I've never seen him angry before, not before your mum left and not even after..." She spoke quietly. Her voice was filled with emotion.

I shrugged. "I really don't know."

"But to go that far... to kill you, I mean. Surely, he wouldn't have, would he?"

"I honestly believe he was just biding his time, dragging it out as long as possible until he got to the main event." I chuckled darkly.

Just as Rose was about to speak, there was a loud noise coming from the corner table. Instantly, all heads turned to the source of the noise to see that Shadow was standing up with the shattered pieces of a coffee cup all over the floor. His eyes, I noticed, were fixed on me, and it was then that I remembered he had been listening.

I could not believe I had actually forgotten he would be eavesdropping. For a moment, I was entirely lost in the memories of my horrific past that not one thought was directed at the vampires sitting in the corner.

"Whoa, he's the sexiest man I've ever seen in my life," Rose suddenly commented, glancing at Shadow and licking her lips.

I had to agree. He was incredibly good looking.

Watching Leah reach over to him and pull him back down, I could see that she was saying something, but I could not hear. I did not have vampire hearing after all. It was a shame, though, for I would have liked to know what she said to calm him down.

"Trust the hot one to be taken," Rose mumbled before turning back to me. "Anyway, I think you should come and stay with me. You know my dad can help, and I don't wanna leave you."

"Honestly, it's fine. I'm safer here than I am back there." At least, I thought I was. I was still holding onto the hope that maybe the vampires weren't going to torture me.

"Are you sure? I don't want to leave you."

"Honestly, I'd really rather be here than anywhere close to him." That, at least, was the truth.

"I wish I could stay, but my dad needs his car back, so you have to promise me you will call and text me every day! I'll come visit you again when I can, but if I don't hear from you, I'm coming back here purely to slap you," she stated as she got to her feet. "I really wish I didn't have to leave."

I stood up, smiling softly. "It's fine. I'll text you later."

"One question, though, before I go. Are you in any pain now? Do you need painkillers?" she asked seriously.

Touched by her concern for me, I pulled her into a hug. "No, I'm not in any pain. Not anymore."

Shadow was still watching me as I spoke.

Chapter Nine

A week had gone by, and I was still stuck in the house. There had been a considerable change in the way that both Shadow and Leah acted towards me, though. They were still blunt with the way they said things, but after learning of my past, it was like they felt guilty or something.

I understood why they were concerned because if I learned that someone had been abused, I would be worried, too. However, when that concern was coming from a man that had kidnapped me, could anyone really blame me for not knowing what to think? Shadow had even told me that he was not going to torture me on account of being abused, which had been shocking enough, really. It just felt like I was being treated like a fragile little doll, and though I was glad of that fact because it meant he was not going to hurt me, I was slightly frustrated by it too.

After my confession to Rose, they had wanted to see the bruises the second we had gotten home. I had shown them, knowing there was no point in refusing—they had been determined to see them, after all. It was then that Shadow realised what I had meant by bruises, and he had seemed relieved to find out that I was not in any pain.

I was still confined to the bedroom, something I doubted would change, but they had allowed me to keep my phone. Just giving me that back made me realise they did not intend to hurt me because if they were, they would not have given it back. I had no idea why they could not just let me go, though. I suspected it had to do with the fact I knew more about them than I should.

As well as giving me my phone, Shadow had also given me my suitcase back the day of my confession. Honestly, I was so happy, I could have screamed. I had assumed it was gone forever.

I knew that I was still in danger, though, in a constant state of impending doom because he could change his mind at a moment's notice and just decide to kill me. Yet as the week went by, he seemed to be a lot calmer, no longer as angry as he had been before. He was actually making an effort to keep his anger contained and had been the one to bring me my meals. I was still locked away like a prisoner, but I no longer jumped every time the door opened.

Being confined to the bedroom came with its disadvantages, though, and it was not because I could not escape. It gave me too much time alone with my thoughts, ones that could be quite dark at times. I found myself regretting that I had stabbed Shadow though it had been necessary under the circumstances. I found myself wishing that I could just die. Worst of all, I found myself wishing I would never be allowed to leave because the harsh reality was that if Shadow told me to leave, I would not have anywhere to go. I could not impose myself upon Rose and her family. That was not right no matter how much she disagreed, and to be honest, a part of me did not want to have to go back there ever again.

I still had not laid my hands on the books I wanted either, and I doubted I would be allowed out of the bedroom to get them. Every meal they brought for me was to be eaten in the room, and then they would come and collect the plate afterwards. I was only allowed to leave the room to shower and use the toilet.

There was a part of me that thought being locked in my own 'prison cell' was better than being in a hotel back home with no idea what to do next. I was confused, unbelievably so, about everything. Since Shadow and Leah found out about my past, they had been kind to me, too kind in fact. I was still on edge, but their sudden kindness was beginning to freak me out a little because it just had me questioning whether they had a plan in mind. I could not seem to figure out what their intentions were, and not knowing was frightening.

So to say I was confused about the circumstances in which I found myself was definitely the understatement of the century. I had no idea what to think or feel. I wanted them to let me go, but if they did, I did not have a place to go. I was scared he was going to change his mind about hurting me even though he seemed to be making an effort not to scare me so much. I was scared of him and what he was, but I was also curious, intrigued even, by him.

It was safe to assume my mind was in total chaos.

***

I was laying on the bed, playing *Monster Busters* on my phone when the bedroom door was unlocked and in stepped a frustrated looking Shadow. I immediately sat up, watching him warily. I had no idea what the source of his frustration was, but it would not surprise me if it were something I had done despite the fact I had been in the same damn room all day.

He barely looked at me, though. Instead, he stormed over to the window and stared out of it. I kept quiet, waiting patiently for him to say something, to explain why he had just burst into the room the way he had.

It was a couple of minutes of an awkward and uncomfortable silence before he finally turned to face me with a clenched jaw.

"We're going out," he spoke through gritted teeth.

"What, where?" I asked, taken aback.

"The neighbours are being too nosy. So get up, grab a bag, and let's go." He clearly was not in the mood for talking, so I shrugged to myself, getting up off the bed. At least I was actually able to leave the room because it was getting a little boring. I did not bother with a bag, though, and instead stuffed some money into the pocket of my jeans and kept hold of my phone. I preferred not to use a bag.

"Ready," I said, looking at him to see that he was already watching me. I noticed he was frowning. His brows furrowed as though something was troubling him and not just the neighbours.

"Let's go then," he said, exiting the room without another word.

I quickly followed behind him, happy that I was finally getting the chance to go outside. I was looking forward to being out in the fresh air for a change.

The second we had gotten outside, I took a deep breath, painting a huge smile on my face that caught Shadow's immediate attention. He looked almost amused by my behaviour, something that instantly made me blush. I was not used to having someone paying so much attention to me even if it was just to keep an eye on me.

Admittedly, I was nervous about being alone with Shadow as Leah was not with us, but I knew this was one of the rare times I would be able to talk to Shadow. Being a curious person, I wanted to know about him. The curiosity was only growing in the past week. It was not every day that you get the chance to meet a vampire, after all, so I definitely wanted to know whether the things I had seen and read were a work of fiction or whether they had a sliver of truth to them.

I held off on asking questions at first because he still seemed frustrated but eventually, after half an hour or so, he seemed a little calmer, so I took that as my chance. The silence that had settled over us was making me feel uncomfortable, so I was desperate to get rid of it.

We were walking down Oxford Street when I decided to try my luck.

"Shadow?"

He looked at me, eyebrows raised. He clearly was not expecting me to talk.

"Erm... how old are you?" I asked nervously.

He chuckled, turning back to the street. "145."

My eyes widened. "Wow, okay. Erm..."

"Is there a reason you're asking?"

I grinned sheepishly. "I'm curious."

"About me?" He seemed surprised by that, glancing at me in confusion.

"About vampires."

"So you want to know whether the films portray us the way we actually are." He guessed, hitting the nail on the head there. I did not reply, though, not knowing what to say.

"Is there anywhere you want to go?" he then asked, changing the subject.

"Waterstones," I told him.

"You're a bookworm then?" he asked conversationally.

I nodded, smiling as I thought about all the books I had read.

"Reading is one of the things that helps me take my mind off the life I have."

Shadow sighed. "About that... I'm truly sorry for what you have suffered. Nobody should ever go through that."

"Thanks?" I replied though it came out more of a question than anything. I was not expecting him to mention that as everything that needed to be said had already been said when he demanded to see the bruises. There was not anything left to say. "That's why you've been so nice to me, isn't it?"

"There's no point in denying I have thought about killing you, but I have never planned on doing it. Who knows? Maybe if you get on my nerves, I'll still kill you. I just won't torture you first," he said, smirking as he saw my horrified expression. "I'm only joking. I only torture those that deserve it."

I decided not to ask about who he thought 'deserved' to be tortured because I was sure I did not want to know. Instead, I asked, "So there are more vampires?"

"Many more."

"Are you friends with them all?"

"Are you friends with all of the human population?" he asked, looking at me with an expression on his face that had me feeling stupid in an instant.

"No." I shook my head, biting my lip as another blush rose to my cheeks.

"Then don't ask such stupid questions." Shadow rolled his eyes, but I saw a flicker of amusement on his face. "There is one thing that you should know about vampires, though."

"What?"

He smirked, a crazy and dangerous look in his eyes. "We're all monsters."

That comment never left my mind for the rest of the day. Even as I purchased the books I had my eye on, I could not stop thinking about his statement. Of course, I believed it to be true, but I was still surprised that he admitted it. I mean, shouldn't he have denied that? I was not sure. I was not sure of much lately. Everything that I had known about life, in general, did not seem to apply to Shadow. He was a murderer, a monster, and a vampire. He was someone who did not abide by the law, choosing instead to go by his own rules. I understood to a degree why he could not follow some of the laws as he needed blood to survive, but he did not have to kill his victims, did he? Couldn't he just wipe their memories? Were vampires even capable of that?

This was why I needed to look up vampires because I had no idea what they could and could not do. Asking Shadow too much always ran the risk of saying the wrong thing.

That was the last thing I wanted to do.

We did not stay out much longer though I did take advantage of the opportunity by asking him more questions. The more I asked him things, the more amused he became, and it actually seemed like he was enjoying answering my questions. I did still feel like an idiot if I asked him something that sounded ridiculous, but all in all, I knew more than I had before, so I took it as a win

Once back at the house with the books I had purchased, I sat down on the bed and took them out of the bag. Grabbing the first one I saw, I settled down to start reading. Opening it up, I glanced at the contents page.

~ ~ ~ Contents ~ ~ ~

Turning the page, I immediately started reading.

Chapter Ten

In this book, we'll be looking at the vampire myth, from where it started in folklore to where it is now. We will talk about how this creature managed to take over the imagination of many, how it has been perceived over the many years since the birth of the vampire legend.

Skipping the rest of the introduction, I went straight to chapter one, "The Vampire Myth." I hoped I would be left with some knowledge about vampires when I eventually finished reading it and not just information I already knew. That would just be a waste of money.

Vampires, in folklore, are creatures that are said to live by feeding on the blood of the living. Vampires are said to be the undead who often visited their loved ones they had left behind. Frequently, they caused all sorts of trouble and murdered others in the neighbourhood they had once lived in and are often described as bloated, dark creatures that are the complete opposite to today's pale-faced vampires that we see on screen.

Communities in the early 19th century were concerned with the dead because the idea of an undead being coming back from the grave to haunt the living had spread among them; superstition was at its highest, and it had filled people with fear.

The superstition did not stop there. As many people believed in spirits, if something were to go wrong, the spirits would naturally be blamed even though they were invoked to help with daily tasks. However, these spirits were considered evil and preferred to wreak havoc instead.

It was believed that when somebody died, their soul would continue to live on, haunting the places they had once lived. To make sure a spirit would leave without causing any trouble, people deemed it important that all burials were carefully observed. This would also explain why they took such care in making sure nobody came back from the dead as a vampire. The hysteria surrounding the vampire myth resulted in corpses actually being staked to prevent the dead from haunting their loved ones.

So, was that how the vampire belief started? Once a soul that lived on after death but soon popularised into an actual body, coming back from the grave?

It certainly seemed likely.

This was definitely going to be an interesting read, I thought to myself. The book then went on to talk about other superstitions and folklore, even going on to mention animals like bats and wolves. Nothing that I had just read helped me understand Shadow any further, which was a little annoying considering I had bought it with the intention of trying to figure out more about him. I just needed to know what was fact and what was fiction because surely, the abilities that vampires had in films or in books had to have come from somewhere—especially since Shadow had one. I still did not know how that was possible.

I had so many questions that I wanted to ask him because I did not know as much as I wanted to. He had been willing enough to answer my questions earlier, but he might not want to answer anymore. I knew he had killed people; he had admitted that to me, anyway. But even if he had not, it was obvious he had. Vampires needed blood to survive, so I did not want him to end up changing his mind about making me his next victim. Curiosity killed the cat, as people say. One wrong move could result in me becoming a vampire's next meal.

Although he had not been too horrible to me since finding out about my dad, the fact still remained that he had kidnapped me and was still refusing to let me go. Obviously, I did not want to get too comfortable with being locked away because he could quickly change his mind. The man was a psychopath after all.

I soon found out just how psychopathic he truly was.

A couple of hours after I had stopped reading, having finished the first chapter, I heard doors slamming and what sounded like a man yelling. I could not hear what he was saying as his words were muffled. I did want to go down to see what was going on, but I could not. The door was still locked... though not for long.

Leah unlocked the door a few minutes after the yelling had started, entering the room and rushing over to me faster than I could blink. Before I could even comprehend what was going on, she had a tight grip on my wrist and was leading me out of the room, not saying a word.

Fear instantly took over me, naturally assuming that he had changed his mind already about keeping me alive. I struggled with all the strength I had in an attempt to get her to release her hold, but nothing worked. With her vampire strength, the only thing that could work was if I had a stake in my possession. I did not. I was left with no choice but try to talk my way out of it.

"Whatever you're planning, don't do it. Please, don't do it. I'm not going anywhere. You've already made sure of that, so there's no reason for you to do this." I begged and pleaded with her.

"Be quiet," Leah spoke in a clipped tone. "I'm only doing this to prove something to you. If you want to make it through this alive, you'd better shut your mouth and do as you're told."

How comforting, I sarcastically thought.

***

Afraid of what was going to happen, I bit my lip to stop from crying out. Leah took me into the kitchen, still refusing to release her grip on me. She probably knew I would try to make a run for it, not that anyone could blame me for that. Her words had only tripled my fear.

The first thing I saw upon entering the kitchen was a man tied to a chair, blood pouring from one side of his face. He looked absolutely terrified; his hands were shaking on the table, and upon seeing us enter the room, his head turned so quickly to face us that I felt nothing but sympathy for him. He was going to be another poor victim of a vampire though I did not know why he had been brought here.

The second thing I noticed was the sheet that was spread across the floor. It was hard to miss, to be honest, considering it took up the whole floor. Seeing that it was stained with something red, bright red, only had my heart racing in my chest. It looked an awful lot like blood.

I almost threw up knowing that because it meant that was the sheet Shadow always used when torturing someone. If he was planning on hurting the man, which seemed likely at this point, then I could not help but wonder what he did. Shadow said he only turned to that if they deserved it. What had this man done? He looked innocent to me.

I hoped that I was wrong, that I had not been brought down here to witness him torturing a man, but really? Why else would I have been brought into the room if not to be a witness? Why would Shadow want me to watch this, though? I wanted to ask him, but I did not dare open my mouth. It was not like I would get any answers from him, anyway. I had more chance of winning the lottery, and we all know that was practically impossible.

The man's eyes widened considerably when they rested on me, a flicker of recognition passing through. Why he was staring at me as though he knew me, I had no idea. I was fairly confident I had never seen him in my entire life.

"You..." he then said, trailing off, his voice barely loud enough for me to hear. His words caused me to frown, trying to figure out how he knew me. I could not seem to remember him from anywhere, though, and that made things even more confusing. He clearly knew me, but how?

"What?"

"Your si—" He was quickly cut off, unable to finish his sentence because Shadow, visibly angry, stepped in front of him. That shut the man up pretty quickly, staring up at Shadow. He was scared, incredibly scared, and I could not blame him. I was too, and I was not even the one currently tied to a chair.

"From now on, if you want to live, you will answer my questions truthfully, and know that if you lie, I will cut off your fingers one by one until you start telling me the truth," Shadow spoke in a low, dangerous tone that had my jaw dropping in shock. Would he really do that? Was he really that into torturing people? Or was he just saying it to gain a reaction because the threat of being hurt could be just as motivating as actually being hurt?

Either way, the man seemed to believe the threat and quickly nodded, his eyes widening even more. Shadow smirked at this and picked up a knife before he sat down in the chair on the other side of the table. Leah kept a tight grip on my wrist though she need not have bothered; I was not going to move. I really did not want to see this, but at the same time, I was too afraid to move. My whole body had tensed up.

"So," Shadow started to speak, running his finger along the knife. "We'll start with the easy questions first. What's your name?"

"Rolan," the man answered immediately.

"Where are you from, Rolan?"

"London."

Shadow was definitely enjoying this; I could tell, and that made me feel even worse, knowing that I could quite easily be in the same position as Rolan. I definitely needed to get away. That was the one thought that circled my mind as I watched the scene in front of me.

"Now, I want to know why you've been standing outside my home for the past couple of days," Shadow then said, but before Rolan could even deny it, Shadow continued. "And I want to know why you were following Violet and me today."

Taken aback by his question, I blinked. What the hell was he talking about? Wouldn't I have noticed if somebody had been following us today?

"I h-haven't." Rolan stuttered.

I felt like telling him to remain calm because him stuttering at that question just proved he was lying. Shadow, realising this too, shook his head, and in mere seconds, he had Rolan's hand on the table, making his fingers easily accessible for him. I really hoped he was not going to do what he said. It made me feel sick just thinking about it, never mind actually seeing it happen.

"Last chance before you lose a finger." Shadow taunted, clearly amused. I could see he was determined to get to the bottom of it. There was an underlying sense of tension coming from him, but that was probably just because he wanted answers.

"I haven't," he said, trying to appear calmer than he was before, clearly realising his mistake. Rolan was shaking by this point, trying to get his hand away from Shadow but there was no way he would be able to get his hand free from a vampire, not when that vampire intended on keeping him in place.

"You're lying."

"I'm not, I swear!" Rolan cried out. "Please, let me go. I've done nothing wrong!"

"Ah, but that's where you're wrong. I know you have been following Violet, and I want to know why. Now!" Shadow's anger was increasing every second the man denied what Shadow knew to be the truth. I wanted to help Rolan somehow, but I was stuck, glued to the spot as I was too afraid of becoming the next victim. Shadow and Leah had been kind enough since they found out about my father, but I was not sure how long that kindness was going to last.

"I don't know her. I swear!"

Everyone knew that was a lie considering he had tried talking to me.

"You've already proved that's not true. You're time is up," Shadow said, raising the knife. Just as it was coming down, Rolan screamed.

"No, wait!"

Shadow halted his movements inches away from Rolan's hand.

"I was asked to find her, that's all! I was given a picture and was told to find her! I swear that's all I know! Please let me go, please!" Rolan begged.

"Who told you to find her?" Shadow questioned. There was a gleam in his eyes that I did not like.

"I don't know," Rolan said, clearly lying. How else would he get a picture of me if he did not see who was giving it to him?

The blade came down so quickly, I could barely process it. Rolan screamed, and Leah ran up behind him, covering his mouth so nobody would hear him. There was blood spurting from his hand and there, on the table, lay a pinky finger.

I clamped a hand over my mouth as my stomach churned and tears built up in my eyes. I knew I should be helping somehow, but I was not sure how to. That poor man, whatever he was asked to do, did not deserve to be tortured. I felt sick, and it was taking everything in me not to throw up all over the floor.

"Stop," I whispered. "Stop, please."

"Not going to happen, sweetheart. I don't approve of lying," Shadow replied, not even the slightest bit bothered. "So, Rolan, are you going to tell me the truth this time?"

Rolan seemed incapable of saying anything now as he cried out over the pain of his missing finger.

"Come on, Rolan, or you'll soon have no fingers at all," Shadow said, leaning forward again, still keeping a tight grip on Rolan's wrist.

"I d-don't know!" He stuttered, eyes locked on his hand.

I kept watching purely because I could not bring myself to look away. I wanted to get Shadow to stop, but I knew he was not going to. He had told me this would happen, that he tortured those he felt deserved it, so there was no getting him to stop until he felt like it—or until he got answers. Whether or not he was following me because someone told him to, I did not care at that moment. What I did care about was the fact I had just witnessed Shadow chopping off one of Rolan's fingers. The fear I felt in his presence, the fear that had gradually been disappearing a little, came back full force. I suppose I always assumed that he was all talk because he had not actually proved he liked hurting people for the hell of it, but now that I had witnessed what he was capable of, I felt well and truly idiotic for ever being intrigued by him in the slightest.

A monster—that was all he was.

Why do I need to know anything else other than that?

It was not until I was about to save Rolan from losing any more fingers that Shadow had raised the knife once again. I opened my mouth to speak, but the knife came down at the last moment, and this time, it was not just Rolan screaming. It was me.

A loud, piercing scream came from me as I stared, wide-eyed, at the scene before me. I could not watch it happen again. I just could not.

"Stop, stop, stop, stop, please, just STOP!" I yelled, sinking to the floor with my hands covering my face. Bringing my knees up against my chest, I curled into a ball, shaking. This was too much for me. It was too much for anyone. I was perfectly fine with watching something like this in a horror movie because it was not real, but seeing it for real, well, it was enough to cause even the strongest man to feel weak at the knees.

I was not aware what happened next as the sight of Rolan's fingers being chopped off was ingrained in my mind. It was the worst thing I had ever seen, and being with my dad, I had endured a lot myself. Watching a man being tortured not only made me feel sick, but it brought back memories of the abuse I had suffered. It also reminded me of the fact of my situation. One wrong move on my part and I could be the next person sitting in that chair.

It was all too much for me.

Feeling dizzy, I was aware that someone was bending down in front of me, but everything was so hazy that I could not focus on just one thing. I felt even worse when I tried to. Images, things I wanted to block out, came rushing to the forefront of my mind, and there was nothing I could do to stop it.

Chapter Eleven

I was put on bed rest after that, once again confined within the walls of the bedroom I had been cooped up in for far too long. I was not sure why they bothered to lock me up again. If there was any reason to stay put, do as I was told, and not try to escape, then it was definitely witnessing what Shadow did to that poor man, Rolan. It was ingrained into my mind, never to be forgotten. Shadow was not bothered by what he had done—I guessed it was not the first time—but I most definitely was bothered by it.

As the days all blurred into one, Leah told me that Rolan had been killed. It made me sick to my stomach knowing that the man responsible was just downstairs, but I could not do anything about it. It would be me being tortured next if I did. What if Rolan had a family though? What if he had a wife and kids who were wondering where he was? They would never see him again, and that was the hardest thing of all to know.

When Saturday came around, a whole three days passing since Rolan's death, Shadow was still trying to figure out who had Rolan following me. Although Leah told Shadow that he should have kept him alive to get more answers, Shadow dismissed that by saying he would not tell anything else and that he was sure he would not have. He had served his purpose and was no longer needed; those were his exact words. I tried to resist the urge to scream at him, tell him it was still a human life he had just ended, but I knew he would not care. He would only be angry at me for opening my mouth and speaking against him.

So although Shadow was trying to figure out what was going on and I did appreciate that he was looking for whoever set Rolan to follow me, I wished he did not have to keep me locked up. I hadn't had any attempts to escape since that day, and I had no desire to even try. I was running on fear alone, too afraid to even take the few steps to the bathroom in case Shadow decided to kill me too.

Whether it was at Shadow's request or her own, Leah had been keeping me company. It was getting extremely boring to be stuck inside the same room all the time, especially when they had turned the Wi-Fi off to make sure I could not get in touch with anyone but Rose. Although I had my laptop, books, and drawing pads, I was more bored than I ever recall being in my entire life. I was scared, I was bored, I was on edge. I could not concentrate on reading or drawing now I knew a man had been killed because of me. Indirectly, but still because of me.

"What are you doing?" Leah asked me as I threw down my drawing pad with a sigh.

I sat up on the bed. "Just thinking."

"That's dangerous, you know," she commented, sitting up straighter from where she sat by the door, guarding it.

"Oh, well," I replied, running a hand through my hair. "I just can't stop thinking about that man. He could have had a family!"

"To be fair, Shadow did give him a chance. All he had to do was answer his questions honestly."

"You really believe that?" I asked, incredulously. There was no doubt in my mind that Shadow would have killed Rolan whether he told the truth or not.

Leah merely stared.

"Does he do that a lot?" I asked, partly curious and partly terrified. I knew it was wrong to be so curious, but I could not help it; up until a couple of weeks ago, I did not know vampires existed. I thought they were a work of fiction and that was that.

"Only if he needs to get answers," she said, glancing at me, seeming to realise instantly what I was referring to. "He won't torture you if that's what you're worried about. I think he realised he can't do that to you after we heard about your dad."

"Why does he care about what I went through?" I frowned.

Leah shot me a look. "Isn't it obvious? You were abused by your dad... isn't that enough reason for him to change his mind? I doubt he ever planned on hurting you that way because he wouldn't have kept stalling; he'd have just done it. I know he appears to be a complete psychopath, and maybe he is, but that doesn't mean he's a horrible person all the time."

"He kills people," I stated.

"Has he hurt you?"

"He bit me."

"He was angry, and when he's angry, he can't always control himself. So I'll ask you again, has he physically hurt you?"

"He smashed my head against a brick wall," I said. "That could have killed me, by the way."

"He didn't know what else to do," Leah told me. Then, sighing, she said, "I told you I was proving a point by making you watch what happened with Rolan. Shadow didn't want you to watch, but I had to make you understand."

"Understand what?"

"That he isn't going to hurt you."

"I find that hard to believe." I snorted.

Leah stared flatly. "He's trying to protect you."

I frowned and shook my head, not believing that for a second.

"Look, I know he kidnapped you, but he did what he thought was right at the time. He doesn't think things through and see the effects in the long run; he never has. He takes action and thinks about the consequences later. Just stop acting as though he will murder you every time you're around him. You're more likely to actually be killed then." Leah looked bored with this conversation now, but I was not done.

"So I have to act like I haven't been kidnapped, that I haven't witnessed him torture someone? That's what you're saying? In order for me to stay alive, I have to act as though none of this has ever happened?"

She thought about it for a second. "Pretty much."

"That's impossible."

"Your funeral," she said, standing up and stretching. "I'm gonna see if he's made any progress. I'll bring some food up later."

Within minutes, she was gone, and I was left alone with my thoughts once again.

***

By the time Leah came back, I had made my mind up to try to act as normal as I could under the circumstances. It would be hard, but if it would stop Shadow from killing me then I had to try, right?

Besides, Shadow had not actually hurt me since that day he bit me. He was even trying to figure out who Rolan was connected to. The more I thought about it, the more I realised that he would not do that if he had any plans to kill me. As soon as he realised someone had Rolan stalk me, he could have killed not only Rolan but me as well. Yet he hadn't. I could just be overthinking everything, but it gave me some hope.

"Shadow wants to talk to you," Leah suddenly said.

"What about?"

"I told him about our little chat," she said, as though it was nothing. "He wants to talk about letting you out of this room."

My eyes lit up at the possibility. "Really?"

"Really. He's in the kitchen. Go now. He's impatient."

"Are you not coming?" I frowned, heading over to the door that Leah was unlocking.

"He wants to talk to you alone. There's no need for me to be there, anyway. He's not going to hurt you," she said, rolling her eyes.

I nodded, taking a deep breath before I headed out of the room and down the stairs. I did not want to keep him waiting long, so I sped up my pace. Once at the kitchen, I stood in the doorway, remembering what happened last time I was in that room.

Shadow must have heard me coming as he glanced up from where he stood, making a sandwich. He told me to sit down, and I did so quickly, making sure to sit on his side of the table. There was no way I was planning to sit on the chair Rolan had once occupied. No way in hell. That was just asking for me to throw up.

"Here," he said, placing a plate in front of me with a sandwich on it.

I looked at him, my brows furrowed. He made it for me? I assumed Leah had made all the meals I have had.

"It's not poisoned," Shadow said, leaning against the counter as he watched me.

Remembering Leah's words from earlier, I started to eat the food, not realising just how hungry I was. I had not eaten since early this morning after all. I was grateful that he had fed me and waited until I finished eating.

"Leah said you wanted to talk to me," I said, pushing the now empty plate away from me.

"Yes, I do," he said, grabbing the plate and washing it before he put it away. "Can I trust you?"

"I think I proved you can."

"You've also proved you'll run at the first chance you see." He raised his eyebrow, turning back to face me.

"I won't run," I stated, shaking my head nervously as unwanted images flashed through my mind. "I promise you that. I won't run."

"Ah," Shadow spoke, smirking and crossing his arms over his chest. "You're more scared of me than you were before."

"Can you blame me?" I shot back, not thinking. My eyes widened. I was hoping I did not annoy him, but he just chuckled at my words.

"I suppose not. If I wanted you dead, you'd be dead."

"I know. That's why I won't run. You've proved you can find me, and I know if I tried again, you probably would kill me."

"Probably," he admitted, still chuckling. "But let's get back to the situation. Until I figure out who is behind you being stalked, I'm going to need your help, so I've graciously decided that you're no longer to be kept locked in that bedroom."

"Why?"

"Rolan was hired to follow you, which means somewhere, there is someone out to get you," he said. "Only you know your enemies."

"I don't have any enemies. My dad kicked me out so I can't imagine him wanting me back now." I frowned.

"There is still a chance he is behind this."

"He doesn't know where I am," I said. Thinking back to what Rolan had tried to say to me right before Shadow had scared him into silence, I added, "You're forgetting something, anyway."

"Go on."

"It sounded like he was going to say, 'your sister.'"

"So she is the one behind this?" His expression hardened. "Why would she do this?"

"That's the thing, Shadow." I bit my lip, staring up at him. "I've never had a sister."

"What about your friend?"

"Rose wouldn't do something like that. It's not her," I told him sternly. Rose may be a little crazy at times, but she definitely was not that crazy.

"Who else knows you are here?" he then asked, seeming more concerned by the second. I could not blame him for that, really; I was beginning to get increasingly more worried myself because if someone was posing as my sister when I have never had one... well, I did not even know anybody that could be behind it.

"No one."

Shadow accepted this, nodding once. "Okay, and you have no enemies?"

"No. I only have one friend."

Shadow frowned though remained quiet for a few minutes. I contemplated what Shadow meant by needing my help because I would not be of much use. I was as in the dark as much as he was regarding this whole situation. I did not know any more than I had told him, so how could I help? It could be something to do with him, for all I know.

I decided to ask.

"Maybe it's an enemy of yours?" I asked, watching him carefully.

"You seem convinced it is."

"The only person that hates me is my dad, but I know he wouldn't waste his time or energy tracking me down when he was the one to kick me out. He probably thinks I'm with Rose, anyway. She's not going to tell him the truth now that she knows what he's like, so it just makes sense that whoever was following me maybe wasn't after me but after you."

"Interesting theory," he spoke slowly.

I shrugged, not knowing how to respond. I kept quiet, letting him think about what I had said. He was bound to have enemies, much more than I had. He was a vampire, after all, one that had been around a whole lot longer than I had. So it just made more sense that he was the one with the enemy, not me.

But if he was the target, what would they want with me?

Chapter Twelve

"Hurry up, will you?! We've wasted enough time!" Shadow yelled in exasperation as he paced the room.

"Just calm down!" Leah called back to him, shaking her head. "It was your idea to wait!"

"We've waited too long!"

Although it was only Sunday, so not much time had passed at all, according to Shadow, we had sat by idly for too long, and now it was time to do something. He was definitely an impatient person, I realised, though I think I had something to do with that. If I had not put the idea in his head that someone was after him and not me, he might not have been so impatient to find out what was going on. He did not rule out the possibility that it had something to do with me, though; he admitted that I had been too much trouble since the second he brought me here and that if I now had a stalker, it would not surprise him. I had to bite my lip because that had annoyed me. I had wanted to remind him why I was in London in the first place, but I refrained from saying anything because it would only make his attitude worse.

"So what's the plan?" I asked, trying to appear calm as I slipped on my Converse. All they had told me this morning was that I was going to be used as bait, and to be honest, I was absolutely terrified as to what that meant. I had no idea what they were planning or what I would be expected to do. I was half-tempted to escape, but the thought of Rolan quickly changed my mind.

Shadow groaned. "Like I've said a thousand times already, you and Leah are to go to Oxford Street again, making sure you are in a public place at all times. I will follow at a distance, hoping to catch a glimpse of someone following you both. Now Rolan is gone, whoever is doing this will have to do the dirty work themselves, or they will hire someone else. Either way, I want answers, and I plan to get some."

"Regret killing Rolan yet?" Leah retorted, entering the room, eyebrows raised.

"Shut up and let's just get a move on."

The journey there was a tense one. Leah and I walked ahead of Shadow, but we did not speak; the atmosphere was too thick with tension that I did not want to ask any of the questions that were flitting through my mind. I was nervous, but most of all, I was scared. What if all of this did somehow link to my dad? What if he did want me back under his roof so he could finish the job? What if someone chased us down the street just to get to me?

I had so many more questions I did not have answers to, and that what was putting me on edge. It was making me edge away from anyone who passed by me a little too close. In fact, I was so frightened of everyone that walked by that I was starting to get strange looks shot my way. That was when Leah grabbed my arm.

"Pull yourself together! Do you want them to know we know?" she hissed, keeping her voice low enough so only me could hear.

"I'm sorry! I can't deal with things like this. Excuse me for not being able to trust you'd keep me alive." It was probably not the best thing to say but being in public made me feel a little braver when it came to voicing my thoughts.

"You still don't get it, do you?" she asked, releasing her hold on my arm. "If Shadow wanted you dead, then you'd already be dead. We're trying to help you, remember? It is your psycho dad that's behind this."

"He wouldn't. I know he wouldn't. He would never risk himself being thrown in jail just to get someone to follow me. I know him, he just wouldn't do it." I was not sure whether I was trying to convince her or myself of that fact. The whole 'sister' thing had really thrown me off.

"And I bet at one point you never assumed he would hit you, and look how that turned out." She snapped.

I was shocked at her words, gaping at her. She was right. I did not know my dad. I did not know what lengths he would go to in order to keep me quiet. If there were any way he knew I was in London, staying with two people, he would know his dirty little secret was in danger of getting out. I would not know what was going through his head then. He could be planning all sorts of things.

"Look, I'm sorry, okay? I didn't mean that. I just—I'm angry at the whole situation. If Shadow had just left you alone that night, none of this would be happening." Leah sighed as we walked around the corner.

"It's fine. You're right." I shrugged, slumping my shoulders. I really had not expected my dad to turn on me. I had put him on a pedestal so high even I couldn't see the top of it, so when he fell off of it... Is there really any wonder why I'm so terrified of people when my own family was capable of so much?

"You shouldn't even be in London. You should be with your friend."

"I'm in more danger there than I am here."

"And how do you figure out that?" Her eyebrows raised.

"After my dad kicked me out, I was in danger from someone else. Shadow said he murdered someone who was going to either rape me or kill me. I don't know whether he was telling the truth, but he had no reason to lie. I was already terrified of him—still am really. So back 'home,' I was in danger from not only my dad but becoming homeless and being hurt by someone else."

"You're in danger here too."

"I'm not fully convinced they are after me," I stated.

"If not you, who?"

"Who do you think?" I retorted dryly. "I am living in his house. If anyone has an enemy, it would be him."

A shadow crossed over Leah's face as I finished speaking, but I did not call her out on it. There was something on her mind; that much was obvious. I was not sure what she could be thinking, and to be honest, I did not really want to ask. I was not sure I would like the answer, especially if she had a hint as to who could really be behind Rolan stalking me. Wanting to know and needing to know are two very different things, and I really did not want to know. It was probably better just in case whoever hired Rolan was after Shadow.

She did not speak as we continued our walk to Oxford Street, nor did she speak when we went for a browse in some of the shops. An awkward and uncomfortable silence settled over the two of us, and I found myself at a loss for what to say. I was not entirely convinced she would even answer me if I spoke to her; she seemed to be in a world of her own, lost in her own thoughts.

The silence continued after that. We walked from shop to shop, doing as Shadow had instructed, but it was not until I was at HMV, looking at the CDs, that I realised she was no longer by my side as she had been only minutes before. A quick walk around the shop told me she was nowhere to be seen.

She had left me by myself.

She went against Shadow's strict instructions and had left me.

What was I supposed to do now?

Exiting the shop, remembering that Shadow was keeping a safe distance to see if anyone was following us, I could not see either him or Leah. Not being able to see him was not a worrying, though, because that was the whole point, but not seeing Leah had me frowning. What was she playing at? Why did she just left me on my own when she knew she was not supposed to do that? Someone was out there, who may or may not be targeting Shadow and anyone who knew him, so for her to just leave... was worrying.

Then I started asking myself whether that had been the plan all along. Maybe they had planned to leave me alone since both clearly believed I was the reason Rolan had been standing outside his house and following Shadow and me. Maybe this really had been the whole purpose of this plan. Maybe they just wanted a way to get rid of me, but if that were the case, why not just do it themselves?

It was not until I was heading back inside HMV in case Leah decided to put in another appearance when I remembered I had both her numbers on my phone. They requested that I put their mobile numbers in my phone, just in case of emergency.

Leah suddenly disappearing out of thin air was probably what constituted an emergency, so I took my phone from my pocket. I tried calling her first, but she did not pick up. That was not entirely surprising, though. I then tried to call Shadow, assuming she would be with him or have at least told him where she was going.

"What the hell are you doing on your phone?" was the first thing he said to me when he picked up after the first ring. There was no hello. He simply got straight to the point. I should not have expected any difference.

"Was this your plan?" I asked, walking around the shop once again.

"What are you talking about? You know this was my plan!"

It was completely idiotic of me, but I could not help the tears that welled up in my eyes. They had done this on purpose. It was their plan all along to put me in danger and let me face it alone. I should not have been so surprised, and yet for some reason, I was. There was no sense to be made of my irrational feelings over having been deserted when there could be another crazed psychopathic vampire after me. At least, that was who I assumed was behind everything. No human could be stupid enough to take on a vampire if they knew they existed.

"Violet? Violet, answer me!" Shadow suddenly spoke, interrupting my train of thought with a start.

"I can't believe you both set this up. You're probably both laughing at how stupid I am, aren't you? I can't believe I was starting to believe that maybe you really did just want to help me. Oh, my God. How fucking stupid was I!" I was on the verge of hysteria because they had been so sure someone would follow us and now I was alone.

I really was an idiot for not knowing that something like this would happen. I had almost let Leah convince me they really were just trying to help, and now look, I was left alone when there could be a vampire waiting to attack. Besides, no captor suddenly decides to let the person they kidnapped walk around their home freely, as though they lived there, no matter how awkward I was. How I could believe otherwise, I don't know, but one thing was for sure: they were amazing actors. They really had me believing they were not all that bad for a split second.

"What are you talking about? Violet, you're not making any sense!" Shadow raised his voice, making me jump.

"I'm talking about you two leaving me alone when you've put it in my head that some psychopath might be following me and might decide to attack! That's what I'm talking about, you idiot!" I cried into the phone. I was so angry and scared—that was the only excuse I could come up with as to why I let myself call him an idiot.

"Wait—you're alone? Where's Leah? This isn't the time for games!"

I scoffed, not pausing to figure out where the sudden burst of confidence was coming from. "Don't act like you don't know! She's with you, isn't she? I know she is."

Shadow's voice suddenly became serious. "No, Violet. She's not with me. She's supposed to be with you."

I paused, raising my head to glance around the shop. "Okay, let's say for a second that I did believe you. If she's not here with me and she's not there with you... then where the hell is she?"

There was silence from the other end, and I knew he was thinking. I began to panic; what if someone had convinced her to leave somehow and were planning to hurt her? As much as I resented her for being part of Shadow's plan to lock me away, she had also been kind to me. She had not actually hurt me, so I could not hate her completely. So knowing that she could be in trouble left me feeling uneasy.

"That's a very good question."

"Just tell me the truth. She's with you, isn't she? This was all one sick joke." Nobody could just leave a shop without being seen, but the more I thought about it, the less I was sure she even came in the shop with me. We had not been talking after that conversation, and I had been trying my hardest to pretend she was not there. I was not sure what to think anymore. It felt like I was going crazy.

"She isn't with me, Violet," Shadow said, dead serious. "I'm supposed to keep a safe distance, remember? I didn't want anyone knowing we're onto them! What did you say to her? Why did she leave?"

"I don't know! We weren't even talking. I'm not even sure she came in here with me," I admitted, biting my lip as I once again glanced around. I spotted someone watching me at the other end of the aisle, and my eyes widened. I glanced back at the row of CDs in front of me, hoping that the person was just someone trying to eavesdrop and not a murderer or something.

"How can you not know that? Are you stupid?!" Shadow yelled.

"We both said some things, and it just got awkward, okay? We didn't speak after that! You're the one that's supposed to be watching us. Shouldn't you know where she was last?"

"There was a crowd in front of me when you went into the shop, so I assumed she was still with you. She knew not to leave you alone."

"So you don't know either." From my peripheral vision, I saw the person that had been watching me walk in my direction. Lowering my voice, I whispered hurriedly into the phone. "Shadow, someone's been watching me, and now they are approaching me. What the hell do I do?"

"Don't move. I'll be there in two minutes."

Chapter Thirteen

"Hey."

I almost jumped out of my skin upon hearing a voice so close to me. Turning to face whoever had spoken, I saw that the man who had been watching me standing with a grin on his face.

I did not say anything, taking in his appearance instead. With his black hair, dark eyes, and dark clothing that did nothing but emphasise his muscles, I wondered if he was the one who hired Rolan. He looked intimidating though whether that was his intention, I was not sure. Just because Rolan made it seem like a woman had hired him did not mean this man was not also working for 'her'—if it even was a woman behind it at all.

As I was questioning everything about him, I realised that I still had not spoken. He was watching me, biting his lip as though he was trying not to laugh.

"Hi..." I trailed off, glancing around the shop. Shadow said he would be here; I had to at least try to believe that.

"I'm Jason. What's your name?"

Don't give him your real name. Make one up! I shouted internally.

"Sophie." I blurted out the first name that came to mind.

He smiled, nodding. "Well, are you okay, Sophie? You look a little freaked out."

"Yeah, I'm fine. Thanks for asking," I replied, smiling slightly. I cast another glance around the room and took a deep breath. Shadow was still nowhere to be seen. "I'm just waiting for a friend."

"A male friend?" Jason asked. Looking back at him, I saw his eyebrows rise, waiting patiently for me to answer. I frowned, why would he want to know that?

I nodded anyway. "Yeah."

"Boyfriend?"

"Yeah." I lied, glancing around again. Surely he would leave me alone now, right?

Wrong.

"I don't believe you," he stated.

"That's your problem."

"Why would any guy leave such a pretty girl on her own?" he asked, taking a step closer. I automatically took a step back.

"He had a phone call."

"You're lying."

"No, I'm not."

"So where is this boyfriend of yours?" Jason asked, a smirk on his face.

"Right here," came a voice from behind Jason, who was immediately pulled away from me.

I let out a sigh of relief when I saw Shadow. I did not even care that he looked extremely annoyed. I was just happy to be away from the creep that had been getting a little too close for comfort.

"Ah, so you're the boyfriend," Jason said as Shadow released his hold on him. "I was beginning to think she was making you up."

"Clearly not, so you can leave now," Shadow stated, coming to stand beside me and wrapping an arm around my waist. I tensed only for a second. Then, I relaxed. I felt safe now as stupid as that may seem.

Jason held his hands up in mock surrender, still looking far too amused. He waved once and then, not waiting for a goodbye, walked away. It was not until he had disappeared from view, exiting the shop, that I allowed myself to relax a little.

"Are you okay? Did he hurt you?" Shadow asked, stepping in front of me and placing both hands on my shoulders as he let his eyes roam my body, searching for any sign of injury. I blushed under his scrutiny.

"No, I'm fine. Was he one of them?" I asked, knowing he'd understand what I meant.

He shook his head. "No, he was just trying to hit on you, I think."

"He had a funny way of going about it," I grumbled. "It was creepy, the way he was watching me."

Shadow moved, standing by my side again, and wrapped his arm back around my waist. Shooting him a questioning glance, he sighed, going on to explain that we had to seem like a couple until we were away from the shop just in case Jason was loitering around. I accepted his explanation; it seemed like a good idea.

So, when we left the shop and saw Jason standing with a group of his friends just outside the shop, I was glad that Shadow was still holding me. Whether or not Jason was a dangerous person did not register in my mind; I just wanted to get away from him. He made me feel highly uncomfortable, so I was glad when Shadow lead us back the way we came.

He did not let me go until we were walking back to his house, deciding that I had been used as bait enough for one day. I did not complain; I was more than happy to put some distance between Jason and me. Shadow had been checking every now and then for a sign of him, just in case he was somehow involved, but neither of us could see him anywhere, so it was clear it was not him.

When we reached his house, Shadow went inside first, searching for any sign of Leah. In our haste to get away from Jason, we have not had the chance to look for her.

I went into the living room, sitting on the sofa as I waited for him to decide what we were going to do next. I did not feel comfortable enough to follow him around or walk around the house on my own, so it was probably better I just wait. When it came to my living arrangements, I was so confused that it hurt my head trying to figure out what I was feeling. I was happy I was away from my dad, but I did not want to be here either. Yet, there was a part of me that would prefer to be here, under the careful watch of two vampires instead of Rose. As much as I valued my friendship with her, I did not want to put her in any unnecessary danger even though her dad could have helped me

"She's not here," Shadow said, entering the room. I glanced up at him, frowning.

"Do you think someone has taken her?" I asked, almost afraid to ask the question.

He shook his head.

"Are you sure?"

He nodded.

"I mean, anyone could have grabbed her there, threatened her maybe…"

"She wouldn't go down without a fight. In which case, both of us would have heard or seen that happen. No, she went silently, so she didn't want to be seen leaving. Question is, where would she go?"

"She left willingly?" I was shocked. She was the one who had been so adamant about acting normal, so why would she just leave? If there was any part of her that thought I was in danger, why would she leave? She said that Shadow did not want me dead, but could she say the same for herself? Maybe that was the reason she left me alone like that.

"What did you say to her?" Shadow suddenly asked, standing by the fireplace opposite me. He folded his arms across his chest, waiting for me to speak.

"Nothing, I—"

"Cut the bullshit. You said neither of you was speaking. I'll ask again. What did you say to her?"

"She was convinced it was my dad behind this, so I told her it wasn't. I know he wouldn't do something like this. I said that it's probably an enemy of yours since I am living in your house, and she just went quiet. We didn't talk after that." I explained.

Shadow began pacing around the room, mulling over my words. He must know who could be doing all of this, or maybe he just had that many enemies that he did not know for sure which one was doing it. I decided to ask.

"How many enemies do you have?"

"Too many." He gripped his hair in frustration.

"So it could be any one of them."

"Perhaps." He did not sound convinced.

"You still think my dad is doing it, don't you?"

His silence was all the confirmation I needed.

"You're wrong. I know my dad. I know Leah was right in saying what she did, but I do know he wouldn't risk getting anyone else involved. He isn't that stupid. If he were, he'd have been caught a long time ago. I don't know why I'm so sure it's not him, but I just know it's not."

"And how do you know he wouldn't? He kicked you out; what if he's decided he wants you back there?" Shadow asked.

I looked at him pointedly. "Just trust me. I know it's not him."

"Then who?"

"You're the one with the enemies, apparently," I said. "How do you know for certain that it isn't one of them?"

"I don't."

"Exactly." I rolled my eyes, leaning back on the sofa and staring at the ceiling. I was sick of all of this. I just wanted to be happy. I was absolutely sick and tired of being on edge all the time, fearing for my life every second of every day. I was scared of everything. I was scared of Shadow and Leah because although they were trying to help, he was the one who kidnapped me, bit me, and locked me up in a bedroom. I thought I was going to be killed, and I was still not certain that thought wasn't playing on his mind still. It would be so much easier for him to just kill me and get it over with, and I was sick of waiting for it to happen.

I actually thought being kicked out would allow me to be free, but here I was, trapped once again.

I had the world's worst luck.

***

Hours later, the front door opened. Shadow was still pacing the floor trying to get hold of Leah as he had been out to look for her to no avail. So he had reduced himself to pacing and calling her phone, but she had not picked up.

Upon hearing the front door, he cast a quick look at me before disappearing out the room in mere seconds.

"Stupid vampire speed," I grumbled to myself as I got up and followed after him.

Leah was just about to enter the room when I reached the door, almost causing us to collide. I stepped back and let her into the room, wondering where she had been.

"Where have you been?" Shadow asked, standing by my side and crossing his arms.

"Following up on a lead." She plopped down on the sofa. "I remembered something, so I wanted to check up on it."

"Remembered what exactly?" Shadow walked over and sat on the edge of the table, facing Leah with a stern expression.

"It was something Violet said. It got me thinking," Leah shrugged. "I'll tell you all about it later."

"No, you will tell me about it now."

I glanced between the two vampires, confusion flooding through me. I had no idea why Leah could not just tell us what she had been doing. It could not have been that bad if she thought she figured something out. Surely, we needed all the information we could get if we ever were to find out what was going on.

"It's not Violet's dad that's been stalking her," Leah said.

I resisted the urge to scream 'I told you so.'

"Then who?" He raised an eyebrow.

"One of your enemies," Leah told Shadow.

"Who?"

"Someone else." She shrugged again.

"Leah," Shadow warned, standing up and taking a step towards her, but Leah was out of her seat the second she saw him approaching her.

"Calm down, Shadow." Leah held her hands up, agitated.

"Tell me who is doing this and why they are targeting Violet."

"Now isn't the time."

"Tell. Me," Shadow spoke slowly, taking another step closer. I could sense the sudden danger in the room, so I pressed myself against the wall, ready to run from the room if I needed to.

"Raven!" Leah burst out suddenly, making me jump at how loud she shouted. "It's Raven!"

Chapter Fourteen

Raven.

Who the hell was Raven?

That had been the question on my mind, but no amount of asking got me all the answers I was seeking. I had assumed by now that I deserved answers since I was clearly a target, but they had only told me two things about Raven.

1. Raven is a girl.

2. She is a vampire.

It was not particularly useful information considering I already assumed that it would be a vampire, but they refused to tell me why she hated Shadow so much. Obviously, they both knew, so I suppose that was better than none of us having a clue.

As a result of Leah's recent discovery, I had been locked back up in the bedroom. It had been a few days since then, and I was beginning to get annoyed, as well as worried. Shadow had proven to me that a locked door would not stop a vampire. What if Raven decided she wanted to kill me for whatever reason she felt justifiable?

I had tried everything to take my mind off the situation. I had called Rose, but obviously, I could not tell her anything, so I spent more time feeling even worse, knowing that not only was I lying to her but that I had to keep track of all the lies that just kept on piling up.

"Are you sure you're okay?" Rose asked when I called her again. "You seem a little off."

"I'm fine, just tired. I haven't been getting much sleep lately," I told her. At least that was the truth. I had been having a hard time sleeping lately because of the situation.

"Well, why don't you go have a nap or something?" She suggested.

"I can't sleep during the day."

"Then I don't know. I have to go now, but remember to ask your grandparents if I can come and stay with you for a while! I miss you!"

I smiled, wishing that was possible. "I will. Miss you too. I'll let you know what they say later. Bye!"

"Bye, bye, bye!"

Once we had hung up, I sighed and lay down on the floor, staring up at the ceiling. I had been leaning against the door after being locked away again. There was no way Shadow would let Rose come and stay, and I could not let her come, anyway. She thought I was with my grandparents. I could not let her know the truth because she would flip and call the police. I should be calling the police myself, but it seemed that Shadow and Leah were trying to protect me from whoever Raven was, and I did not want them to kill any innocent people just because I called the police. I may not have control in much, but that I did have control over, and I refused to let innocent people die because of me.

I knew that I needed to escape, only this time making sure I would not be found. I was not quite sure how I was going to achieve that considering how easy it had been for them to find me last time. I did not know how many friends they had to help them, and I was not sure where I would even go. I didn't have enough money, anyway, so I couldn't go to another hotel—not that I would even want to. So where would I go? I didn't have any family or friends in London.

It was in times like these when my thoughts ran away with me, and I found myself thinking of things I never would usually think about. It seemed like no matter which direction I turned, I was stuck somehow. There was only one definite way out of this, and that was death. I was not suicidal, though—not actively suicidal, anyway—and yet even knowing that, I still found myself thinking about it. It was better to go out on my terms rather than anyone else's. I had no idea what Raven was planning or if it included me or not. So how was I supposed to know I was even going to live much longer?

I didn't, and not knowing scared me.

***

Hours later, the clock on the wall ticking on by, I still had not moved from my position on the floor. I had been drifting in and out of sleep, still unable to sleep properly. It was true that I could not sleep during the day, not unless I were ill.

So when the door flung open, coming into contact with my head, I almost jumped out of my skin. The pain was instant, and I raised a hand to rub the spot that was hurting and groaned.

"What the hell were you doing in front of the door? Shit, are you okay?" I heard a frantic voice ask. Seconds later, a head popped into my line of vision, and I saw Shadow, glancing down at me with a mixture of anger, frustration, and worry.

"The door just hit my head, and you're asking if I'm okay?" I retorted.

"Well, you're clearly fine," he stated with a roll of his eyes. "You're lucky I saw you on the floor, or I'd have walked into you too."

"Thanks for seeing me after you flung the door open," I replied sarcastically. I couldn't help myself.

"If you weren't laid in front of the door like an idiot, you wouldn't have been hurt. Now sit up." He rolled his eyes again.

I did as he said, still rubbing the spot that the door came into contact with. Shadow must have used a lot of force to open the door as the pain had not dulled.

"Close your eyes." He ordered, moving to sit on his knees.

Closing my eyes, I tensed. I was not sure what he was going to do, but when I felt his hand grab mine, moving it out of the way, I understood immediately. He was going to take the pain away. Although I wanted to open my eyes and see how he did it, I kept them shut.

He pressed two fingers against the spot that hurt, and I winced.

"Sorry," he mumbled. "There's a bump already."

"Great," I responded.

Suddenly, I felt something wash over me, something that I could not explain. I felt warm inside and a little dazed. It was something I had never felt before, but as the feeling grew and grew, the pain in my head decreased until I could not feel anything other than the amazing feeling I felt when Shadow was using his ability.

A smile formed on my face, and I opened my eyes, staring straight at Shadow who was deep in concentration. When I was sure there was no more pain, I called his name, but he did not reply. He was still rubbing the spot on my head, but I was sure there was not a bump anymore. I would have been able to feel it, wouldn't I?

I raised my hand and placed it on his chest, catching his attention immediately. His eyes stared into mine with an intensity that had me quickly moving my hand.

"Thank you," I said, smiling and staying still. It was the little things he did that made me feel more comfortable in his presence despite everything he had put me through since he brought me here. I was sure the fear would not ever fully disappear until I was certain that he would not put me in harm's way, but it was no longer an overwhelming fear that had me wanting to run whenever I saw him.

I wasn't sure why. I could not explain if I had to, but I found myself staring into those eyes that once evoked terror in me. Those grey eyes sucked me in, and I found myself feeling something strange, something entirely new to me. I was drawn in by those eyes. Before I could comprehend what I was doing, I leaned forward. Shadow, who had not moved or spoken since I thanked him, leaned forward too until we were centimetres from each other. One move and my lips would touch his. I found myself wanting it too, wanting to know what it would feel like to kiss him. But I couldn't. He had kidnapped me; I could not allow myself to think such thoughts.

That last thought was enough to bring me back to reality, and I quickly moved back, shame and embarrassment flooding through me. My heart was racing in my chest, and my hands were shaking.

What was I thinking?

Shadow blinked, shaking his head.

He was out of the room before I could apologise, leaving the door wide open in his haste to get away. I was not sure how much time passed by as I sat there on the floor thinking over what had just happened. I had been so close to kissing him, but that was not what bothered me. It was the fact I wanted to kiss him. I could not let myself feel like that. I could not.

I was not going to develop a case of Stockholm syndrome.

No way.

I ran out the door with no hesitation.

Chapter Fifteen

Racing down the stairs, I knew that wherever Shadow had run off to, it was not anywhere in the house because he did not stop me. Neither did Leah, which only led me to believe that I was completely alone in the house. I was able to run straight to the front door, flinging it open and rushing out of it without being stopped by anyone.

That had been far too easy.

I did not stop running, though. With everything piling up in my mind, I just had to get away. What had I been thinking? How could I even want to kiss him? He was attractive, but he had kidnapped me and threatened to kill me on multiple occasions. It should not be so easy to forget that. So why, at that moment, had I?

I was so embarrassed and ashamed of what almost occurred that I did not want to go back to the house. Not yet. It may be the safest place for me at the moment since there was someone after me, but I could not go back. In a few hours when I have managed to calm myself down, I would have no choice, but until then, I needed to get far away from Shadow.

I should have known it was not going to be that simple.

About an hour after I ran off, my phone rang. Of course, it just had to be the person I was trying to stop thinking about. It seemed I was never destined for good luck. Sighing at the caller I. D, I ignored the call. I did not want to speak to him. I was still too embarrassed.

I kept rejecting the calls each time he rang—a grand total of twelve times. I assumed he was going to yell and threaten me for escaping again, and that was something I was not in the mood to hear. The more I thought about it, the more I realised I did not want to go back. Raven had an issue with Shadow, not me, so he could sort it out. Going back meant being locked away again until it was 'safe' for me, but how could I trust my captor? How could I trust him after everything he had put me through? Leaving my dad's house was supposed to be the turning point in my life, the point where things got better. It was never supposed to be filled with monsters like Shadow. I would rather live my life blissfully unaware that vampires even existed if it meant I could finally live my life and be happy. That was all I wanted.

Was that too much to ask?

"Hello again," a voice spoke, causing me to flinch, not expecting anyone to speak to me. I half-expected it to be Shadow, but when I turned my head, I saw someone else. Someone I was not pleased to see because it only meant one thing.

Ric.

"Go away," I told him, jumping off the bench I had been sitting on, backing away slowly. There was no way I would be able to outrun a vampire, but that did not mean I was going to stand around and let him take me back. It was obvious why he was here.

Ric frowned, holding his hands up in surrender. "I'm not here to hurt you."

"Shadow sent you, didn't he?" I asked, taking another step back.

He did not answer, but his silence was all the confirmation I needed. I took another step back as Ric took one step forward.

"I don't want to go back." I shook my head. "Just tell him you haven't seen me."

"I can't do that. I'm sorry," he replied, seeming genuinely apologetic.

"Yes, you can!" I yelled as tears welled up in my eyes. I felt like an idiot for being on the verge of tears, but everything happening lately was proving to be too much for me, and I could not cope with it all. The stress was getting to me bit by bit, and I was tired of it. I was tired of everything.

Ric, noticing the tears in my eyes, quickly stopped trying to get to me. His eyes went wide, and it was obvious he had not dealt with a lot of crying people before.

"Look, please don't cry," he said. He held his hands up again. *Trust the vampire not to be able to handle tears*, I thought to myself, casting my eyes to the ground.

"Just leave me alone," I told him, deflated of all energy. The idea of sleep seemed extremely comforting right now. I could do with a month of sleep if not more—anything to get me away from this nightmare I was living.

The thought almost made me laugh. People are supposed to have nightmares when they sleep, not when they are wide awake. I was the exact opposite. Sleeping meant I could finally escape my troubles, but I would always wake up into a nightmare. I was living a nightmare that I could never even dream of.

"I have to take you back. He's got everyone looking for you." Ric tried to reason with me, but it was not working. I was adamant that he leave me alone, despite his protests.

"Why can't he just leave me alone? Why can't everyone just leave me alone?"

"Because he's worried," Ric said.

"About me?" I raised an eyebrow. "Yeah, right."

"He told me that Raven is after you. That's enough reason right there to be worried about you. That girl makes the rest of us look like saints."

"What are you talking about?" She wasn't after me. She couldn't be after me. I didn't even know her!

"I'll let him explain. I just have to bring you back."

I started backing away, keeping my eyes on Ric so he would not do anything while my back was turned. It was then that I walked into something, and upon spinning around, I saw a man I had never seen before.

His eyes told me that he was a vampire. Those veins, those quickly darkening eyes... And when he opened his mouth, letting me catch a glimpse of the fangs, I knew I had no choice now.

"You're coming with us whether you like it or not," the man said, flicking the dark hair away from of his eyes. He had a messy hair style, I noticed. It looked as though it had not been combed in months.

"Alec, put your fangs away. Do you want to catch everyone's attention," Ric hissed, approaching the two of us. I tried to walk around Alec so I could get away, but he grabbed my arm, pulling me tightly to his side so I could not move.

"Let me go!" I yelled, struggling to get away.

"Not going to happen, sweetheart. You're going to Shadow."

"Does everyone just follow his orders!" I snapped, though a part of me was genuinely curious. Everyone was so quick to do his bidding, and I just did not know why.

"If we value our lives, then yes," Ric answered for me.

Alec, on the other hand, snorted. "It's called loyalty."

"You're all scared of him," I stated, finding it hard to believe when they are all vampires.

"Unless you're a newborn, you get stronger the older you get," Ric informed me. "Shadow is the oldest out of us all."

"Shouldn't it be the other way around? The younger, the stronger?" I asked, cocking my head to one side in confusion. I stopped struggling. My curiosity was piqued.

"To humans, maybe."

"Let's just go, shall we?" Alec asked, appearing bored. "I haven't seen Leah in a few weeks."

"That's your fault for being away." Ric rolled his eyes.

"Yeah, yeah, I had no choice. Now, let's go," Alec said, pushing me forward and telling me to walk.

The walk back to Shadow's was an awkward one. There was an unsettling silence that ensued, making me feel as though something bad was going to happen. The way that the two of them glanced around our surroundings every couple of minutes did not help me feel safe at all. What if they decided to kill me?

It was safe to say I was a paranoid person, but nobody could blame me. I had been through hell and back in my life; it would be a miracle if that paranoia ever subsided.

***

"DO NOT FUCKING RUN AWAY AGAIN!" Shadow yelled the second I was forced through the front door by Ric and Alec.

I flinched upon hearing his voice. The anger behind it, the expression on his face... It reminded me all too much of the days when I lived with my dad, and I automatically took a step back, bumping into Ric.

"Shadow, calm down. You're scaring her," Leah said, placing a hand on his shoulder as she gave me a soft smile before she saw

Alec. Smiling hugely, she ran over to him, jumping into his outstretched arms.

Seconds later, they were kissing, so I turned away, giving them a little privacy.

Shadow took a deep breath before speaking. "You can't keep running away, Violet. Have you forgotten that Raven is after you?"

"Why would she be after me when I don't even know her? It's more likely she's after you."

"She will use you to get to me," Shadow stated.

I frowned. "Why would she do that?"

"Rolan was sent by her to keep tabs on you. She knows you're human."

"So she got him to follow me to get to you? That doesn't make sense. What are you keeping from me?"

"Nothing."

"Stop lying!" I burst out, my emotions once again taking full control. "You never tell me anything! I'm sick of being kept in the dark when it's my life that's in danger all the damn time! How am I supposed to trust you'd keep me safe when you won't tell me what she wants?"

Shadow walked towards me, not stopping until he was centimetres from my face.

"Raven is a psychopath that will do anything to get what she wants. That is all you need to know," he spoke sternly.

Shaking my head, I sighed. I knew I would not get anything else out of him. Not unless he wanted to tell me, and it was obvious that was not the case.

"I don't want to be here anymore," I whispered, glancing at my feet.

"You're not leaving. It's not safe for you to be alone."

"Safe?" I raised my head, narrowing my eyes at him. "I haven't been safe in years! Being kicked out was supposed to be my happy ending, a fresh start, but no... I just had to get kidnapped and put in even more danger. You say I'm safe here, but you're the fucking reason I'm in danger! I don't feel safe anywhere. How can you not get that!"

By now, everyone was watching us with Leah having pulled herself away from her boyfriend. She gasped as she heard me speak, not expecting me to say so much. Even Ric and Alec looked uncomfortable, not knowing where to look or what to do. I stared at Shadow, but the unreadable expression on his face once again gave nothing away.

"You think you will be safe out there?" Shadow finally spoke, stepping back and pointing to the front door. "You wouldn't last the night. Raven kills without remorse."

"Just like you then." I spat, not knowing where the sudden confidence was coming from. I really needed to shut the hell up before I got myself killed.

He chuckled darkly. "I have done nothing but try and keep you safe. It's my job to make sure that you are."

"Then take me back." I did not need to explain any further for him to understand where I meant.

Shadow rolled his eyes. "That's not happening. Raven will kill you the second she see's you alone. She will rip you limb from limb just to prove a point."

"You've been threatening to kill me since you brought me here. Why would you care about what happens to me?"

Shadow's mouth twitched. "You've grown on me. You're not quite as annoying as you were before."

"Well, thanks for the compliment," I said sarcastically though I was fighting to keep the smile from my face. I was weirdly touched by that, happy that he did not find me a burden like I had been used to being to everyone. It made for a nice change. "But I'm still nothing to you. We're just stuck with each other, so why would she come after me?"

Shadow remained silent though he appeared annoyed by my words.

"Is that really what you think?" Leah asked, taken aback. She appeared to be hurt over my words, but I did not understand why.

"Well, yeah…"

"I thought that you, that maybe… I thought we were friends," Leah replied.

"Friends?" I asked in disbelief. "You've kept me locked in a bedroom with nothing to do all day because you won't give me the Wi-Fi password so I can entertain myself. You walk me to the toilet and wait outside the door, so I don't run. It feels like I'm in prison."

"I'd rather you be in a prison than in a coffin," Shadow said, stunning me into silence with his words. It sounded as though he cared about what happened to me, but how could that be true? How could he possibly care about what happens to me? I could not fathom it.

"Maybe compromise then?" Ric jumped in. I turned to face him to see that he was staring at Shadow sheepishly.

"What?" If Shadow's glare was anything to go by, he was not impressed by that.

"Compromise. Give her the password because we all know that people her age are obsessed with the internet. If you let her have free reign, then maybe she won't keep running off. Stop following her every move. Instead, she can just tell you that she's going to the toilet or something. The less this feels like a prison for her, the less afraid of you she will be."

I was beginning to like Ric all of a sudden. That was the smartest thing he had said.

Leah considered it for a moment. "He's right, Shadow."

"No." Shadow shook his head, folding his arms across his chest. "She's locked in that room because no one but us can get in there."

"A locked door doesn't stop a vampire." I could not help but snap.

"She's right," Ric told him.

"Fine. No more being locked away, but you do as I say and when I say it," Shadow said, glaring at me.

I nodded instantly, hoping that maybe it would not be so bad now. Fingers crossed.

Chapter Sixteen

Although Shadow was not impressed by the fact he had to let me walk around without a chaperone, he had no choice in the matter. He knew I would only try to escape again—and I would. I did not want to be anywhere anymore. I did not feel safe. I did not understand why he could not just take me to Rose so I could stay with her because surely if Raven knew that Shadow had 'gotten rid of me' so to speak, she would not be inclined to chase after me? Then again, I did not know what she had against him in the first place as they still refused to tell me that part, so I did not have a clue about anything. I was left in the dark, and I hated it.

I was given access to the internet, something that helped me pass the time a little. All I did was go on social media or watch videos, but it was better than nothing. Leah usually sat beside me watching everything I did, though, just in case I told someone. Why they thought I would when nobody would believe me, I did not know, but it just proved that as much as I did not trust them, they did not trust me either.

Alec had been in and out practically every hour whether it was to see Leah or to speak to Shadow. He rarely spoke to me; whenever we were in the same room as one another, he did not seem to know what to say. It was not like I wanted to make conversation with him either, so it did not bother me too much. I kept to myself, only speaking when spoken to.

"Raven is outside!" I suddenly heard Leah yell from the hallway, rushing into the living room where the rest of us were. I was at the corner of the room, sitting on the floor and out of the way, reading the vampire book I had gotten when she rushed in, looking panicked.

Shadow was instantly on his feet, casting a quick glance at me before he disappeared. I heard the front door open and Shadow yelling. There was a female voice yelling back.

She was in the room before anyone had the chance to jump up. She stood, a manic grin on her face as she looked around the room. Everybody stood up, even I stood up on shaky legs, leaning against the wall for support.

"Where's this bitch then?" Raven asked, glancing around the room when her eyes zeroed in on me. Glancing up and down, I shrank back against the wall. "What a cute little pet you have, Shadow, though I'm sure you could do better."

"Get out, Raven," Shadow said, standing behind her.

I felt exposed as I stood there, trying to remain calm but knowing it was impossible. There was no way I could feel even remotely calm. Raven was definitely not what I was expecting, whatever that was. She had bright purple hair that was tied back into a high ponytail with tendrils of hair escaping to frame her face. As she walked further into the room, her hips swaying, she did not take her eyes off me, and I gulped nervously.

I was trapped, and she knew it. She could reach me before I could reach Shadow or Leah, or even Alec.

"Get out, princess. Can't you see you're not welcome here?" Alec said, walking around the room slowly until he stood in front of me, protectively. I was shocked at the gesture as he gave me the impression he did not care what happened to me, but either way, I was glad that Raven's gaze was no longer on me.

Okay, Violet, think escape options, I told myself. Escaping a psychotic vampire was definitely going to be tricky, but if I could escape two, surely I could escape another? Would the others even let me run if I had the chance? I had to try. There was a window two steps to my right, but I would need to open it first before I could jump out, and by the time I'd opened it, Raven would catch me. That would be hard, but I could not cross it off completely. Maybe if Shadow grabbed Raven, I could make a run for it, but then what? Where would I go?

The more I tried to think of an escape route, the less sure I was that I would be able to pull it off. I did not even know if Raven had any friends that would be willing to help her since I did not know anything about her. She could have the place surrounded, for all I knew!

So I resigned myself to the fact I could not escape this particular situation and sighed, glancing at the floor with the book still tight in my grip. *Maybe I could hit her with it*, I thought, *if she came too close*. It was times like these that I wished I had something sharp in my possession so I could at least try to fight back. If I could stab Shadow, then I could do it to Raven too, as horrible as it would undoubtedly make me feel later. I just was not cut out for hurting people though I suppose nobody ever really knows what they are capable of until they are backed into a corner.

Oh, the irony.

While I was having an internal debate, Raven was walking around the room with that same manic smile on her face. She really did look psychotic, and I could not help but notice.

"So why have you been keeping this pet around, Shadow? You'd usually have killed your pets by now," Raven commented, turning to face him so her back was to Alec and me. "All those people you've taken and killed. What's so special about this one?"

"That's why you're doing this, isn't it?" Shadow asked. "Because she's still alive."

I peeked over Alec's shoulder and saw Raven shrug. Leah was frowning, glancing at Raven in confusion.

"So it was you that had Rolan follow her. Why a human, though? You had to have known what I'd do to him." Shadow continued. "All this time and you're still hung up on something that isn't going to happen. Quite pathetic, don't you think?"

He was taunting her, deliberately trying to wind her up. It worked. Raven charged towards him, but Alec was quickly rushing forward in vampire speed, grabbing her by the arms to drag her back. Raven thrashed around in an attempt to escape Alec's grip, but it was no use; he was not letting go of her anytime soon.

Shadow stalked towards her with a dangerous look on his face, and instantly, images of Rolan came to mind. I blinked, shaking my head, and focused all my attention on the scene in front of me.

"Let me go, Alec!" Raven yelled, trying to kick him.

"No can do, princess," Alec said, twisting her arms even more. "As much I'd love to be the one to kill you, I think I'll let Shadow do the honours."

Raven stopped struggling as Shadow came to a stop in front of her. The smirk on his face, the one I had seen many times, chilled me to the bone as all the blood drained from my face. I could not witness someone else being tortured; I just could not. At that moment as he spoke to Raven, he was more dangerous than could I ever recall. Being scared of him was something that would not disappear until I was one hundred percent sure he was not going to turn and kill me just for bringing all this trouble to his door. At that moment, I knew he was no longer messing around.

I should not have been surprised. He is a vampire; it was what he did. He killed people to survive but tortures them for fun. He was just as psychotic as Raven was, if not more. I could not forget that, no matter the way he treated me. I had to remember just how frightening he could be.

"Now, you're going to listen to me, and you're going to listen well because if you don't," Shadow spoke threateningly, leaning into Raven. "I will make you wish that you had never met me. I may have turned you, but don't think for one second that means I won't kill you because I will. If you push me that far, I will do it, and I won't hesitate. You are nothing. You are nothing to me. You're not even worth my time, but you have forced my hand. You couldn't just leave it alone, could you? You're that desperate, you will go to any length to get my attention. Well come on then, Raven, you have it now. What do you want with Violet?"

Raven did not respond straight away, probably too shocked that Shadow had spoken to her like that. I was not as shocked as I should have been. I was expecting it, but it still did not stop me from gasping, afraid that he might just kill her where she stood.

My gasp seemed to bring Raven to her senses.

"Come here," she said to Shadow, smiling sweetly.

Shadow did not move.

"Come here so I can tell you," she said.

Shadow sighed, leaning closer to her so she could whisper in his ear. Whatever she was saying, she clearly did not want me to know as the others were surely going to hear it as well with their vampire senses and all.

What I did see, however, was Shadow's reaction to it, and that was enough to send my heart racing into a frenzy. My eyes had been locked on him since she started whispering to him, so I saw the way his hands formed into fists by his side and the way he pulled away with a murderous expression on his face—jaw clenched, his rage clear as day.

It happened in the blink of an eye.

Chapter Seventeen

He snapped her neck like it was nothing but a twig. If it were not for Alec still maintaining a tight grip on her, she would have fallen straight to the floor. She slumped over, and that was when I let out a sob, clamping a hand over my mouth.

"Is she..." I gulped. "Is she dead?"

"I can't believe she just said that." Leah shook her head, sadly.

"What did she say?" I asked, almost afraid to hear the answer.

"Nothing you need to worry about," Shadow said, taking Raven's body from Alec and slinging her over his shoulder.

I rolled my eyes; I expected that. I remained silent as Shadow disappeared with Raven's body, not even bothering to ask where he was taking her. Now that I could think a little clearer, I knew she was not dead. It took more than a snapped neck to stop a vampire after all, and I shuddered to think of what Shadow had planned for her now. I was not cut out for this. I really wasn't.

Then, a thought occurred to me. Did that mean I could go home? Did that mean Shadow could take me to live with Rose? I hoped it meant I could because Shadow could just kill her now. I had no reason to stay here any longer. I did not have to be a prisoner anymore because it was not like anyone would believe me if I started screaming I had been kidnapped by a vampire. They would laugh in my face and think I was crazy.

So when Shadow entered the room again and walked over to me with a stern expression, I waited with bated breath for him to say I was allowed to leave.

Unfortunately, that never came.

"From now on, I'm not letting you out of my sight until this is all over," he told me.

I was confused. "What? Can't you just—"

"No." He cut me off with a shake of his head.

"Why?"

"Yeah, Shadow." Alec jumped in suddenly, annoyance plain on his face as he wrapped his arms around Leah. "Why is she still alive after that?"

"You heard what she said. I'm not taking any chances." He snapped.

My frown deepened. What were they talking about?

"You're keeping her alive?" I asked, tentatively.

"Yes," Shadow responded.

I let out a breath. No matter what Raven was trying to do, there was a part of me that was glad she was not dead. I was not sure why I felt like that, I could not answer anyone who asked, but I just was. Maybe it was just a matter of my sanity, knowing she had not been killed to prevent her from harming me.

"What's going to happen now?" Leah asked, glancing at Shadow.

"I don't know," he replied.

Leah snorted. "Great plan there, Shadow. Really, truly great."

"Now isn't the time for sarcasm, Leah. If you've got nothing to offer, then just leave. I'm not in the mood today."

Leah shook her head with an amused smile on her face.

"Well, Alec and I are going out to meet Ric so try not to kill Raven while we're gone," she said before leaving the room. Alec said his goodbyes, following Leah until they were both out of the room. When the front door opened and shut, I slumped against the wall again.

"I'm never going to leave here, am I?" I asked, not expecting an answer. Sighing, I closed my eyes and tried not to cry because that was the last thing I wanted to do. Opening my eyes, I blinked a couple of times, just as Shadow moved to lean against the wall next to me.

"Do you want to leave?"

I nodded.

"Where would you go?" he asked.

"To live with Rose."

"And risk seeing your father?" He looked at me with a raised eyebrow.

He had a point. As much as I would love to live with my best friend and her family, I did not want to risk bumping into my dad. I would not know what to do or say, and there was the possibility that he would want me back if he actually saw me in person.

I shook my head. "I don't know where I'd go. I just want to be safe."

"You're safe here," Shadow stated.

"Am I, though? I mean, Raven is after me for some reason. That's not exactly me being safe, is it? And I can't forget the fact you kidnapped me either."

He rolled his eyes. "If I wanted to kill you, I wouldn't be trying to protect you."

"That may be true, but I can't stop thinking about it. All I've done lately is think."

"Then stop." He shrugged, as though it was that simple. I guess to him, it really was that simple.

"I can't. When I was living with my dad... I would think and think and think until I couldn't stop. I started to think that maybe—" I suddenly cut myself off, surprising myself by how much I was about to reveal to him.

"Started to think what?" He inquired.

I shook my head and stared at the floor. All thoughts I had been desperately trying to push to the back of my mind came rushing forward. Once again, I was left feeling like everything was all my fault, like I was the reason everything was happening. It was true as well. If I weren't here, I wouldn't be burdening Shadow, Leah, and even Alec and Ric. Shadow would not have had to spend all his days figuring out what was going on. He would not have had to kill Rolan or snap Raven's neck.

I stopped short, eyes wide. The realisation that I was the reason Rolan was killed was all too much for me. Tears welled up in my eyes before I could stop them, and I took a deep breath. I was the reason Rolan was dead. It all came back down to me. How could I live with that?

Not wanting Shadow to see me cry, I ran. I knew if he wanted to, he could stop me in seconds, but thankfully, he did not. I ran straight out of the room and up the stairs, heading for 'my' bedroom. Once inside, I shut the door and slumped against it, staring straight ahead.

How could I live knowing I was the reason a man was dead?

That thought haunted me and would continue to do so.

***

I was not sure how much time had passed, but I was not feeling any better. I had managed to stop crying, but I could not stop thinking about poor Rolan. What part he played in this whole mess no longer mattered to me because he had not hurt me. He may have been following me but that was all, and in comparison to what I had suffered at the hands of my dad, being stalked was nothing. So I could not help but feel sympathy for Rolan and the family he may have had. I think that would be what haunted me most of all, knowing that out there somewhere, could be a little girl or boy wondering where their father was.

A knock sounded at the door, and I sighed, wishing I could just be left alone no matter how much I knew it was not going to happen. Standing up and stretching as I had been sitting down in the same position for far too long, I then turned and opened the door, only to reveal Shadow.

"You're staying with me," was all he said. He turned on his heel and walked away.

Staying with him? What on earth did that mean? I quickly followed after him, wanting to ask him, but he had disappeared. I stood in the middle of the landing and looked around, but he was nowhere to be seen.

"What?" I asked myself.

I was about to leave when a door opened behind me, so I turned and saw Shadow, leaning against the open door, motioning for me to follow him. I did so, partly out of confusion and partly out of curiosity because I knew that the room he had just come from was his bedroom and I was curious as to what it looked like. Was it filled with dark colours to suit him? Or was it brightly coloured? I was curious to find out.

It turned out to be a combination of light and dark colours. Cream walls gave the room the light it needed, but all the furniture was black. The bed, the wardrobe, the chest of drawers, the tables, everything was black. Even the lamp shades that sat on either of the bedside tables were black. Oddly enough, I liked it. It suited him. Dark and mysterious, just like him.

"What do you mean I'm staying with you?" I finally asked after a few minutes of me wandering around the room.

"I told you. You're not leaving my sight until this is over with," he stated.

"So I'm staying in here?" I frowned.

"Raven is in this house. Do you really think I'm going to let you sleep alone when she's tied up downstairs?" He sat on the edge of his bed, looking up at me as I stood in front of him.

"Erm..." I trailed off. When he said he was not going to let me out of his sight, this definitely was not what I was expecting. In fact, this was the last thing I ever thought would happen.

He rolled his eyes, "I'm not sleeping in the bed with you if that's what you're thinking. I'm not going to be sleeping, you are."

"You don't need to sleep?" I asked, curiosity taking over. I was way too fascinated with vampires, I thought to myself as I waited for him to reply.

He shook his head. "Not if we don't want to. We usually do. It passes time."

I moved and sat beside him on the bed. "So you act like a normal human?"

"What were you expecting? Sleeping in coffins and burning in sunlight?"

I blushed at the amusement on his face. Then, a thought struck me.

"Why don't you burn in sunlight?"

"A witch we know cast a spell to prevent that from happening."

"Of course, witches exist, too," I muttered to myself.

"You don't seem surprised," he commented, the amusement clear.

I shot him a look. "I'm living with vampires. I think I can accept witches exist too."

He suddenly started grinning. "When we had the witch come to help us, Leah actually wanted us to have rings made that would prevent us from burning."

"Like in the Vampire Diaries?" I asked, cocking my head to one side.

"Exactly like that," He chuckled. "She likes to watch all the vampire shit on TV just to see how they differ from us."

"So she wanted you all to wear a ring?" The thought was too amusing to me, and I fought to keep the smile off my face. "With a stone and everything?"

He nodded.

"What stone did she ask for?"

"Onyx."

"That would have been a pretty ring," I said, seriously.

He pulled a face. "Pretty? Couldn't you have said something else? I am a man, you know."

"What does it matter? You don't even have one!" I laughed, unable to help myself. Shadow was definitely the most dangerous person I had ever come across in my life, and that was including my dad as he paled in comparison, but to know he still got offended over me calling a gemstone pretty... It was too amusing.

It did not hit me until later that we had actually been getting along without me fearing for my life. In fact, talking to him then, I soon realised I was not scared at all.

Chapter Eighteen

"Why do you think she's doing this?" I asked Shadow. It was one of those rare occasions that he was not interrogating Raven like she was a criminal. From what I hear, he had not gotten very far. What he wanted to get from her, I did not even know, but the frustration on his face show that she had not told him anything worth knowing.

"Because of me," he simply replied.

"If it were that simple, you'd have killed her by now." I shook my head, not buying it. There was something more to it, I was sure. I just could not figure out what that was yet.

"You don't need to know."

"I do when it's me she wants to kill," I stated, sitting up on his bed. True to his word, he had not left me out of his sight since he had tied Raven up. I was not allowed back in the other bedroom; I had been staying in Shadow's, much to my protest. The first night was the most awkward because it was extremely hard to go to sleep when you know there is someone else in the room, just watching. It was incredibly uncomfortable too, but I learnt to just get on with it; there was no hope of me ever having space. *So much for me having "free reign,"* I thought bitterly.

"All you need to know is that it's not going to happen. Nobody is going to kill you."

"Nobody but you," I whispered under my breath.

"You keep saying that as though I'm actually going to kill you. Maybe I should." Shadow turned to face me, his fists clenched. "Then this whole mess would be over with."

I did not reply.

"You've been nothing but a burden ever since I brought you here. And to think I was saving your life? Ha! I should have just killed you when I had the chance, or better yet, left that man to have you for himself. You could be his little pet to do with what he pleases." Shadow seethed, taking a step toward the bed. I instantly got to my feet, afraid. My eyes were wide, and my hands were shaking as I watched him warily.

I would be lying if I said his words did not have a profound effect on me because it did. I was terrified. I was panicking, though I desperately tried not to let it show. No doubt he had picked up on that too with the state he was in. His words struck a chord in me. It was something that my dad would say. After all, he had just basically told me he should have just let a man rape or murder me so nobody could blame me for being so scared. It reminded me all too much of my dad.

Apart from, you know, the fangs and all.

Still, it was scary enough being reminded of my dad in the presence of someone that could break every bone in my body, so I shifted a little, trying to get within reach of the door. My actions did not escape Shadow's notice if the smirk on his face was anything to go by. He looked highly amused to see me so scared, so worried for my own life, that I could not believe he had seemed to be a normal human being not that long before.

"Maybe I should kill you myself or let Raven get a hold of you. I'm sure she'd love to have the pleasure of killing you." Shadow spat, his anger increasing the more I backed away from him.

I wanted to say something, but words seemed to fail me. I was not sure there was anything I could say to help diffuse the situation. Any attempt could make things worse, and that was the last thing I wanted. I was now more aware than ever how I got into this in the first place. Try as I may to be nice to Shadow and even attempt to be his friend—of sorts—I knew now that I was kidding myself. At the end of the day, he was still a monster. How could I think we could get along? Shadow could be nice one minute and change in seconds. I could not figure him out. Who knows what goes on the mind of a vampire.

Suddenly, he turned around and punched the wall behind him, making me jump. It was something that was all too familiar to me. I jumped back, almost stumbling in my haste to get away from Shadow, to put some sort of distance between us.

I was reminded all too much of my dad, and that terrified me. Being kidnapped by a vampire may be something I could not forget, but it was easy to put it on the back of my mind considering he had saved me from a fate far worse. It was not all that hard to forget the fact he had bitten me either because it was what vampires do, and I should not expect anything less from them. But to be reminded of the one person that was supposed to love me no matter what, support me no matter what... well, that was too much. I could not cope with that.

As his back was turned, I grabbed the door handle and flung the door open. I was aware that Shadow would follow me, but I just needed to get away from him. Images of things I longed to forget made things hard for me as I rushed down the stairs. I went straight over to the front door and opened it, but I did not run away. I knew better than to do that. I just needed some space to clear my head.

Instead, I stood outside and tried to get rid of the images flashing in my mind. The harsh words my dad would spit at me in a fit of anger right before he attacked me... Every word he said, I could still remember. The insults... everything. All of them were running through my mind, and I could not do a damn thing to stop it.

I sank down to the ground, breathing heavily and curling into a ball, not caring if anyone saw me. I was too busy drowning in all my pent-up emotions and memories I longed to forget.

Someone touched my shoulder, making me jump. I raised my head from my knees to look at the person. It was Shadow, just as I presumed it would be. I knew he would not risk me running away again even if the threat was tied up somewhere in the house. He said he would keep an eye on me, and he had been doing exactly that, so it was obvious he would not let me leave.

His anger had subsided, I noticed, as he bent down with a look of concern etched onto his features. I looked at him with teary eyes, breathing heavily. I was not sure what he was going to do to me, if anything at all, but his threats were not going to leave my mind. It was too similar to the things my dad had said, all the times he had threatened me.

I shook my head as I whispered, "Leave me alone."

"Look, I'm sorry for what I said. I would never let anyone touch you like that. I'm just so pissed off with this situation that I took it out on you," Shadow explained, but I shook my head again. I was not sure whether he was telling the truth or not.

"Go away." I rested my head on my knees again and stared straight forward.

Shadow sighed and sat down beside me, leaning against the front door after he closed it. We sat there in total silence, watching the world go by.

Eventually, though, Shadow got bored with the silence and started to speak.

"Why did you run off like that?" he asked.

I frowned, looking at him though he was not looking back; he was avoiding my eyes.

"It doesn't matter." I turned away.

"I want to know."

"Tough."

"You know, you're really not helping yourself. How can I be expected to protect you when you keep running off?"

"Do you not remember what you said to me?" I asked in surprise. "That was… I can't even explain."

"I wasn't actually going to let Raven have you, and you can't honestly believe I would kill you after all the trouble I've gone to in order to make sure you're safe." He looked at me in disbelief.

I shrugged. "You've said it often enough."

"If I wanted you dead—" he started, but I quickly cut him off.

"Yeah, I know. I get it. But it just reminds me of... Well, never mind. Besides, it's not even about you threatening to kill me."

"Then what is it about?"

I did not answer. I wanted him to figure it out for himself. He was not stupid; he knew what he had said. Whether he meant it was an entirely different story. I was about to stand up when he spoke.

"That man I saved you from. Him? That's what this is about?"

I bit my lip.

"I didn't mean it. I would sooner rip off a man's dick if he even tried to force himself on you, or any woman for that matter," he said, and this time, when I looked into his eyes, I believed him. He was sincere, I could just tell.

I smiled softly. "I'm sorry for overreacting."

His eyebrows raised. "Overreacting? You've been too calm about all of this, in my opinion. Sure, you get scared, but considering you didn't know vampires even existed a month ago, you sure aren't acting like anyone else would if they'd been kidnapped by a blood-sucking monster."

"I guess deep, deep down I know you wouldn't hurt me though I do have my doubts," I said, honestly. "And of course, I'm scared. I've been taken away from everything I knew and placed in the middle of something I wasn't even aware of. It's like I've been thrown into an entirely new world, and I'm lost. I'm lost, confused, and scared, and I don't know what to do."

"It's natural to feel that way, you know? I can't let you leave because then you're at risk of being killed and because you know too much, but that doesn't mean I'm planning on killing you, no matter how much I state otherwise. I want you to know that. It may be hard to believe after you've witnessed what I did to Rolan, but I'm not going to kill you. I'm trying to protect you."

"Why?" I asked suddenly, curious of his reasoning. I could not understand why he would want to protect me. It just did not make sense. I could not wrap my head around it.

"Because you've been hurt enough already. I don't want to add to that," he admitted, shaking his head.

"Why?"

"Upstairs, in my room," he said suddenly, straightening up a little. "That's why you ran, isn't it? I reminded you of your father?"

I blinked, surprised he had figured it out but nodded anyway. There was no use in lying to him, and to be honest, I did not want to. I found myself wanting to talk to someone about it. I had kept everything in for far too long that I had let it destroy me emotionally.

"It wasn't the threat of being killed. I'm sorta getting used to hearing you say that. It was what you said about leaving me to that man because that's what I was to my dad. Granted, he never raped me, but he did with me what he pleased, and I was powerless to stop it. I felt like a rag doll when it comes to my dad, his personal punching bag, and I never want to feel that way again." A tear spilled over halfway through my speech, so I quickly wiped it away.

Shadow shook his head. "For what it's worth, I am sorry. It makes me so mad even to hear what he did to you, and I don't even know the details. I want to kill him, I really do. I won't, though, for you."

"What makes you think I'd care whether he was dead or alive?" I asked, aware of how cruel that sounded.

"The same reason you didn't ever tell the police about him; because he's your father."

"Stupid, isn't it?" I asked with a humourless laugh. "Everything he put me through and I still can't turn him in."

"It is stupid. You don't owe him anything, so why didn't you?" he asked, frowning as he stared at me.

I shrugged. "Because I know it's my fault he is the way he is. If I didn't drive my mum away, then she'd still be with my dad, and they'd be happy. He wasn't always abusive. He used to be really nice, and he always made me laugh. I can't turn him in because I'm the reason he is so unhappy with his life. I can't be the reason he goes to jail. I just can't. No matter how stupid or pathetic that makes me, I won't ruin his life any more than I already have."

Shadow, completely shocked by my words, stood up and grabbed me, pulling me up. Standing in front of him, I was completely confused as to what was going through his mind, especially when he took my hands in his and stared straight into my eyes with a determination on his face that had me at a loss for words.

"It was not your fault, Violet. That man changed all on his own. It had nothing to do with you. As for the reason your mother left? That isn't your fault, either. If she loved you or your father that much, then she would not have left either of you. That woman is just as responsible for how he turned out, but it is not your fault. Don't blame yourself, Violet. It's not your fault. Whatever he has said to you, they are all lies. He's trying to blame someone because he won't blame himself. That's all it is. It's what weak men do when they can't own up to the mistakes they've made."

He actually believed I was not to blame, I thought as I watched him speak.

Every word, to him, was the truth. He said it with such conviction that even I was having a hard time denying it. I had gone on so long thinking my dad was telling the truth that the possibility he was lying to me had never crossed my mind—until now. Was I the reason she left? Was anything he said to me the truth?

Trying to contain the tears was proving to be even more difficult than I originally thought, and they made their way down my face quicker than I could wipe them away. Shadow, upon seeing the tears, sighed and pulled me into him, wrapping his arms around my waist as I wiped the tears again.

"Why did he have to do it?" I asked Shadow as I cried into his shoulder. "Why did he have to hurt me like that? All those times he punched me or kicked me or strangled me, what did I do to deserve it, Shadow? He left me broken, and I don't know why. I thought he was right, that I was the reason she left, but now I don't know. I don't know anything anymore. I'm a mess."

"I might not be the best person to be having this conversation with as all I can think about is torturing him the way he tortured you, but I do know this: you're not broken. You're stronger than you believe you are, a lot stronger. I'm willing to bet thousands of pounds that he was the reason she left, not you."

I remained silent, mulling over his words. I found myself wondering whether I was really to blame for all that had happened. I found myself wondering things I had never wondered about before, and it was all because of Shadow.

"Thank you," I whispered.

Chapter Nineteen

Things changed between Shadow and me after that. He was a lot more understanding than I had given him credit for. Now he knew how I felt about certain things, he had been trying his best to watch what he says but, more importantly, he was trying his best to make sure I was alright. It was like we had turned a corner, that we could get along without him threatening to kill me every ten minutes. Of course, he still got angry and would threaten me, but I was learning to just brush it off. He was right; if he wanted to kill me, then he would not be trying to protect me.

I was feeling a little better about everything after the talk with Shadow, though I had a long way to go before my emotional wounds would be mended. I knew I was far from being fixed, but I was just happy to have been able to open up a little. I had kept everything inside for so long that it was breaking me down little by little but now, I felt as though one day I would be okay. That was all I could hope for.

"Violet!" I heard my name being called from the kitchen, so I got up from the sofa and walked into the kitchen to see that Leah and Alec deep in conversation about something.

"Yeah?" I said, glancing at the two of them.

Leah smiled as she looked at me, jumping up to come over to me and give me a hug. I awkwardly hugged her back, wondering what she wanted me for. I had not seen her in a few days because she had been staying with Alec, so I was a little surprised to see her so suddenly.

"How are you?" she asked me as she pulled away, going back to sit opposite Alec at the table. The same table where Rolan—No. I shook my head. I could not keep thinking about that. I could not. It would drive me insane.

"I'm okay," I replied.

"Good. That's good. That's great!" Leah said, grinning hugely. She was too happy, and it was beginning to make me feel uncomfortable until Alec spoke up.

"Leah, relax, would you? You're creeping her out."

"Oh, shut up! I'm allowed to be happy! Raven is locked up somewhere, you're back with me, and Shadow is actually trying to get on with Violet! It's a wonderful day!" she said to Alec, that grin still on her face.

Alec shook his head at her in amusement. "You're such an idiot."

"Yeah, but I'm your idiot," she replied, winking as she got up to go and sit on his lap. When they started to kiss, I took that as my cue to leave. The whole interaction was a little strange, that was for sure.

I went back into the living room and sat back down, grabbing my phone. I was going to call Rose as I hadn't heard from her in a few days. I wanted to catch up, but as it turned out, I did not have to call her as I had a message from her. I quickly opened it up.

I'M COMING TO VISIT YOU, BITCH! I'm coming tomorrow, so you better be ready because I've missed your ass! I'm so excited!

What?! I can't wait to see you. I've missed you too! Are you driving here or getting the train? Where are you staying? I hurriedly typed and hit send.

Although I was extremely excited now that I knew I would be able to see my friend, the one person who gave me a sense of normalcy in this crazy new world I had been thrown into, I was internally panicking. Shadow would not let me leave the house without a chaperone. It was not just because of Raven, but because he was afraid I would run. There was no way he would leave me alone, and yet there was no way Rose could see me with him or any of the others.

While I was having an internal debate on what I could do, my phone vibrated in my hands, signalling that I had just received another message.

I'm driving, duh! My dad so very kindly lent me his car again after a lot of persuading... I will be setting off bright and early tomorrow! I'm so looking forward to seeing you, you can show me around, and who knows, maybe I'll find a hot rebound guy while I'm there? ;) See you soon!

I thought you'd already had a rebound guy? What happened there? See you soon! I replied.

Let's just say the guy had no idea what he was doing.

Rose and I chatted back and forth for a while longer. All the while, my panic was increasing. I would have to explain to Shadow what Rose had planned though I was not sure how he would take it. We may be getting on well recently, but that did not mean his anger issues just disappeared. They were still there, waiting for the chance to come out to play.

I stood up, deciding to just get it over with. It was better than waiting until tomorrow to tell him. We would need some sort of plan, anyway. At least this way, we would have the night to think something up.

"Where's Shadow?" I asked Leah and Alec, entering the kitchen again.

"Oh! I forgot!" Leah said, turning around but still remaining on Alec's lap. "That's what I called you for. He's interrogating Raven but said that he would be taking you somewhere later. He didn't say where, though."

I was confused. Shadow had not mentioned anything to me about it, but then again, I had not actually seen him all day. I could not help but wonder where he was taking me because as far as I was aware, he had no reason to take me anywhere. I was curious though and, as much as I hated to admit it, I was also pretty excited.

"If I were you, I wouldn't go looking for Shadow until he's done interrogating Raven. You don't want to get on his bad side. Trust me," Alec said, looking at me with a grim look on his face.

I nodded. I was not planning on going to look for him. I did not know what room he had her locked up in, so I certainly was not going to go and search the place. It was a big house, so I was not sure where he was keeping her. All I knew was that there was no way in hell I was going to witness him torturing someone else.

***

Shadow did not appear until a couple of hours later, walking over to the sink. I caught the sight of blood on his hands and grimaced, turning away and resuming my conversation with Leah and Alec. I really did not want to know what he had done to Raven. It would make me sick, literally—or I would faint. It could go either way with me.

"Has she said anything?" Alec asked Shadow, glancing up at him with a curious expression on his face.

"Yes and no," Shadow replied, turning around and leaning against the sink, drying his hands with the tea towel that had been left on the side.

"What does that mean? Either she did, or she didn't." Leah chimed in with a curious expression on her face.

"It means that she's been saying the exact same thing all the time." Shadow paused for a second, deliberating on whether or not to continue. Eventually, he proceeded. "I do have to let her go, though."

That had both Leah and Alec standing to their feet in an instant while I remained seated, wondering what was going on. Let her go? That was not a good idea at all. She would just kill me like she has wanted to since this whole thing started. Why would he let her go?

"You know why I have to, so shut the hell up!" Shadow yelled as Leah and Alec shouted at the top of their voices. It made me cringe hearing how loud they were being.

"What else has she said?" Alec demanded, lowering his voice though it was clear he was still incredibly pissed off.

"You know what," Shadow replied, in a clipped tone.

"I know what she's threatened to do, but you know you can't rely on her word. She's a pathological liar, Shadow, and you damn well know it!" Alec spat.

Shadow, pushing himself off the counter he was leaning against, stepped up to Alec, getting right into his face. I edged away from the two of them, not wanting to get in the middle of a vampire fight.

"You heard what she said that day. I am not taking any chances, Alec, so if you don't like it, you can leave." Shadow had spoken in a hushed tone, but he had a dangerous look about him. A dangerous look that I did not like—not one bit.

"What did she say?" I blurted out before I could stop myself.

Shadow's eyes flickered towards me though he did not look any less dangerous. As he walked towards me, I took a few steps back, feeling my heart start to pound relentlessly in my chest.

"You want to know what she said?" he asked, smirking.

"Don't you dare," Leah warned him. "Don't you think she's been through enough?!"

"Shut up, Leah." Shadow rolled his eyes though he did step away from me. I let out a breath I had not realised I had been holding, relieved that he was no longer in my personal space. It made me nervous, incredibly so.

He did not tell me anything after that, which should not have surprised me. It was annoying. I had a right to know what she had said. If it was about me, I definitely had a right to know, but none of them seemed willing to let me in on it.

I sighed, shaking my head. "Fine, don't tell me then. It's not like I've not been kept in the dark about anything before, is it?"

"Violet—" Leah started, but I quickly cut her off.

"Rose is coming to London tomorrow, by the way. That's what I needed to talk to Shadow about. She's going to want to stay with me, and we all know that can't happen. So, what do we do?" I asked, immediately catching all their attention as they glanced at me.

"What did you just say?" Shadow seethed, glaring at me.

"Erm... Rose... You know? My friend... Well, she's coming here... tomorrow." I stumbled out, not liking the look on his face. The phrase 'if looks could kill' came to mind as I watched him anxiously.

"As if I didn't have enough to worry about!" Shadow suddenly burst out, making me jump back in fright. "As if I didn't have enough on my plate already, and now I have to worry about you mouthing off to your friend or running off with her?!"

"I'm not going to tell her anything," I stated. "I wouldn't. You'd kill her if I did. I'm not stupid."

"Well, you're acting pretty stupid right now." Shadow shot back.

As much as I hated to admit it, his words actually hurt. I turned my gaze to the floor, I did not want to look at him any longer.

"Just tell her she can't come. It's that simple," Alec spoke up in an attempt to diffuse the tense atmosphere that had loomed in the room.

"I can't." I looked back up, meeting his curious gaze. "If I tell her not to come, she'll come anyway."

"Where does she think you are?" Leah asked.

"At my grandparent's house."

"Then tell her she has to stay at a hotel because you've got no room for her." Leah nodded to herself. The more I thought about it, the more I realise that could actually work. "If Violet stays with Rose in the same hotel Ric works at, at least he can keep an eye on her while we sort things out here. You know it's not safe here for Violet now Raven is locked up here, Shadow, so you have no choice in the matter now. Violet will stay with her friend."

I nodded, liking the idea the second Leah stopped speaking.

Shadow, however, did not.

"I told you that Violet is not leaving my sight until this mess is sorted out, and I am not changing my mind on that," he spoke through gritted teeth.

"You don't have a choice, mate. Raven will keep to her threat if you don't listen to her," Alec said, pulling Leah to him and wrapping his arms around her protectively. She leant into him, a small smile on her face as she glanced up at Alec, and I found myself frowning, wishing I could have someone to protect me like that.

I quickly shook my head. Now was not the time to be thinking things like that, I told myself. I had bigger things to worry about.

"Look, Rose can't see any of you with me." I started, capturing their attention once again. "You don't know her. She will question you on everything just to make sure I'm safe around you. She does know I was kidnapped, remember? She just thinks I escaped. If she sees any of you with me, she will jump to conclusions. I know she will."

"So we stick to my idea." Leah nodded.

"It's the best plan, mate," Alec said to Shadow, who still was not pleased though he knew he wasn't going to win.

With a sigh, he stormed out of the room.

Chapter Twenty

"You're acting like a child!" I yelled at the top of my voice, not able to contain my annoyance any longer. Shadow knew the score; he knew I had to meet Rose alone no matter how much he despised the idea. Rose was my friend, and I would be safe with her. So why he was acting like a petulant child, I was not sure, but it was starting to grate on me; that was for sure.

"I'm trying to keep you safe!" Shadow yelled, his jaw clenched as he struggled to contain his anger.

I scoffed. "Funny that because if you'd just left me alone that night, then none of this would be happening."

"If I'd left you alone that night you would be dead." Shadow scowled.

"Better dead than being stuck like this!" I snapped, shaking my head as I tried to calm down. Shadow just did not understand that I had to meet her alone. She had already seen him once; she was sure to recognise him again. She never forgot a face and especially a good looking one. That would cause the questions to start, questions even he knew he could not afford to be asked.

"You want to know why going out there unprotected would be suicide?" Shadow spoke, determination taking over him. He stalked towards me with hands clenched into fists by his side, never taking his eyes off mine.

My breathing hitched when he stopped in front of me, inches away from my face. I knew he was trying to scare me, and unfortunately for me, it was also working.

"You want to know what Raven said so badly?" he asked again, his breath hitting my face. In any other circumstance, him being this close to me would cause an entirely different reaction, a more pleasant one.

"What?" I asked, trying not to let him know just how scared I actually was.

"She has friends, as hard as that is to believe. She has friends that wouldn't hesitate to kill every single one of us in this room if we killed her that day. Those very friends have very strict, very clear instructions on what to do should we ever kill her." He lowered his voice, and for some reason, that only added to the tense atmosphere. "Those instructions are to hurt you in the worst way possible, and let me tell you something: all those friends of hers are male, and they just love a vulnerable, human girl who is utterly defenceless against them."

It did not take a genius to figure out what he was trying to say, and the fact he did not even need to spell it out for me should have been the first sign. I should not leave unprotected. I should stay with Shadow or at least let him come along.

I did not.

"Shadow, what the fuck is wrong with you?" Alec's voice suddenly made me jump.

"She wanted to know." He shrugged.

"Don't fucking lie." Alec spat. "You want her to be afraid, don't you? You want her to rely on you, so you don't have to fucking worry every god damn second about where she is because you actually do care."

"Of course I care!" Shadow turned on him. Leah, I noticed, jumped up from the sofa and placed herself in between the two guys though she said nothing.

"So you terrify the poor girl even more?" Alec rolled his eyes.

"I am the only one that is doing anything lately. All you two do is laze around all day while I am the one trying to sort this whole shit out. So don't you dare lecture me, or I swear, I will kill you."

"Go on then, kill me," Alec said, stepping around Leah and getting in Alec's face. "But if you do, I can tell you one thing for sure. Leah would never forgive you. You say you're trying to sort everything out, and maybe you are, but I don't see Leah or myself trying to terrify Violet into doing what we say. She listens to us because we aren't terrifying her every second. Ever wondered why she runs from you all the time?"

Alec had a point, but he was wrong about one thing. I didn't just listen to him or Leah. I listened to Shadow because I was afraid of him. I was aware of how much he wanted to kill me, and I knew he would not hesitate in doing so. The thing with Alec was that he seemed to realise when to draw the line and knew not to cross it. He knew the boundaries and respected them. He was a good person at heart, but he did not know me well enough if he thought I would not run from him or Leah if I had enough reason to.

"Just shut up!" I shouted suddenly with eyes wide. The arguments between the two of them were ridiculous. They were constantly trying to one-up the other. It was stupid. The testosterone levels were ridiculous, and I was sick of hearing it. I was already terrified of everything, anyway; why did they have to make it worse by arguing with each other every second? It was not going to help anything. It would undoubtedly make them worse, not just for myself, but for Leah, too. If Shadow killed Alec, she would break.

Not being able to take the arguing a second longer, I pushed past them all.

"Where the fuck do you think you're going?" Shadow asked me as I headed for the door.

"Away from you!" I said, not bothering to turn back to look at him. Once in the hallway, I ran over to the front door. I knew Shadow would want to chase me, but I was hoping he would not. I needed the time away from all the vampires. I needed space. So, rushing out into the fresh air, I did not stop until I was sure they were not following me, not even stopping to think about the danger I was in being alone.

Only an idiot would run towards the danger rather than away from it.

Apparently, I was an idiot.

***

"What is wrong with you?" Rose asked in exasperation as we left yet another clothing store. We had been shopping for around an hour, and I had been trying to enjoy myself as much as I could, but I could not help letting my eyes wander, glancing around nervously for any sign of Raven's friends. Shadow's words had not left my mind. If his intention was to terrify me yet again, then he had succeeded. What made it worse was the fact I literally had no idea what her friends even looked like. It could be anyone.

"What do you mean?" I asked Rose furrowing eyebrows.

"I'm talking about you looking over your shoulder every few minutes. What's wrong?" she asked. She was irritated; it was obvious, but could she blame me after everything I've been through?

"I'm sorry," I mumbled, casting my eyes to the ground as we walked down the street. "I'm just nervous. I was kidnapped, remember?"

"Yeah, but you also got away." She pointed out.

"They brought me to London, Rose," I spoke bitterly. "That means they live here. They could be anywhere just watching me. Excuse me for watching my back."

A guilty expression took over her face as she glanced at me. "I'm sorry, Vi. Really. I've just got a lot on my mind."

You and me both, I thought bitterly.

We kept on talking as we headed to the hotel Rose was staying at. Shopping had not been of much use to Rose, who had not found a single item within her price range and had to leave empty-handed. We did end up buying some food, though, but that had been pretty much it. So, with a dejected sigh, she had announced that we may as well go to her hotel and binge on room service while she told me about her boy troubles. To be honest, I was looking forward to it. Not only had I missed Rose, but I had missed having a sense of normalcy in my life.

We never reached the hotel.

Upon seeing someone standing in front of an alley that we were just about to walk by, I stopped dead and grabbed Rose's arm, clinging onto her for dear life. I had no idea how I knew, but I just knew that the man watching us with a smirk on his face was one of Raven's friends. I could feel it in my bones.

"Hey, what's wrong?" Rose asked again, not having spotted the man yet.

"Maybe we should get a taxi?" I suggested, not taking my eyes from the man. He was only a few steps away from us, five at the most, but no matter the distance between us, we would not be able to escape him. Outrunning a vampire was impossible after all.

"What, why?" Rose asked. From my peripheral vision, I saw her frowning and then she craned her head to look in the direction of my gaze. I heard her gasp. "He looks... dangerous."

"Yeah..." I trailed off.

"Do you know him?" she asked.

"No."

We took a step backwards, silently agreeing that heading back was the better option, but we did not get very far. We bumped into someone else. Rose squealed as we turned to face who stood in front of us, and when my eyes landed on the familiar purple hair, I gasped.

"Did you miss me?" She smirked.

I did not even get a chance to reply before she grabbed Rose and me, taking us into the alley.

Chapter Twenty-One

"LET ME GO!" Rose yelled, thrashing around as she tried to get the man to release the grip he had on her. It was a useless attempt, though. He was not going to let her go anytime soon.

I glanced at Raven, who stood in front of me with her arms folded across her chest. She was just watching me, clearly amused by how scared I was at that moment. She was enjoying my fear, and that just made me all the more scared. What was she going to do now?

"Now then, little Violet," she spoke suddenly, grinning wickedly. "What do I do with you? Should I kill you or torture you… or should I let my good friend here have his way with you?"

My eyes widened. Shadow really had been telling the truth.

"What do you want with us, you sick fuck?" Rose yelled, still trying to get away.

Raven craned her neck to look at her. "Oh, it's not you I want. You're just collateral damage, really. It's Violet that I want."

I shrank back, wishing that I had not run out the way that I had. I was definitely regretting that decision now. I hoped that Rose would get out of this alive; I really did. She had not done anything wrong. She did not deserve to die like this. She did not even know what was going on. She was completely innocent. I did not particularly want to die myself, but that was what Raven wanted. There was no way that I was getting out of this alive.

I was not sure how I felt about that, to be honest.

"What's so special about you then, Violet?" Raven asked me, causing me to frown. What was she on about now? "Shadow never keeps humans alive. He was reckless. He would kill people and leave their bodies for their family members to find. He certainly didn't keep one as a pet, and he certainly never tried to protect them. So, Violet, what is so special about you?"

"Who the fuck is Shadow?" Rose asked me, though I didn't reply to her. My mind was on other things. Was Shadow really like that? Did he really just kill people as though they were nothing to him but a walking blood source? Did he really care so little for human life?

I should not have been so surprised. What he did to Rolan should have been the biggest sign that he truly cared nothing for human life, but I could not help but make excuses for him. Rolan had been following me, and we had not known what for. We had not known what he was up to. And no, nothing Shadow did was right, but I had come to terms with the fact that he did things in the only way that got him answers and that he would not allow anyone, much less me, to talk him out of it. Yet, as I thought about it, I knew there was a part of Shadow that enjoyed the way he tortured people. The look on his face as he was torturing Rolan proved it.

So was Shadow really that bad? If he still was like that, why would he protect me? What was so special about me?

"There's nothing special about me," I told Raven honestly. "Please, just let us go. We've done nothing wrong. Whatever your issue is, talk to Shadow, but please, let us go!"

"Not happening, sweetheart." She smiled, condescendingly.

"Let go of us, you purple headed dinosaur!" Rose yelled. I bit my lip. Now really was not the time for Rose and her sarcastic comments, but it almost seemed like it was her defence mechanism. Whether or not that was true, it would surely get us killed that much sooner.

Raven, who did not seem to understand the reference Rose made, turned to her. I saw her face transform—the veins appeared, her eyes darkened, and her fangs were put on display—showing Rose that she was not just an average human with a grudge but an evil psychopath that would not hesitate to rip our throats out.

I also saw Rose's reaction to this.

She was terrified. Her eyes had widened considerably, and her face had paled. She looked as though she was about to faint at any given moment. I was concerned. What was going to happen now? Rose now knew about vampires, the one thing I never ever wanted her to find out about. She would freak out, she would scream, and she would cry. It was in her nature to be dramatic.

I was surprised then when instead of the reaction I was expecting, she took a deep breath and appeared to not be as affected as I thought. I knew it was an act. She was trying to appear tough while on the inside, she was freaking out, but I would rather her show it than keep it inside. It was creepy to see her so calm. It was the complete opposite of who she was.

"As you can see, I'm a vampire, not a dinosaur." Raven smirked though she did appear to be slightly disappointed at the lack of reaction coming from my friend. That, perhaps, was the reason Rose tried not to show how she was feeling. She did not want Raven to know.

"Look, can we just get on with this before they figure out you escaped?" The man that was holding Rose suddenly spoke, his eyes glittering dangerously. It was daylight, and there were still people milling around as they walked down the street, so I knew they would not be dragging this out too long. They would want it over and done with before they were caught. Whether or not they would be, I was not sure, but it would not make a difference as they would surely kill whoever caught them, but then the murder count would go up, and that was something I did not want, not when Raven only wanted me. It would be easier just to hand myself over to her.

"WAIT!" I shouted, capturing Raven's attention as she turned back to face me. She pushed me against the wall harshly, sending a wave of pain down my spine. I hurried to speak. "Let my friend go, and I will stay put. I won't move. I won't scream. I won't do anything to risk being caught, but you have to let my friend go."

"You think I'm stupid, huh?" Raven shook her head. "You think I don't know your friend will run and get help? I'm not stupid, honey, so don't test my patience. It's already wearing thin."

Even Rose could not deny that. She would not leave me alone.

"Let her go!" I begged, feeling the tears springing to my eyes as the fear started to take over. I was trembling all over by this point, breathing a little heavier. It was clear that we were not getting out of this situation, that we would both end up dead. Somehow, although I was terrified for my own safety, I was more worried about Rose. She had people who cared about her, a family who loved her. She had to get back to them safely whereas I had no one. Sure, Shadow and Leah and to some extent, Ric and Alec had become friends to me, but I still did not trust them, and I knew they did not actually care. I have no clue why Shadow was keeping me alive, but I could only assume it was to drag it out long enough for me to put my guard down, and then he could kill me without a struggle. I would not see it coming. I was not sure if I was right, but then again, I was not sure of much these days.

"No can do," Raven replied.

"Look, you're wrong if you think Shadow cares about me. He locked me up in a bedroom for weeks, so why would he care? He's planning on killing me. I know he is. He doesn't care, and I'm not special. Whatever the reason that you are doing this, you're wrong. You don't need to kill us!"

"I'm doing this because of Shadow," Raven suddenly hissed, leaning in closer. I tried to shrink away, but I could not; I was trapped in her grip, and she showed no sign of letting me go anytime soon. "He means something to me. He turned me, you know? He turned me into a vampire and then just left me to deal with it alone. Quite harsh, don't you think? That was why I vowed to not only ruin his life but ruin the lives of those around him. It's too bad about Leah, really, but if I have to kill her, then I will."

I hated to admit it, but there was a part of me that sympathised with Raven. Just leaving her to deal with such a dramatic change alone was both harsh and cruel, but no amount of pain could justify her actions. I had been through a lot, but I still would not ruin my dad's life as she was attempting to do Shadow's.

"You're in love with him," Rose suddenly said, causing both mine and Raven's heads to turn to look at her. She was still acting as though this was not bothering her, but I could tell it was. If I looked closely enough, I could see her hands shaking.

"What did you just say!" Raven asked, cocking her head to one side.

"You're in love with him, this Shadow guy. No one goes to such lengths because you want revenge on a guy who left you. Not unless you're in love with him." Rose explained.

I was taken aback by her words. Raven, in love with Shadow? I could hardly see it myself, but then as Rose explained, it did make sense. If it was true and Raven really did love Shadow, that would mean she really was intent on killing me especially if she had gotten it into her head that I meant something to him. Which I did not. I definitely did not. Yet she clearly did not believe it.

"I've had enough of this!" Raven suddenly spat, narrowing her eyes as she then turned her attention back to me. "Adam, keep that bitch quiet. You can have your turn after."

I knew then that it was time. She was going to kill me and then she would kill Rose because god forbid she had a witness to what was about to occur. By now, I was paralysed with fear. There was no hope in hell of me ever managing to get away now because even though Raven had me pushed against a brick wall, I still could not move my legs. I was terribly scared. It was ridiculous that I was too helpless to fight back. I wished that I could. I wished there was something to prevent what was going to happen.

She had me trapped, and she knew it.

It was not until she came closer and moved my hair out of the way, showing my neck, that I knew I was in deep trouble and if I wanted to get out of this, then I would have to try. I did not manage to get myself under control until I saw her face nearing my neck, putting her fangs on display.

Moving my arm as fast as I could, I punched her straight in the side of the head. She hissed and backed away, leaving a satisfied feeling spreading through me. That feeling did not last long, however, as she soon recovered from the shock of it.

It only took two steps for her to grab my neck and push me even harder against the wall. I cried out in pain, but she did not stop. She repeated this once more before sending me flying through the air and crashing into the opposite wall before crumpling to the floor. Vampire strength, I noticed, was something that would definitely come in handy to me right now.

I could hear Rose screaming, seeming to forget what she was trying to accomplish by appearing calm. She was screaming and now, she was yelling, yelling at Raven to let me go and to stop. Adam, the man who held Rose's arms behind her back, was grinning.

I felt dazed. Everything was spinning as Raven pulled me up from the heap I was in, pushing me against the wall once again. I hoped, and I prayed that she would not throw me against it again as the pain was already unbearable.

She did not.

Instead, she smirked. As much as I wanted to beg for my life, I knew there was absolutely no point. Raven would not listen. Psychopaths did not listen. They did what they wanted when they wanted, so it was clear that nothing I could say was going to convince her to spare our lives. She was intent on doing this and seeing it through.

She placed her hands on my shoulders and inserted her one leg in between mine, trapping me against the wall again. She leaned in like she had before, and I swore I heard her sniff my neck. It came as a start to realise she was not sniffing out the perfume I wore but rather the blood running through my neck.

I gulped, teary eyes meeting Rose's terrified ones.

The thing about death? It was inevitable, and yet it comes so unexpectedly. The last thing I was expecting when I met up with Rose was meeting death face to face, greeting it like an old friend. When Raven sank her fangs into my neck, and I was struggling to get away, battling to stay conscious, I knew I would soon be seeing the grim reaper up close and personal.

I tried to scream or to even speak at all, but my voice seemed to fail me. The pain was excruciating though familiar. Pain was not something I should be used to, but that was just how unlucky I was, I guess. It felt as though I was on fire, and she had to clamp a hand over my mouth to stop the screams. She successfully managed to drown out the noise I was making, but it did not matter; I was losing consciousness, I could barely breathe. It was hard to stay focused when the blood was literally being drained out of me.

"Raven, that's enough." I heard Adam speak suddenly.

She did not listen. She continued to suck the blood out of me as my head rested against the wall and my eyes fought to remain open.

I was going to die. This would be how I meet my death: drained of blood by a jealous vampire. It did not seem real, almost.

She was suddenly ripped away from me, and I sank to the floor, not having the energy or the strength to stand. Adam was the one who had pulled her away, and for a split second, I was grateful to him for it. Rose, now free of Adam's grip, rushed to my side with tears streaming down her face.

"Violet!" she screamed, gripping my shoulders tightly as her long nails sunk into my skin. "Violet!"

I could hear Raven and Adam yelling back and forth to one another, but I could not make out what they were saying. I was drifting in and out, struggling to keep my eyes open as I clamped a hand over my neck in a feeble attempt to stop the blood pouring from me if I even had much left. Rose, on the other hand, was now taking her jacket off and she moved my hand, pressing the jacket against my neck.

"Oh my god, oh my god, what do I do? Violet, you need to stay awake. I'll call a hospital and the police, and oh god, who else do I call? They'll think I'm crazy if I tell them what happened!" Rose was becoming hysterical. I would have reassured her if I could.

People say your life flashes before your very eyes in the last few seconds of your life. They were wrong. All I could focus on was the pain, the unbelievable amount of pain that I was in though the people I would miss did come to mind. Rose... even Shadow and Leah, to some extent. All three of them had helped me in some way after all.

I found myself wishing that I could see them again one more time before I died. I wanted to thank them. It was only now that I realised just how much they had tried to help me. I also wanted to comfort Rose, who was still hysterical, but I could not. I could barely breathe, let alone talk.

All I could utter were two short words before I passed out.

"Call... Shadow."

***

Shadow's POV

"What the fuck do you mean she's escaped?" I asked, trying to keep calm as Alec shifted awkwardly, clearly uncomfortable about the situation. "You were supposed to be watching her."

"I was, but Leah needed me. I wasn't long, I swear, but by the time I got back, Raven was gone!"

I pinched the bridge of my nose and breathed in deeply. *Stay calm*, I told myself, *don't flip out.*

"There's something else..." Alec trailed off.

"What?"

"She knows Violet is unprotected."

Anger coursed through my veins faster than I could throw Alec up against the wall, gripping his shirt tightly. I glared at him, my fangs on display. How could he let this happen? He was supposed to be watching her, and now she was out there, after the one person I was trying my hardest to protect.

Alec pushed me off him, shaking his head. "Shadow... calm down, okay? We're gonna find her. I promise."

I did as he asked, calming myself down before I could let the anger take over any further. Leah would never forgive me if I killed the love of her life, as she frequently liked to remind me. Besides, getting angry at him was not going to help us find Raven or Violet.

"Find Raven." I ordered Alec. "I'll find Violet."

He rushed off when I finished speaking, knowing better than to stand around talking. I followed him, hoping that I could find Violet before Raven did.

Why the stupid bitch was so obsessed with me, I had yet to figure out, but I put it down to being in love with me. I mean, I was not big-headed or anything, but I did look good. I have had a lot of girls throwing themselves at me in my extremely long life so it would not surprise me if she were. Raven was just too obsessed for her own good, and it was not going to end well for her. If she even thought of hurting a hair on Violet's head, then I would end her miserable existence faster than she could beg me to stop.

I knew I was to blame for this, considering I had been the one to bring her here, and I was the one that Raven had the fixation upon. All I wanted to do was protect her, though, and I was going to continue to protect her in any way I could. I may be a condescending, cold-hearted arsehole, but that did not mean I did not have a soft spot for her. She was just too hung up on the murderer thing to realise I was not going to go through any of my threats.

Nobody was going to hurt Violet; I would not allow it. She had been through too much, and I refused to put her through any more pain. She did not deserve it.

***

I had been looking for Violet for ages now with no such luck. I had no idea where she was. She was not answering her phone, and it was safe to say that I was beginning to get a little worried. Why the fuck wasn't she answering her phone? What was the point in me giving it back to her when she was not going to answer the damn thing?

I was still mentally cursing her when my phone started to ring. The caller I.D told me it was Violet, and relief instantly flooded through me—until I answered the phone.

"Where the fu—" I started to speak but was quickly cut off by an extremely annoying, extremely hysterical voice on the other end.

"Oh my god, oh my god, oh my god," the voice kept repeating before it sounded further away, almost like they had pulled the phone away from them. "Violet, keep your fucking eyes open, or I swear to God I will slap you!"

Hearing that, I halted in the middle of the street, pressing my fist against my mouth. That did not sound good.

"What's going on?" I asked, moving my fist away from my mouth, hoping that I was wrong in assuming Raven had caught up to her first.

"Oh, God! You're Shadow, aren't you?" The hysterical girl was back. "She told me to call, and oh God, you have to help us! Please, you have to help! Some purple bitch came, and vampires are real, and Violet was bit, and now she's bleeding, and oh God, I'm freaking out!"

Upon hearing that, I felt like somebody had just punched me in the stomach. I felt like everything was crashing down around me, and I was helpless to prevent it. What was that feeling? I did not know, but finding out was the last thing that was on my mind right now.

"Put your hand over the bite mark and press down hard. Where are you?" Trying to sound like I was not panicking myself was easier than I thought it would be, and after the hysterical girl, who I soon realised was Rose, told me where they were, I was running down the street in hopes that Violet would still be alive when I got to her.

I reached the alley in no time, and upon seeing the figures, one huddled over the other, I faltered—I did for a second before I realised that standing around was not going to do anything. So I ran over and bent down beside them.

Rose turned to look at me with a frown on her face. I looked at her, seeing the tears that were rolling down her cheeks and the wide-eyed, horrified expression on her face, and I just knew I was going to have my hands full trying to get her to calm down.

I could always kill her, but I knew Violet would never forgive me for that either.

I turned to Violet. Whatever words I was about to say got stuck in my throat as I stared down at her unconscious body. I was breathing hard by this point though I was not sure why. It was not like I needed to breathe. I was dead after all.

"Well, do something!" Rose cried. "Don't just sit and watch her, you idiot!"

Gritting my teeth together, I refrained from taking out my anger and frustration on her. She was just worried about her friend, I reminded myself. There was no need to kill her. Not yet.

"Violet," I called her name softly, moving Rose's hand from her neck to inspect the wound. Raven was going to wish she had never crossed me; that was for sure. "Violet."

She did not answer, so I pushed my feelings to the back of my mind. I could think about that later. All that mattered now was making sure Violet was okay.

I picked her up bridal style with her head flopping back as I stood up. She looked dead already, and if it were not for the fact I could hear a heartbeat, I would have lost what little control I had.

"Where are you taking her?" Rose asked, following me but watching me warily. "Hang on a minute! I remember you! You were in that coffee shop! Oh, my God! Are you the one that took Violet? Get off her, you psycho!"

I turned to her, showing my fangs. That was enough to make her face pale, her eyes widen, and a terrified expression to cross her face.

Good, I thought smugly, *that might shut the bitch up.* How could Violet even stand to be around her? She was pissing me off already. Perhaps I could just snap her neck and blame Raven?

The thought was becoming more and more appealing by the second especially as she continued to stare at me.

"Are you coming or not?" I snapped, glancing back at Violet to see that she still had not woken up. My chest tightened, but I ignored it. "I need to get her somewhere safe, and you're already pissing me off. So either follow me or stay here and get killed. I don't care either way."

She followed me, keeping a safe enough distance from me while trying to be close to Violet at the same time.

I ignored all the strange looks I received from carrying a limp Violet in my arms, and I soon heard Rose telling people that she had passed out and that we were taking her to the hospital. With the way that Violet was in my arms, the bite mark was hidden, but I could feel blood sticking to my clothing. The smell of her blood was almost enough to make me stop and bite her myself. After having already tasted her blood once, I could not lie and say I did not want to taste it again.

My jaw clenched as I tried not to let the smell get to me, but it was hard to do so. As I stared down at her face, however, I found it was a little easier to ignore. She looked so peaceful that she could have been mistaken for someone just sleeping. If I had not known the truth, I might have actually assumed that myself.

The second we arrived back at my home, I set her down gently on the sofa. Then, taking my phone out of my pocket, I called Alec.

Thankfully, he picked up on the first ring, but I did not even give him the chance to speak.

"Get back here now," I hissed down the phone, standing back to let Rose sit by her friend.

"Have you found Violet?" he asked immediately.

"Raven got to her."

"Shit." Alec cursed. "We're on our way."

"Good."

"And Shadow?" he spoke just as I was about to hang up.

"She'll be okay."

Hanging up, I knew I should have healed Violet right then, but I could not. I was so overcome with anger that it was controlling me. I had only one thing on my mind, and that was having the pleasure of killing Raven.

Walking over and bending down by the sofa, I looked at Rose. "My friends are on their way. They will make sure Violet is okay until I get back."

Kissing the top of Violet's head, I then stood up and stormed out of the room, heading to the front door.

I was going to kill Raven, and I was going to love every damn second of it.

Chapter Twenty-Two

"Give her some space." I heard Leah snap harshly.

"What the hell is going on here?" That was definitely Rose, the hysterical tone making it obvious. "Vampires? Really? Next, I'll be bumping into Edward Cullen in Tesco!"

"Calm down, would you?"

"No, I will not calm down! I just watched my best friend get the blood sucked out of her. I thought she was dead, you moron!" Rose yelled.

My eyelids flickering as I came to and saw that Leah and Rose were both watching me as I was laid out on the sofa. The pain was still present though it had dulled considerably.

"You're awake!" Rose screeched, visibly relieved.

"Lower your voice," Leah hissed, covering her ears as she moved away. Looking at me, she then smiled softly. "I'm glad you're awake. I was worried about you."

"Worried? Ha!" Rose laughed darkly. "You people are the reason she is in this mess!"

"Rose." I warned weakly, seeing the hurt expression on Leah's face. I struggled to sit up on the sofa as I did not have enough strength, so both Rose and Leah had to help me. When I was seated, they sat on either side of me as Leah checked the wound on my neck.

"Where's Shadow?" I asked before I could stop myself, disappointed that he was not here when I woke up. I found myself wanting to see him though I could not figure out why.

"Your friend called him using your phone, so he went straight there," Leah told me. "His face when he brought you back... God, Violet, he was so worried. He put you down, got Alec and Ric, and left."

"They went after Raven." It was not a question, merely a statement, but Leah still nodded anyway. I could not help but think of Shadow. He was worried about me? Although I found it hard to believe, I was slightly happy to hear it.

"I hope they kill her when they find her," Rose said, an angry expression on her face.

"They won't." Leah shook her head.

"And why the hell not?" Rose demanded.

Leah did not answer her question, piquing my curiosity. Shadow did not strike me as the type to care about Raven considering he had spent so much time torturing her for information. It definitely did not make sense, but I said nothing. He will have his reasons.

Feeling a little more strength gathering in my body, I attempted to stand up. I needed a glass of water and some painkillers, but the second I tried to take a step forward, I almost fell, nausea washing over me. If it had not been for Leah catching me at the last moment to prevent me from crashing into the table in front of us, I would have only ended up in even more pain. My body was certainly feeling the effects of being thrown against a wall and coming in contact with the floor. How many blows to the head could a person sustain before getting some serious damage? I had no idea.

"You need to rest. Wait till the guys get back and then you can go to bed," Leah told me.

"Aren't people supposed to stay awake if they've hit their head?" Rose asked instantly, seemingly way too pleased to know something Leah clearly did not.

"Did Shadow heal me?" I asked before they could start arguing again, recalling the time he had healed the injuries I got from my dad. There had been no pain at all after he had healed them but now, after I had been bitten—for the second time—I still felt pain. It was still there. I could not ignore it though I could not figure out whether the pain was coming from the bite wound or my bruised body.

"No, I had to," Leah spoke with a grimace. "Shadow taught me the basics, but I'm nowhere near as good. Does it still hurt?"

"She was thrown against a wall." Rose jumped in. "You only did some weird healing thing to her neck."

Leah bit her lip. "I don't want to risk trying again. I only know how to heal bite wounds because of… Well, never mind. I'll go get you some painkillers."

When Leah got up and exited the room to get me something to take away the pain, leaving Rose and me alone, that was when she jumped into action. She stood up then leaned over so she could pull me up, draping my arm over her shoulder. She hoisted me out of my seat, and I almost fell back down but managed to steady myself at the last minute.

"We need to get out of here," she whispered in my ear, so low that I had to strain to hear her. I wanted to tell her that we were safe here, but I knew she would not listen. There was no way she would. She thought I was in danger here, and I could not exactly tell her otherwise after what had occurred. I was in danger, just not in this house. I knew that now.

I let her lead me out the living room and into the hall. There would be no reasoning with her, so it was best to just go along with it though I did not exactly want to. I would rather stay put because I really was in pain and did not have my full strength back. As Leah had said, I needed to rest.

It was not as though we even got very far. Although Rose only meant well, she had to be fooling herself if she thought Leah would not hear the front door being opened. Just as she had opened the door, Leah was suddenly there, standing in front of us and not looking very happy.

"Move," Rose told her, trying to appear as though she was not affected by Leah's sudden appearance out of nowhere.

"No can do," Leah said, momentarily showing Rose her fangs which immediately caused Rose to stumble back in shock. Whether she knew Leah was a vampire or not, now she really could not deny it. "As you can see, if you run, I will catch you before you even make it to the end of the street. Now, Violet is in no danger in this house. She has been living here since Shadow brought her here over a month ago. So, Rose, get back in the living room and sit your ass back down like a good little girl."

It was the first time I had witnessed just how intimidating Leah could be. She had always been happy-go-lucky when I was around her, rarely showing her more dangerous, intimidating side. Seeing it now was like a slap in the face, and this time, it was not only Rose that took a few steps back. Having been bitten by vampires twice now, I was not sure how I was ever able to feel comfortable around them, even if I did not entirely hate them.

Rose complied with Leah's orders, taking me back into the living room and sitting us both back down on the sofa we were on before. I noticed there was a glass of water and two pills on the table now, so I snatched them up, swallowing the pills immediately and washing them down with the water. I did not stop drinking until there was nothing left in the glass. I had not realised how thirsty I actually was.

Placing the glass back down, Rose then started to speak.

"Hang on a minute. You just said Violet has been here the whole time... She has been with her grandparents."

"Erm, actually..." I trailed off, knowing that she would now want to know everything, without leaving anything out. She turned to me with a hurt expression on her face as she realised that I had lied to her about my whereabouts.

"Why didn't you tell me?" she asked in a small voice. "I could have helped you."

"I was scared," I admitted. "I was scared that you would come after me if you knew, and I didn't want you to get hurt doing that. I'm sorry. I know I should have told you—I wanted to, but I couldn't. I wanted you to be safe."

"But you're not safe!" Rose burst out, standing up and placing her hands on her hips. "You've not been safe ever since you were brought here!"

"She is safer here than anywhere else." Leah chimed in. Rose turned her then.

"Say that to the bite mark on her neck!" Rose snapped. "You're coming back home with me, and that's it. You can stay with me, I told you my family wouldn't mind, and they don't! At least we can help you, Vi!"

I stood up, trying to figure out what to say. I was not used to arguing with Rose. We hardly ever had a disagreement, not about anything that mattered, anyway. The only disagreements we have had were about petty stuff that in hindsight, did not really matter at all.

Rose looked at me, her eyes shining with unshed tears. "I just want you to be safe, Vi. You're my best friend, and I can't lose you."

"You're not going to lose me," I told her, stepping forward and bringing her into a hug. At that precise moment, I heard the front door open and slam shut again. Rose and I pulled apart, knowing that it would be Shadow.

When he entered the room, glancing at the three of us, I could not help but notice that his eyes lingered on me the most. Before I knew it, he was standing directly in front of me. Rose gasped in shock, automatically stepping back to put some distance between her and Shadow.

"You're awake." Shadow breathed out. A big smile was on his face that had me momentarily stunned. I was hit by just how handsome he looked when he was not smirking like I was used to seeing. When he was smiling, like he was now, he looked even more handsome than he ever had, and all I could do was blink back at him.

"How are you feeling?" He asked as he placed a hand on my neck, tilting my head so he could get a better look. "Does it hurt? Who healed it?"

"I did." Leah jumped in, coming over to us. "You were in such a hurry to find Raven that you forgot. She's still in a bit of pain, but she's taken some painkillers for it."

"Still in pain?" he asked sharply, eyes narrowing. "What else happened, Violet?"

"I..." I trailed off, not really wanting to tell him. I knew it would only make him angry.

Rose, on the other hand, had no problems informing him of everything that happened because apparently, she had not gotten around to it before when he had found us. I was right; he was not pleased to hear what Raven had done, but I assured him that I was okay now. Well, I would be as soon as the painkillers kicked in.

"You didn't find her, did you?" I asked quietly, not liking the thought that Raven was out there still.

Shadow shook his head grimly. "No."

"What are you going to do when you do?" Leah asked carefully, almost as if she was afraid of the answer.

"Well, I hope you kill the bitch! She was going to kill my best friend!" Rose stated, crossing her arms over her chest.

"Shadow..." Leah trailed off with a pleading expression on her face.

"I'm not going to kill her."

"You're not going to kill her? Are you serious?" Ric, who I had not noticed was in the room until now, spoke up. He stood beside Alec, who also looked unhappy to hear what Shadow had said.

"I think it's time you realised that she isn't going to change. She is obsessed with Shadow. She's not going to change, Leah. I'm sorry, but it's true," Alec said, walking over to Leah and pulling her into his side.

I frowned, not understanding what he meant by that. It did also remind me of something that Raven said to me, and I gasped, attracting all attention as I clamped a hand over my mouth in shock.

"Raven said something to me..." I trailed off as everything she said suddenly came back to me.

"What? What did she say?" Leah asked eagerly.

"She told me why she's doing this. She said that it's too bad Leah's involved but if she has to kill her too, then she will. I didn't think anything of it at the time, but now that I think about it, it really doesn't make sense."

Leah looked devastated. She fell back into Alec, who wrapped his arms around her tightly, trying to soothe her. Shadow looked angry, and just like Rose and I, Ric looked confused.

"Why is she doing this?" Shadow suddenly asked, trying to contain his anger. It was hard for him to do so as he very clearly had anger issues—unless it was just a vampire thing. I could not be too careful with what I said, and stupid me realised that too late as my words clearly affected them.

"She wants revenge."

"So she's not in love with him?" Rose asked, frowning. That was her initial theory, but I was not going to dismiss it completely because Raven could have feelings for Shadow for all we knew.

For some strange reason I could not fathom, the thought unsettled me.

"She wants to ruin your life because you ruined hers," I continued, my mind clouded with thoughts. "Because you turned her and then just left her to deal with it on her own. She wants to kill everyone around you for revenge, so you're alone too, I guess."

"That's when she said she would kill Leah too if she had to?" Ric asked, gaping at me in shock.

With furrowed brows, I nodded.

"Well, shit." Ric breathed out.

"Wait, wait, wait." Rose shook her head. "There's one thing I'm not getting. Why is that purple bitch perfectly fine with killing my best friend but not Leah, someone who I assume knows Shadow for longer?"

That was the million-dollar question. I could not understand it, no matter how much I tried.

That was until Leah dropped a bombshell.

"Because she's my sister."

Chapter Twenty-Three

Silence.

Complete and utter silence.

Raven and Leah... are sisters? The thought was not something I could comprehend. In fact, the more I repeated those words in my mind, the less believable they became. They were polar opposites. Not just in appearance but in personality, too. They looked nothing alike, apart from their face shape and nose, but that was as far as the similarity went.

I was sure I looked a sight staring at Leah with wide eyes and my mouth open, but I could not help it. The revelation had knocked me for six; I had never expected that to be the reason. Not in a million years.

Rose was the one to break the silence though it was not with a sympathetic word. I should not have expected any different, really.

"That doesn't even surprise me. I told you that you're not safe here, Violet, and this just proves it!" she said, coming to stand by me, pushing Shadow out of the way. Now, that was something that was surprising in itself. Not that long ago, Rose was absolutely terrified at the thought of being in the presence of a vampire, but now she was pushing one around as though they had been friends for years. I suspected that fear had something to do with her bold actions as it dominates us in ways we never thought possible. Fear was the catalyst for her actions, and she was certainly taking advantage of that.

Shadow took a step toward her, his anger bubbling over, but I quickly stepped in between the two, and the movement caused my head to spin. All this standing up was not doing me any good, and I swayed a little on my feet. Shadow, spotting this, quickly wrapped an arm around my waist and guided me to the sofa where he then proceeded to sit down beside me. He kept his arm around me, and it was surprisingly comforting, so I relaxed into him.

"Oh, you've got to be kidding me!" Rose threw her hands up, watching us with scrutinising eyes. Confused, I glanced at her, but she did not elaborate. Instead, she said something that had everybody protesting. "We're leaving."

Shadow was instantly on his feet, standing in front of me as though he were protecting me from Rose. It was ridiculous because I had nothing to fear from Rose. She was my best friend after all, so if I could not trust her, then who could I trust? She had never let me down, and I knew she never would, so why Shadow was suddenly being overprotective, I did not know.

"She's staying put," Shadow told her sternly.

"Like hell she is!" Rose spat, stepping towards him. "She hasn't been safe here at all, despite what you think!"

I probably should have reminded her that she was, in fact, yelling in the face of a vampire with anger issues but, to be honest, I think she was trying to forget that particular detail. It was because of that that I just let her get on with it; it was obviously her way of coping with the situation. Besides, it was actually amusing to see someone standing up to him for once.

"The best place for Violet is here, but you're more than welcome to leave if you wish," Shadow spoke with a hint of a smirk on his face, almost daring her to continue.

"She can come and live with me where none of you will be near her! How can you expect me to leave her here when you're the ones putting her in danger?"

She had a point there, not that I voiced that out loud. I had been in danger from the very moment I was brought here, despite Shadow's various protests that he was trying to keep me safe. I would want to say it was not his fault but, well, it kind of was.

"She is not leaving this house," Shadow said, running a hand through his hair in frustration.

"You can't stop her from leaving if that's what she wants!"

I was still trying to wrap my head around the fact that Leah and Raven were related, so I was not in the right frame of mind to be making any serious decisions. Coupled with the fact that I felt dizzy every time I stood for a lengthy amount of time, I was not in any fit state to leave.

Yet, somehow, I did not think Rose was going to be okay with that.

"Look, Violet is staying here whether you like it or not. Now, you're more than welcome to stay here with her, but she is not leaving," Leah stated.

"Rose," I started, waiting for her to look at me before I continued to speak. "I can't leave. Not now, anyway. I feel dizzy standing up for too long, so we'll stay tonight. Tomorrow, we can talk about leaving."

Rose was not happy to hear that she would have to stay in a house filled with vampires, but she knew she had no choice. She was not going to leave me on my own after everything that had happened tonight, and I could not expect her to. It was better that she stay here so we could talk.

"Fine." She finally relented.

Shadow sat back down, facing me with determination. I watched him warily, wondering what was going through his mind. He placed a hand on the side of my head where it had come in contact with the floor.

"There's a bump," he muttered, his eyes meeting my own almost tenderly. "Where else is the pain?"

After telling him that there was a slight pain in my back and shoulder, he told me he would sort it after, but I told him not to bother. There really was no need now that I had taken something for it.

Accepting this, he still placed his hand gently on the side of my head, and I then felt that same feeling that I did when he used his ability, and my eyes closed automatically. That same warmth spread through my body until the pain was no longer there and I no longer felt dizzy. I felt so much better that I could not resist smiling. I heard Rose asking what was wrong with me, but I did not respond; I was lost in the warm feeling I felt.

He then stood up, bending down to pick me up in his arms and carrying me effortlessly. Rose immediately began protesting, and I knew that deep down, I should not have felt so fine with this either, but I did. I was not entirely sure what to think about that. I should not feel this comfortable in his arms, and yet, when I rested my head against his shoulder as he carried me from the room and up the stairs, all I could feel towards him was gratitude. There was no fear. I was not scared of him at all. He had saved me after all. I might not have known the details yet, but I did know that if he had not turned up to help after Rose called him, I would probably have been killed. I was grateful towards every single person in this house. Leah had saved me by healing the bite wound, so I did not lose any more blood, and Alec and Ric worked to find Raven so she would not continue to be a threat. They really were protecting me—all of them. I now owed my life to people that I should have been terrified off, but I could not bring myself to be scared.

Entering the bedroom, Shadow kicked the door shut before walking over to the bed, setting me down gently on the edge of it. I immediately fell back, exhaustion washing over me. Having some rest did not seem like such a bad idea, to be honest.

The bed suddenly dipped, signalling that he had sat down beside me, so I sat back up, looking at him.

"Are you okay?" he asked, eyeing me carefully as though he was searching my face for some hint that I wasn't.

"I'll be fine." I shrugged as though it was nothing, as though I had not been attacked by a crazed vampire. I was not sure whether I was trying to convince myself of that fact as I was the furthest thing from being fine.

"Will you, though?" he asked. His hands balled up into fists, causing me to frown. "You were attacked. You could have died, Violet."

"But I didn't," I told him.

"That's not the point!" He burst out, looking at me with an incredulous look on his face. "Your friend is right. I tried to keep you safe, but all I've been doing is putting you in danger!"

I stopped him right there, overcome with the urge to comfort him. Placing a hand on his shoulder, I shifted my body, angling it so I faced him.

"I've been in danger for years, Shadow. The only difference is that now, I actually have people looking out for me, trying to keep me safe from it. When I lived with my dad, I thought he would eventually go too far and kill me, and you know what? I actually looked forward to that day because it meant it would finally be over... that I wouldn't be in constant pain anymore. I was too scared of what he'd do to Rose if I ever told her, so I kept quiet. It was hard, but to be honest, I wouldn't have changed it. I wouldn't have been here now if something had been different. I know I'm in even more danger, but I now have people trying to protect me from it."

Shadow wrapped an arm around my shoulder and pulled me into him, winding his other arm around me and holding me in his arms. I rested my head against his shoulder again, waiting for him to speak.

"I hope you never feel that way again."

"So do I," I admitted.

"I wish I could kill Raven," he then said.

"She's going to come back, isn't she?" I asked, voicing out the one thing that had been on my mind. Raven would know I survived, and then she would come back for me just because she was determined to ruin Shadow's life.

"I won't let her get to you again." He vowed, tightening his grip on me. His voice had taken on a dangerous tone.

"I know you won't," I replied, and I believed it too. I knew he would not let her get to me again though I was not sure why. I could just feel it.

"You're not leaving tomorrow," he stated suddenly.

"I know." I agreed. "I'll have to speak to Rose. Even I know the safest place for me is here and not in a hotel where Raven can get to me easily. I'm scared, though. What if Raven goes after Rose as well?"

"That's not going to happen. I won't let it," Shadow stated, shaking his head. "I know I didn't bring you here under the best circumstances, but I am only trying to protect you. Your friend is going to have to stay as well. I'm just sorry you both can't leave."

"Don't apologise. There's no need to." I shook my head, thinking of my life. If I had a choice between living with my dad, wishing for death or staying here and being in the midst of danger, I'd chose the latter every time. "I would rather be here than back there. There are too many memories; I can't go back."

Shadow sighed. "You deserve a much better life, Violet. I hope that one day you will have that, I really do."

I smiled. I could not resist. It was in moments like these that I realised Shadow was not the monster he liked to show he was—that I assumed he was. I knew that he loved to torture people as I had witnessed that first hand, but I also knew hc had a caring side, one that he just did not show very much. I wished that he would; the other side of him, the one I had seen most, had me fearing for my safety all the time.

"Can I ask you something?" I asked suddenly, glancing at him as he looked down at me, still wrapping his arms around me. I did not even try to move.

Shadow nodded in response.

"Why did you turn Raven and just left her?" It was something that had been on my mind ever since she said it to me, and I needed to know. Was he really that cruel? The things she said about him, it just would not leave my mind.

"Because I wanted to."

Of all the things he could have said that was the last thing I had expected him to say. I should not have been surprised because he had shown me time and time again that he could be heartless, but it shocked me nonetheless.

I pulled myself away from him and jumped up, backing away as my heart pounded. He wanted to? That was his reasoning behind leaving someone to deal with the change alone, to deal with being a vampire alone? Raven could have turned out entirely different if only she had Shadow there to help her through it or at least give her some advice. She was the way she was because he wanted to leave her, and that just did not sit right with me. It made my stomach churn just thinking about it. If he could be that heartless to someone he actually knew, then what did that mean for me?

Shadow stood up too, confusion written all over his face as he took a step towards me, but I instantly took one back. All I saw in front of me was a monster. That was what he was: a heartless monster that just did not care about anyone or anything.

I started thinking about what Raven had told me about him, about leaving the bodies for their families to find. That was a cruel thing to do. Did he do that with Rolan, too? I never asked because I did not want to know, but now I could not stop wondering. How could anybody be that cruel, that inconsiderate of someone's feelings?

"You're a monster," I whispered.

Shadow nodded though I did not miss the hurt that flashed in his eyes.

"How many people have you killed?" I blurted out, needing to know how many had suffered because of him. Whether knowing the exact number would help me or not, I sincerely doubted, but I still had to know.

"I can't remember," he replied, honestly.

Taken aback by his honesty, I said, "How could you do it? How could you kill people just like that?"

Shadow caught on quickly. "What has Raven told you?"

"That you used to kill people and leave their bodies for their families to find."

"Of course she would tell you that." He retorted sarcastically.

"What do you mean?"

"Raven will say anything to make you run out that front door and never look back. Why? Because then she has you right where she wants you."

"So she lied?"

"No, she didn't lie." Shadow shook his head, and I was sure this time. The guilt on his face was not a figment of my imagination. He really did feel bad. "I was like that but, Violet, I have not done that in years. I did not have the luxury that Raven had. I was turned by a man that molded me into the person he wanted me to be. I hated him, but I had no choice. So I rebelled whenever I could, killing people and not caring who found them, but I do regret it. I regret it every single day."

There was something about the way he spoke that had me believing his words. The more I studied him, the more I could see that he truly did regret what he had done. At least, that was what I thought. He was either an incredibly talented actor, or he was actually telling the truth.

Deciding to give him the benefit of the doubt, I stopped trying to get away from him and instead asked him to explain what he meant.

"Sit down then. You're going to want to," Shadow told me with a sigh. Quickly doing as instructed, I turned to face him once again and waited for him to speak. It did not take long before he did. There was a faraway look in his eyes as he stared in front of him, not really seeing anything. "I was turned in 1871. I was only twenty-three. It was not a random attack though I wish it had been. Viktor, the man that turned me, claimed he had plans for me. I remember it like it was yesterday... the smug look on his face when I was turned. He did not care that I was in pain. He didn't offer any sympathy because it was not in his nature. You call me a monster, but he makes me look tame in comparison."

As Shadow paused, taking a deep breath, I noticed that his hands, clenched tightly, were shaking in a rage. It was obvious he was picturing it happen in his mind so without even pausing to think about it, I grabbed his hands in mine. His grey eyes flashed to me immediately as I squeezed his hands in comfort and smiled at him, encouraging him to go on. Although I could not imagine the pain he must have gone through, I did know something about pain and could—to some extent—understand.

"Well," he continued to speak, clearing his throat. "He used to taunt me constantly. He could kill my entire family in minutes, and he threatened to do just that at every opportunity. He liked to get me all riled up to see me lash out because when I did, I killed people. I tried to kill him, but it never worked, he always saw it coming. I didn't care about who else I killed, though, and I sometimes had to kill people for him. Everyone I killed, I pictured it was him: Viktor. I hated him for what he had done, and he didn't care because he had me exactly where he wanted me."

"Shadow..." I trailed off, tears building in my eyes.

"During the many years I was with him, I was more his pet than anything, hence the name. I did everything he told me to do because I had no choice. In a way, I knew I owed him for giving me this ability that I could use for good but that, of course, wasn't his plan at all. The things I had to do... I can't talk about that. The more I stayed with him, the more I was expected to do and eventually, I just went along with it because I knew what the alternative was. But one day, I'd had enough, and I killed him when he least expected it."

"What happened then?" I asked him, maintaining my grip on his hands. I felt him squeeze mine tightly in return. I knew he needed comforting, and I hated myself for not being able to.

"The damage was already done. His words would echo in my mind, and so I killed more people. I became more sinister. Viktor would sometimes make me kill people in their homes and leave them there, knowing that the family would soon arrive and see the body of their mother, their father, or their brother and sister, and that was something that stuck. It was sick that I liked doing it, but he had gotten to me. He'd created the ultimate killing machine, just like what he wanted. I didn't realise I wanted to change until I heard a little girl crying one day about her father that had been killed. I still don't know if he was one of my victims, but it hit me. I couldn't continue being a dead man's bitch, so I changed. What I was like still haunts me every day."

It chilled me to the bone to hear about how cruel he had been, more so than I could ever have thought. It was truly frightening to hear it even though I understood he had had no choice. Whoever Viktor had been, he did not seem like someone I would ever want to know.

All I could do was reach up and pull him into a hug, knowing that he definitely needed one. He could not be strong all the time. I finally saw the cracks in the walls he had up. Shadow tensed at first, clearly not expecting me to be so bold, but he soon relaxed, once again wrapping his arms around me.

Then, as I pulled back to look him in the eyes, ready to speak, he did something that I certainly was not prepared for.

He leant down and kissed me.

Chapter Twenty-Four

Things with Shadow and I were tense after that. He was avoiding me, and I was avoiding him though the kiss was always in the forefront of my mind. I could not deny it now; I like Shadow. After everything that he had put me through, I have done the one thing I was so adamant about not doing. How could I have been so stupid? I was kicking myself over it. Nothing good could possibly come out of having feelings for him, and yet every time I thought about that kiss, I could not bring myself to care.

The kiss had not lasted very long—it was more careful than passionate as if neither of us was sure it was what we should be doing, but at the same time, neither of us cared. His lips were soft, so soft that I found myself wanting to kiss him again.

I was in too deep. Developing a case of Stockholm Syndrome definitely had not been on the cards, but as people say: sometimes, the things that happen unexpectedly can often be the best thing to happen to you. At least, that was what I was trying to tell myself.

If any of the others noticed anything different about Shadow and me, they did not comment on it, and for that, I was grateful. I did not want anybody knowing Shadow and I had kissed anymore than he did. I knew we were going to have to speak to one another about it eventually, but for now, I was content on avoiding him as much as I could under the circumstances.

Rose stayed with us but she would soon be leaving. After a long and serious discussion, we had all managed to convince her that leaving would be the safest thing for her. She did not like it, not one bit, and yet there was nothing that could be done. She could not stay; she would be in danger, and I knew that she was not coping with this very well at all. Nobody could blame her. There were some days that even I found myself struggling to believe that it was all real and not a figment of my imagination, and I had been here over a month now.

"Hey, are you okay?" Rose suddenly asked me, coming to sit beside me on the bed. She had been sharing a room with me since she refused to stay anywhere else. She had only been here a few days, but she was already turning into an overprotective mother who kept asking their child how they were feeling every five seconds. It was sweet, really, and I valued her friendship, but she could be a little overbearing at times.

"I'm fine," I told her, smiling.

"Are you ever going to tell me what's going on with you and Shadow?" she asked suddenly. I was taken aback by her question, gaping at her. I was not aware that anyone had noticed anything different as he was busy trying to track down Raven before she came back to finish the job.

"Nothing is going on." I shrugged off her question, hoping that she would believe me and drop the subject.

"You seriously expect me to believe that?" she asked with her eyebrows raised. "The way he was with you the other day, there is definitely something you're hiding from me."

I sighed, really not wanting to get into it. "Rose, there's nothing going on with me and Shadow."

"So why don't I believe you?" she asked, sceptically.

"I don't know." I shrugged.

"You like him, don't you?"

For a second or two, I considered lying to her. I considered telling her straight up that I had no feelings towards Shadow whatsoever. I considered telling her that I had no idea what made her think such a ridiculous thought. I even considered telling her that the whole vampire thing had gotten to her mind and that as a result, she was seeing things that were not really there.

Too bad I couldn't. I wanted to tell her to talk to somebody about it because I had no idea what to do now. I could not act on my feelings because he was avoiding me, a sure sign that he regretted what happened even though he was the one to initiate it. Was I expected to tell him how I felt or keep it to myself until I got over it? What was expected of me now? I had no idea.

That was why I told Rose.

I told her everything. I left nothing out. It was about time I be honest with Rose. I knew she was still upset I had kept her in the dark about so much even though I had managed to get her to understand I had no other choice. I think she was just happy to finally know everything, to be honest.

"How are you so calm right now?" Rose asked, shock clear on her face.

I shrugged. "I don't really know. I mean, I'm absolutely terrified of everything, but at the same time, things really can't get much worse than when I was living with my dad, can they? I don't think they can, anyway."

"So you'd rather be here with a bunch of vampires that can snap your neck than be with your dad?" Rose raised an eyebrow.

I nodded, not even needing time to think about it. "You don't get it, Rose. My dad, he was awful to me. I would rather be anywhere than with him."

"I'm sorry." Rose sighed, pulling me in for a hug. "I'm just trying to understand."

"I know," I replied.

"So, tell me about this kiss!" She wiggled her eyebrows suggestively with a huge grin on her face, and I groaned, shaking my head and covering my face with my hands. I could already feel the blush rising to my cheeks.

"No way!"

"Come on! It's not every day I hear about you kissing some guy, so come on, tell me. What was it like?" she asked, enthusiastically.

"Fine!" I said, moving my hands to throw a pillow at her, but she quickly caught it, placing it on her knees so she could rest her elbows on it. "Well..."

If I had been thinking clearly, I would have remembered that everybody in the house would have been able to hear everything I said.

Unfortunately, I forgot about that entirely.

***

"Why is she just standing there?" I heard Leah ask as Rose and I entered the living room to see her standing with Shadow and Alec by the window, staring out of it.

"What are you doing?" I asked them, confused.

"Raven is outside." Alec informed us.

Hearing that she sent a shiver down my spine. It was obvious she had come to finish the job. She was determined to get rid of not only me but the others as well to make sure Shadow truly would be alone, but after hearing about what he had gone through, I was also determined not to let that happen. Don't get me wrong, I was absolutely terrified of her, but Shadow needed his friends around him.

If he was alone, I knew he would go back to being that monster he used to be, and I did not want that for him. He was better than that.

Where my feelings were concerned, I really was in deep, I thought to myself.

Walking over to the window and standing behind them, I had to stand on my tip toes so I could catch a glimpse of Raven outside. Rose went and sat on the sofa; she did not want to be too close to a vampire, as she frequently liked to remind me. It had only been a few days since we had been attacked, so I could not blame her. She was still processing everything after all.

Placing a hand on Shadow's shoulder so I would not fall, I felt him tense up, but I did not move my hand. My gaze was locked on the figure outside, who just stood watching the house. Raven was dressed all in black, stuffing her hands into the pockets of the coat she wore. Her purple hair was the only way I could tell who she was as it flew around her face, showing just how windy it was out there.

"What is she up to?" I asked, brows furrowing as I looked at her.

"I don't know, but she's up to something, that's for sure." Alec commented, shrugging his shoulders.

"I'm going after her," Shadow stated, pushing past me to get to the door. Leah stopped him, grabbing hold of his arm to prevent him from leaving.

"Wait," she said. "What are you going to do?"

"What I should have done the second she came here," he replied with an angry expression on his face as he looked her in the eyes.

Leah shook her head. "You promised me."

"She tried to kill Violet." Shadow snapped. "And don't think for a second she wouldn't kill you too just to get to me."

"Shadow, please!" Leah begged, and I was not sure whether I was seeing things or not but it looked as though she was on the verge of tears. I understood why. I mean, it was her sister Shadow was threatening to kill. Then again, Leah had not seemed to care about Raven until recently, so I was definitely confused about how she was feeling. I made a mental note to talk to her later to see if I could help. If anyone could relate to how she felt, it would be me.

"Shadow, don't," I jumped in, wanting to help the situation. I walked over to him and Leah, shaking my head. "You can't kill her. You know you can't."

"Yes, I can."

"No, you can't," I said, casting a quick glance towards Leah, who was watching me gratefully. "She's Leah's sister. You can't kill her. There has to be another way to get her to stop."

"She won't stop until she has what she wants."

"Well, I say kill the bitch." Rose chimed in, not moving from her spot on the sofa. "Kill her before she kills everybody and yes, that includes you, Leah. She doesn't give a shit about you."

Leah was enraged to hear Rose speak so carelessly and was about to go for her if it was not for me jumping in the way at the last minute. Trying to put some space between them, I pushed Leah back a little but kept my eyes on her just in case.

"Rose is right." Shadow nodded. "Raven doesn't care about anyone but herself."

"Finally, someone agrees," Rose muttered, tapping away on her phone.

"She's still my sister," Leah argued.

"She tried to kill Violet!" Shadow argued back, raising his voice.

"Don't even start with that!" Leah yelled, pointing a finger at him. "You've been avoiding her for days so don't act like you even care about her now."

"You think you know everything." Shadow shook his head though there was a smirk on his face. It was obvious what he was thinking about, especially as his eyes flickered towards me before looking back at Leah.

"Shadow, just don't. Whatever Raven is planning, we need to stick together. You can't kill Raven—you know you can't. We need to think of another way." I tried to reason with him.

"There is no other way. When are you going to get that?" Shadow turned to me in a fury. I tried to appear calm, knowing he was angry at the situation and not me, but it was hard to do so when he was glaring at me.

"Everybody, just calm down. This is exactly what Raven wants," Alec said, sighing as he finally wandered away from the window. "She's just left, by the way."

It did not escape my notice that Leah visibly sighed upon hearing that. I felt bad for her, I really did. Knowing how she was feeling, it was easy for me to understand her. As much as I hate my dad, I would not want him dead. The same thing goes for Leah's feelings towards Raven. It was hard to turn your back on your family completely.

"I will kill her," Shadow warned Leah before he stormed out of the room.

***

Shadow's POV

Violet really did confuse the fuck out of me. One minute it seemed like she was accepting the situation she was in, and the next she was pointing at me and calling me a monster. I understood. After the thousands of people I had killed, I even agreed with her.

Still, that still did not make me any closer to figuring her out.

I had not planned on telling her about Viktor. I had not wanted her to ever find out about him or my life after I was turned. I knew what I would see on her face if I did tell her, and for some reason I could not fathom, I did not want to see that look on her face. Yet when she had asked me about Raven and called me a monster, I felt the need to defend myself. I was so overcome with the urge to explain myself, to make her understand. Apparently, seeing that disgusted look in her eyes made me feel something I did not like at all.

After I had explained, and she had hugged me, looking at me in a way she had never looked at me before, I could not help myself. I had to do it. I just had to.

I kissed her.

I had expected her to push me away or slap me. With Violet, it really could have gone either way. I was not expecting her to respond to my kiss, but she did, and our lips moved together as feelings I had long forgotten rushed forward.

I may be a killing machine, but I was capable of feeling lust. I had felt lust a lot in my lifetime, but I had never experienced whatever the fuck it was I felt as I kissed her.

However, lust was definitely a part of it, and I struggled to keep that at bay. If I gave into it, there was a ninety-nine percent chance I would have thrown her down on the bed and taken her right there. As a vampire, everything was heightened, every feeling was so much stronger. That was why I had to remind myself that I was not an animal, that I could control the lust because, if I did not, it would only scare her off. I did not want that. I had been enjoying it far too much to let her run from me just like that.

Who knew one kiss could make me feel so much? I thought to myself, wandering the darkened streets. Who knew one small, human girl could cause such a reaction in me. Even now as I searched for my next victim, I could not stop thinking about that damn fucking kiss and how soft her lips were.

It was safe to say that I wanted more. I wanted more than one fucking measly kiss. I wanted to pull her to me and kiss her like she had never been kissed before. I wanted to kiss every inch of her body until she was panting and writhing beneath me, begging for more. I wanted her completely.

"Shit!" I cursed aloud, the realisation hitting me like a ton of bricks. I paused in the street with hands clenched into fists. I had always known I felt something towards Violet that I was not used to, but this was different. I had assumed it was a protective instinct, not something different, not something more.

Of all the stupid things I had done...

Shaking my head, I cleared my mind of all thoughts involving Violet and continued my search of the streets for someone walking alone. It had been a while since I had last fed, so I really needed blood now. It took all my strength not to go for Violet.

Fuck, I cursed mentally. There I go again, thinking about Violet! What the fuck?

Suddenly, from my peripheral vision, I saw movement, so I quickly turned and stalked towards them. It was a man who was clearly drunk, mumbling incoherent things as I approached him. In fact, he was so drunk he did not even notice me until I was directly in front of him.

He opened his mouth to speak, but I did not give him the chance to. Showing my fangs, I grabbed him by the hair and pulled him towards me. Sinking my fangs into his neck, I fed, satisfied that he was not trying to scream. He was that drunk; he probably thought he was getting a blowjob.

Moving my hands to keep him upright, his body soon went limp, and upon noticing the lack of a heartbeat, I knew he was dead. I threw the body over my shoulder so I could bury him somewhere later.

For now, I needed to find somebody else. The thirst for blood I felt so strongly was nowhere near close to disappearing anytime soon. I needed more blood. I needed to quench the thirst before I went back home.

***

I tried to avoid Violet after that and instead, went out and fed more often, trying to find Raven. It took all my strength not to grab Violet and have my wicked way with her. It did not help that I had heard every tiny detail of her conversation with Rose, so I knew exactly how she felt about everything that had happened since I brought her to London.

I also heard exactly what she thought of the kiss. Hearing her tell Rose that she enjoyed it and that she liked me caused a huge smirk to cross my face that just would not go away. As much as I despised Rose, I was grateful that she chose to harass Violet for answers because otherwise, I would never have known. Violet was avoiding me just as much as I was avoiding her, if not more, but at least I knew why.

Avoiding her was hard, though, and when she placed a hand on my shoulder so she could glance out the window, I tensed. *Don't go there*, I warned myself, *Control your dick.*

I focused all my attention on Raven, who seemed to think it was perfectly okay to just stand outside my home like a fucking creep. How could I ever think she was hot enough to fuck? It made me shudder to even think about it now. She was even a creep in the bedroom.

"I'm going after her," I said, not even glancing at Violet as I pushed past her to get to the door. I pictured Raven sinking her fangs into Violet's neck, and it made me feel so much anger, my arms were shaking as my hands were clenched into fists. I was going to kill Raven. That was a promise.

"Wait!" Leah suddenly grabbed hold of me to prevent me from going anywhere. I let her stop me even though she was nowhere near matching me in strength. "What are you going to do?"

"What I should have done the second she came here," I answered her truthfully, feeling the anger coursing through my veins. I was going to torture Raven the way I wished I had when I had her locked up. I was going to torture her until she begged me to stop and then, only then, would I end her miserable life. I was going to chop off every finger, every toe, pull out every tooth until it sunk into her pathetic little head that she would not win. Not against me.

"You promised me," Leah said.

I glared at her, not understanding how she could still try to protect her pathetic sister even though she knew Raven would kill her. Without a doubt, Raven would kill Leah. It amazed me that they were even related at all as Raven was so bitchy and Leah was so whiny.

"She tried to kill Violet!" I snapped, trying to contain my anger a little so I did not take it out on the wrong people. Then, just for good measure, to make sure the message sunk in, I said, "And don't think for a second she wouldn't kill you too just to get to me."

Leah continued to beg me to spare Raven's life, but I was not listening to her. She was only adding to the anger already fuelling me. Things would not end well for her if she did not quit now.

So when Violet, of all people, jumped in to agree with Leah, I was so shocked that some of the anger dissipated. Of all people to have agreed with me about Raven's fate, it should have been Violet. She had been attacked by her, almost killed by her. What the fuck were they on to think Raven deserved a life? Everybody else seemed in total agreement with me that Raven had to go. Even Alec agreed with me, and he was the love of Leah's life, for fuck's sake! You would think that would get Leah to see it from our point of view, but apparently, her head was still firmly stuck up Raven's arse.

More fool her.

I tried to get them to see sense, I really did, but they were not having it. Violet seemed to think that because of Leah, Raven had to stay alive. She was an idiot for thinking that. How could she not see that I was only doing what was necessary to keep her safe? How could she not see that her safety was all that mattered to me? You would think kissing her would make her see that there was something going on between us and that was why I wanted to keep her safe, but she seemed just as oblivious as she always was.

She was so oblivious that she agreed with Leah.

I need a drink, I thought as I stormed out of the room.

Chapter Twenty-Five

"We need to talk."

The famous, dreaded words.

When Shadow told me we needed to talk, it was clear that the only thing we needed to talk about was the kiss that I had been having a hard time forgetting. Wanting to talk to Shadow about it was the last thing I wanted, especially as I knew he would only be telling me what a mistake it was. That was something I did not need or want to hear.

Leah had stopped talking to him, refusing to even acknowledge his existence until he agreed to keep Raven alive even though we all knew that could not happen. While I did understand the way Leah was feeling, I knew that Raven could not be stopped any other way. I had told her we would find one, but I was not stupid. The only way to stop a vampire is death.

Since trying to reason with Leah was not going to work and Rose was still trying to convince me to leave, I could not avoid speaking to Shadow. Alec and I were not the best of friends. We were civil with one another, having the odd conversation here and there, but other than that, that was as far as it went.

That was how I found myself sat on Shadow's bed as he paced back and forth in front of me. I had my hands on my lap, glancing at them because I did not want to look at him. I did not want to see the look on his face when he told me what a mistake kissing me had been. Even though I knew how stupid I was for developing feelings for Shadow, that did not mean I wanted to hear him reject me, whether it was what I needed to hear or not.

"We need to talk," Shadow repeated his earlier words, still pacing around. "We can't keep avoiding each other."

I sighed, knowing he was right. It probably was better to just get it over with.

"What happened that night... the kiss..." He started, struggling to find the words to say as he pinched the bridge of his nose in frustration.

"It's fine. I get it," I said, rolling my eyes. He did not care about my feelings before when he was scaring me half to death, so I could not understand why he was trying to sugarcoat it now. It was ridiculous.

"What?" he asked, halting his pacing to look at me.

"It was a mistake, it won't happen again, blah blah blah," I replied, finally glancing up at him. The confusion was clear though he said nothing. He was just looking at me, watching. It began to make me feel slightly uncomfortable until he finally spoke.

"Good," he said, clearing his throat. "I'm glad you understand. That was easier than I thought."

I rolled my eyes as I jumped up from the bed, wanting to leave. "What were you expecting? For me to cry and beg you that it wasn't a mistake?"

His silence spoke volumes.

I chuckled, not being able to help myself. "Sorry to disappoint, but that's not going to happen. I knew that you would say it was a mistake. It was obvious. So don't worry about it. Let's just forget it ever happened."

As I turned and left the room, shutting the door behind me, I heard the distinct sound of a fist slamming against the wall and a curse that followed. I tried not to think anything of it. I really did, but it stuck in my mind for the rest of the afternoon.

It was not until around eight PM that Shadow finally came back downstairs. The rest of us had been trying to figure out what we were supposed to do now because we had to be ready to fight just in case Raven came back unexpectedly, something that was highly possible. It would only be a matter of time before she would once again try to kill me, but this time, I wanted to be prepared.

Having to rely on people I was only just getting used to was hard because I did not want to just sit back and let them do all the work—not when I was the one Raven seemed to have it out for most. I wanted to be able to help somehow even though I could not do much in comparison to them. I had just grown sick and tired of just having to sit around waiting for Raven to come back. When she did, I wanted to be able to fight back, I wanted to be able to defend myself.

That was how I ended up agreeing to self-defence lessons with Shadow as my tutor, but Leah and Alec would be helping when they could. I was not sure when Ric would turn up again because he had not been around much, but Alec had told me was busy trying to find out about Raven's friends. Even Rose was going to have the lessons too though how long she would stay here was another matter entirely. I could not blame her if she decided to leave; it was too much for her.

As it was already getting late, we decided to wait until tomorrow for the first lesson. Shadow was still angry over our conversation, not that I could understand why. I put it out of my mind as much as I could. I did not want to be questioning his motives all the time because it got too much. I would start overthinking, and that was when I would start wondering whether he had any good intentions at all. It was a ridiculous thought. He had done nothing but try to keep me safe after all. Granted, he threatened to kill me, but in a twisted way, I was used to his threats, even the ones that went into detail.

"What are you thinking so hard about?" Rosc asked as she sat beside me on the floor. She had been trying to avoid being too close to the others on account of what they were.

"Nothing," I answered quickly, a little too quickly.

"Liar," she replied, crossing her legs.

I sighed. "Everything really."

"But mainly Shadow," she stated, a smirk growing on her face.

"No." I glared at her, knowing that the vampires in the room could hear our conversation. *Damn vampires.*

"Really? What did he want you for, anyway?" she asked.

"To talk about the kiss."

She grinned. "What happened? Did you kiss again? Ooh, come on, tell me something! I'm living my love life vicariously through you."

"I don't have a love life," I told her with a shake of my head. I saw Leah look over at us with a grin on her face, causing me to blush. I doubt I would ever get used to them being able to hear everything we said.

"But you could."

"I'm not going to have a love life," I told her sternly.

"Can you two go somewhere else if you want to talk about your love life," Alec complained, craning his neck to look at us. I did see the hint of a smile though and knew he was not finding the conversation too annoying.

"I don't have a love life," I repeated, sighing in exasperation.

"Whatever it is, can you talk about it somewhere else? It's really annoying."

"Just like you then," Rose muttered under her breath.

"You know? You're really blunt for somebody who can't even bare to be around us." Alec commented suddenly, his eyes darkening. It was no secret that he was annoyed by Rose and her comments, he never tried to hide his contempt for her. He hated her just as much as she hated him.

"What can I say? It flares up in the presence of assholes." Rose bit back with a smirk on her face, satisfied by her comeback. I rolled my eyes at the two of them, annoyed that they could not at least try to get along for my sake. Alec and I may not be the best of friends, but we had a mutual respect for one another, and I had been hoping Rose and Alec could have the same. Apparently, they had other ideas because they would rather annoy each other than talk in a civil manner.

Alec made a start towards her, not taking too kindly to being called an asshole. He did not care what his friends called him, but if it was someone he did not like, then that was when you had to watch out because he would kill them. He bared his fangs, and that was all it took for Rose to jump to her feet suddenly out of fear.

Leah quickly pulled him back and thankfully, he did not protest and instead let her pull him away and out of the room. He did not stop glaring at Rose until he disappeared from view, though. When he did, Rose let out a sigh of relief before turning to me.

"I can't stay here anymore," she admitted, biting her lip.

I sighed, nodding. I had been expecting it. This was too much for anyone to bare, including myself, but I had more time to come to terms with it and, because of the situation with my dad, I knew that being here was the safest option for me. Besides, I actually liked the vampires now whereas it was clear that Rose never would. Although we had managed to convince her to leave—she had planned to leave at the end of the week—but I knew she would want to leave before that. It was obvious. Nobody would stay somewhere they did no feel safe.

"I know," I replied, pulling her into a hug. She wrapped her arms around me tightly, resting her head on my shoulder. "Do what you have to do."

"I don't want to leave you here alone."

"We've gone over this. I'll be fine."

"I don't trust them," Rose said, pulling away to look me in the eyes.

"Then trust me," I stared back. "They won't hurt me. I know they won't."

They're vampires, Vi! Hurting people is what they do!"

I sighed. It was useless arguing with her. Nothing I could say would sway her decision. Her mind was already made up, and nothing would change that. All I could do was accept it.

"What are you going to do?" I asked her, changing the topic.

"I'm leaving tomorrow," she stated, nodding to herself.

"You're not going to wait till the end of the week?"

She shook her head sadly.

"Okay, well… if that's what you want."

"It is." She nodded.

Tomorrow, Rose would be leaving. It was the best thing for her to do, but I would miss her, definitely. The hard part was knowing I might not be seeing her anytime soon; she clearly had no intention of ever coming back here, and I had no intention of ever going back there. So when I would see my best friend again was uncertain, but the main thing was that she would be safe. That was all that mattered.

Chapter Twenty-Six

"Call me when you're home," I told Rose, squeezing her tightly as I hugged her. Tears were welling up in my eyes already, and she had not even left yet.

When it came to goodbyes, I turned into an emotional wreck. Thankfully, I was not the only one; Rose was a blubbering mess, too. Tears were streaming down her face as she tightened her grip on me. I knew she felt guilty for leaving me here, but no amount of guilt she may be feeling would sway her decision.

"I promise." She responded, finally pulling apart.

I took a step back, standing beside Leah who merely smiled at Rose before turning her attention to Alec, who did not even acknowledge Rose's existence. Pretending she was not there seemed to be easy for him. I rolled my eyes at his behaviour. Who knew vampires could be so annoying when they were not being so scary?

Shadow stepped forward to help Rose with her bags, being the gentleman that he definitely was—not. He was the furthest thing from a gentleman, but he did have his moments, I suppose. It probably did have something to do with the fact he wanted Rose out of his house, but it did not matter. Rose would be safe. That was what I had to keep telling myself.

I did not watch her leave; I could not stand to. The tears that I had been desperately trying to keep back spilled over onto my cheeks, running down my face. I was never good when it came to saying goodbye. I knew that Rose and I would still remain in contact, but it would be hard to when we were both so far from one another. We could—and would—speak online, but it would not be the same as her actually being here.

I bit my lip, shutting the front door, and turned around to face Alec and Leah. Shadow having carried Rose's belonging out. I leant against the door and sighed, wiping my eyes on the sleeve of the hoodie I wore.

"Thank fuck she's gone." Alec suddenly breathed out. The instant he finished speaking, Leah elbowed him harshly in the ribs, causing him to wince. He glanced at her in confusion before glancing at me, apologetically. "Sorry."

I shook my head and walked up the many stairs to the bedroom I was staying in. However long I was going to be here for, I was glad that I could at least be left to my own devices when I was in the bedroom. Was it mine? It probably was. I mean, nobody else stayed there. I had asked Leah before if it was hers, and she had said no, only that she had stayed in there once or twice. So I could probably claim the bedroom as my own, which I did. Either way, when I shut the bedroom door behind me, they all knew to leave me alone.

Sitting on the bed, I ended up thinking about Raven and how we would stop her. Death was the only way, but getting Leah to agree to that would be impossible—it just wasn't going to happen. Leah would never agree to kill her sister, the same way I would never agree to kill my dad. No matter how much pain and suffering they had put us through, they were still family. Or maybe we just had better morals.

Did vampires even have morals?

When a knock sounded on my bedroom door, I merely glanced at it, not even bothering to get up and open it. It did not matter who it was. I was not in the mood to talk to anyone. Not yet. I needed to be alone with my thoughts.

I should not have been surprised when the door opened, and in stepped Shadow with a grim look on his face. He shut the door before he came over and sat beside me though he said nothing. I did wonder why he had come to see me if he was not going to speak, but I did not ask. I was too tired. It was as though everything had finally caught up with me, leaving me feeling more exhausted than I could ever recall being before.

"Are you okay?" Shadow suddenly asked.

I shrugged. "Yeah, I think so."

"You think so?" He raised an eyebrow.

"Well, I know it's better that Rose has gone home, but I'll miss her. I doubt I'll see her much now, if at all because I'm never going back there. She'll never come here now she knows there are vampires crawling the streets. I don't know... It's all just proving to be too much." I sighed, fiddling with the ring on my finger.

"Look, she's safe, and that's what you wanted, right? So don't think about when you'll see her. There's always text messages and things," he said.

"Yeah, I know. It's just not the same."

Shadow sighed, bringing his hand up and running it through his hair. I watched the movements of his hand, wondering why he had bothered to come check on me. I could not make sense of anything he did. From kidnapping me to saving my life... nothing he did make any sense. It gave me a headache trying to figure him out.

My scrutiny did not go unnoticed, however, and he was quick to call me out on it.

"What is it?"

I shook my head. "It's nothing."

"There's clearly something on your mind so spit it out." Shadow rolled his eyes.

I bit my lip. "It's just..."

"Just what?"

"I don't... I don't understand you…"

His brows furrowed, frowning at me.

"I mean, you kidnapped me and yet... all you've been doing in trying to help... apart from when you bit me... and were scaring me all the time..."

"That's what this is about?" He took a deep breath. "You still think I kidnapped you?"

"Well, you did..." I trailed off, unsure on how he could not understand it. That was exactly what he had done.

"If I remember correctly, you were wandering the streets after being kicked out. Let's not forget that I also prevented someone from attacking you. If anything, I did you a favour."

"Did me a favour?" My eyes widened, staring at him in disbelief. "Sure, in the long run, but... I'm in more danger now than I ever was there."

"So you'd rather I just let that guy do with you what he wanted?" Shadow snapped, completely missing the point.

"Of course not, but you didn't have to kidnap me!" I burst out. All my pent up frustration at the situation was coming out before I could stop it. How could he actually think he had not kidnapped me? If it were not for him, I would not have a psychotic vampire seeking me out for revenge. I would not be trapped in a house with no way out because leaving would mean that the said psychotic vampire would catch me and kill me, draining my body of blood.

Shadow was on his feet in a matter of seconds, glaring at me. He was not happy anymore. He was angry. The look on his face caused my heart to race in my chest, and I gulped nervously.

I probably should have just kept my mouth shut, to be honest.

"After everything that's happened, you still think bad of me, don't you? Okay, I may have kidnapped you, call it whatever you fucking like, but you wouldn't even be alive if it wasn't for me. I have done my best to protect you, but you still can't see that, can you? You know what? Fuck it. I give up. Why should I help such an inconsiderate bitch like you when you clearly don't appreciate it?"

He had stormed out of the room before I could even so much as blink, leaving me completely bewildered by his reaction. That definitely had not been what I was expecting because no matter what way you looked at the situation, he had brought me here against my will. But for him to storm off as though I had offended him... Well, that was confusing because I had not.

Had I? I had only said what had been on my mind. He wanted to know what was on my mind, and all I did was tell him. So why was I in the wrong now?

I suddenly felt guilty. Maybe I should apologise. I had not meant to upset or offend him; I was just confused about everything. I never knew what to expect with him, so was it really any wonder that I could not figure him out? One minute he was protecting me, and the next, he had his fangs buried in my neck. One minute he was being caring, and the next he was angry. It was exhausting trying to keep up with his mood swings.

Despite all that, I did not like knowing he was mad at me. That was the part I hated the most.

Chapter Twenty-Seven

I should go after him.

I should apologise.

I should do something.

But I remained on the bed because something else had captured my attention, and I could do nothing but stare down at my phone, shaking my head in disbelief. I could hardly believe I had received such a message, yet the proof was staring up at me.

Are you okay? it said.

Of all the messages I could have received from this particular person, I never believed in a million years that I would see those exact words. Death threats, sure, but this? No way.

After the initial shock wore off, the anger settled in, and the grip I had on my phone tightened. How was I supposed to move on from the things I had suffered if it kept haunting me? How could he even think he could send a message like that as though he actually cared about my well-being? How could he even think he had a right to contact me at all? After everything he had put me through, he now has the audacity to send me a message asking how I am? No. No way. I could not allow myself to be sucked back into the tragedy that was my dad. It would not end well; it would be asking for trouble. I could not trust him, and I certainly could not forgive him.

Deciding I would try to take my mind off it, I went downstairs so I could get a drink. I needed to be active, or I would end up overthinking everything.

Once I had reached the kitchen, I poured myself a glass of coke and drank it all straight away. Shutting my eyes tightly, I breathed in deeply. I could not get that message out of my head. It was in times like these that I wished I could just get so drunk that I forget my own name, let alone everything that was wrong with my life. So when my eyes landed on the bottle of wine that Leah had left on the counter, I made a beeline for it. I was not thinking. I had only one thing in mind, and that was how much I wanted to forget. I needed to forget, or I would explode.

I sat down on the kitchen floor with the bottle of wine, drinking straight from the bottle, not even bothering with a glass. It wasn't like I would need one.

Somewhere along the way, tears blurred my vision, but I did not bother trying to blink them back. Trying to forget everything was not that easy when I was alone. Being alone was never a good thing when you had too much on your mind after all.

"Stupid dad, stupid Shadow, stupid vampires," I muttered, taking another swig from the bottle.

"Why are we stu—Are you drinking?" The door to the kitchen suddenly opened, and in walked Leah, who stopped short upon seeing me sitting on the floor clutching her bottle of wine as though it were a newborn. It was safe to say that I was not planning on letting go of it anytime soon.

"Go away," I told her simply before turning back to the bottle. The taste was not very appealing to me, but I did not stop drinking it. I was downing the bottle as though it was the last drink I would have for a while.

"No way," Leah said, coming over to me and swiping the bottle away from my clutches. "I'm cutting you off."

"Give it back!"

"Why are you drinking, anyway?"

"It's not important."

"Is it about your argument with Shadow? If it is, I wouldn't worry about it. He'll calm down eventually," Leah told me.

"Why does he get so angry with me? He did kidnap me! He is the reason I'm here!" I wailed as a stray tear streamed down my face before I had the chance to wipe it away.

Leah sighed, sitting next to me and resting her head on my shoulder. "You think he kidnapped you, but he thinks he saved your life. I mean, in a way, it was sort of both."

"How can it be both?" I asked, taken aback by her words. It was either one or the other.

"Because he did take you against your will—"

"He smashed my head against a brick wall, knocking me out." I cut her off sharply.

"Yeah, that," Leah winced. "So yeah, it was kidnapping. Then again, he had just killed someone to save your ass from being raped, so I guess he was saving you too."

"He didn't need to bring me here or knock me out for that matter. He could have just let me go to a hotel like I was planning." I reminded her.

"And he was wrong to do that, but you're here now, and there's nothing you can do about it. Besides, where did you expect Shadow to take you? He didn't know where you were heading. He thought you'd just been kicked out, and that you had nowhere to go. How was he supposed to know otherwise? He may have kidnapped you, but at the same time, he saved your life because you definitely didn't have enough money to last at a hotel, and you damn well know it."

It was quite possibly the longest speech Leah had ever given in the time that I had known her. She was usually the sarcastic one, the one that would wind Shadow up just because she could, and here she was, explaining Shadow's reasoning behind taking me. As much as I hated to admit it, she did have a point. That night, Shadow had not asked me where I was going; he had no reason to. We were total strangers; he had no reason to ask. So I suppose, in some twisted way, Shadow really had no choice but to bring me here.

I suddenly felt guilty, guiltier than I had before.

"Where is he?" I asked her, sitting up a little straighter. I had to talk to him now. I had to apologise.

"I don't know. He'll be back soon, I'd have thought."

I had no choice but to wait for him to get back, but I was not the most patient person in the world when it came to something I was eager to do. I wanted to just to get it over with.

***

After a long shower where I mentally prepared my apology speech for Shadow, the water started running cold before I actually got out. I always preferred to have long showers because it gave me the time to think properly, to sort through my thoughts.

By the time I had gotten out, got dressed, and dried my hair, I was confident about the speech I had prepared. I only hoped Shadow would actually accept it because I could never be too sure with him.

I spent the remaining time waiting around with Leah for him to get back, reading a book on vampires. I was not sure why I bothered because it still had not given me much information that was actually useful, but it helped pass the time. I just wanted to get the apology over and done with so I could relax a little. Knowing Shadow was angry with me made me uncomfortable.

I did not get the opportunity to apologise to him because when he eventually came back around nine PM, he was visibly enraged. His hands formed fists at his side, and he was breathing deeply. His fangs were on show, and his eyes were darkening.

Instantly alarmed by his appearance, Leah and I both shot up out of our seat. Alec had gone out earlier with Ric and had yet to return, so it was just the three of us.

Leah walked over to Shadow tentatively, almost as though she was afraid he would take his anger out on her. I knew that Shadow would not hurt her, but with that dangerous look in his eyes that seemed to be focused on me, I could not say the same thing for myself. What had I done this time? This could not be about earlier, could it?

"Shadow?" I called his name, warily. "What's wrong?"

Three words were all it took to put me in a state of panic, just three words. It was crazy, absolutely crazy how just three words could cause such a reaction. It was strange how three words could cause such a reaction. Hearing 'I love you' causes joy. Hearing 'I miss you' causes happiness. Hearing 'I hate you' causes anger. Just three words and they had the power to change your emotions in an instant.

Those were not the three words I heard, however. I would have actually preferred to hear one of those. At least, I could have handled that. The words I heard were much different, ones that had me stumbling backwards, clamping a hand over my mouth as my eyes filled with tears. I could not believe what I was hearing, and yet the look on his face told me I had not imagined it. He really had said it.

"Raven has Rose."

Bad things were supposed to come in three's, right? That's what people say. Three bad things, and I already have had two of mine in just one day. I was dreading the third because one thought lingered in my mind, one I could not escape no matter how much I wanted to. There was only one way things could possibly get worse than this.

"What the hell do you mean? She left this morning!" Leah burst out.

"Oh, my God! Raven has Rose. She has my best friend. Oh god, she's going to kill her, isn't she? We have to do something! We have to save her!" I panicked. Just the thought of Raven having Rose had me freaking out because who knows what Raven was planning.

"Calm down." Shadow was suddenly in front me, placing his hands on my shoulder. "We are going to save her, but you're staying here."

"What? No!" I yelled, staring at him in alarm. There was no way I was going to be left behind. I was going to help save my best friend, and that was all there was to it.

"I'm not letting you anywhere near Raven when it's you that she wants," Shadow spoke through gritted teeth. "She's already tried to kill you once. I am not letting that happen again."

"You don't get to decide when it's my friend that's in danger," I retorted, glaring up at him. He did not even seem fazed by my words, rolling his eyes instead.

"If I have to lock you up to make sure that you stay safe, then I will do it," Shadow replied.

"Shadow, please," I begged. "This is my best friend we're talking about. She was supposed to be safe from all of this. I have to help her, please!"

"Violet, you're staying here. I need to make sure you're safe and here is the safest place for you." He tried to reason with me.

As Shadow and Leah started talking about the rescue mission, all I could think about was Rose. She had to be alive. She just had to be. Raven had her reasons for doing this. In her mind, her actions were completely justified, and that was worrying because who knows what lengths she would go to just to get her point across. It was clear she was not the talking type of person, preferring to act on her emotions rather than talking them through.

Please let her be alive, I thought to myself, wiping away the tear that fell. If something happened to her because of me, I would never forgive myself.

Chapter Twenty-Eight

I had begged and pleaded with Shadow to let me go with him, Alec, and Ric to rescue Rose despite the fact I could not actually protect myself against Raven should she decide to come after me. I had tried to explain that if they kept Raven busy, I could get Rose away, but he just was not listening. He refused to change his mind. I had even considered following them, only to remember it would not work out well considering they would be able to hear me coming, literally.

Stupid vampires.

That night, they came up with a plan, excluding both myself and Leah, and the next day, they were off before either of us could complain about being left behind. Leah clearly was not happy either if the glare she shot them was anything to go by.

I was stuck in the house with only Leah for company though I knew she was only left behind to make sure I did not escape. I had heard Alec say as much though I did suspect whether his decision had something to do with the fact she was related to Raven.

I was not stupid, though. I knew I was better off remaining where I was safe. The fact my best friend was in danger was the only reason I wanted to do my bit to help.

It was almost torturous to be stuck in the house with nothing to do but panic, questioning whether Rose was even alive. It was agonising, and any attempts to distract myself failed miserably. Nausea washed over me, and my head hurt, but I could not even sit still long enough to rest. With each tick of the clock that went by, it was another second with no word from Shadow or the others.

As well as worrying for Rose's safety, I even found myself worrying about Shadow. What would he do when he saw Raven? Would he kill her or was he going to let her live? What if Raven had all her friends and were waiting, expecting him? What if Shadow, Alec, or Ric got hurt? Worse still, what if they were killed? Never being able to see Shadow again... the thought was almost too much for me to bare.

The only distraction I had was Leah, who tried to take my mind off everything by talking about lighter topics, but even she knew it was useless. The only thing that would make me feel any better would be to see the three of them walk through the door with Rose behind them.

"What if something goes wrong?" I asked Leah as I paced around the living room, biting my lip hard enough to draw blood. Probably not the best thing to do considering I was in the presence of a vampire, but I could not bring myself to care.

"Nothing is going to go wrong. They have it all planned out perfectly. Everything will be fine." Leah tried to lift my spirits, but I shook my head; I was not convinced. She did not know if something was going to go wrong or not. She was just guessing. For all we knew, Raven had already killed them all, and we were just waiting for something that was not going to happen.

I wished that thought had not entered my mind. It only succeeded in making me feel even more worried than I had been minutes before, something I had not thought possible.

I felt like I was going out of my mind with worry. I was worried about Rose, I was worried about Shadow, hell, I was worried about Alec and Ric! I was not sure what Raven had planned, but it was obvious that she would have something planned. She would not go down without a fight.

It was not even like she was going to gain much by doing this. Shadow did not care about Rose. None of them did. The only reason they went after her is because of me. They would have been more content in letting Raven do whatever they want with her, especially Alec. It would have made more sense for Raven to try to take me hostage since she seemed to think I was special to Shadow. It could not be further from the truth. It seemed laughable to me, but what did I know?

"Will you stop pacing already?" Leah suddenly burst out. "You're driving me insane!"

"Sorry," I mumbled, sitting down on the sofa and taking my phone out of my pocket. No text messages. No missed phone calls. Nothing.

I bit my lip. What if something had actually gone wrong? What if Rose was not even there? How did Shadow even know Raven had Rose, anyway? In the midst of all my panic, I had not even questioned how he knew. I just assumed he was telling the truth because he had no reason to lie.

"How much longer are they going to be?" I asked Leah, staring at her.

She shrugged. "As long as it takes to save her."

"What if something has gone wrong? What if they aren't coming back? What if Raven killed them all?" I asked, voicing my worst fears.

"The three of them are much stronger than Raven and any of her friends. They can take them single-handedly. So don't worry. They'll be fine."

"What if Rose is dead?" I asked, tears springing to my eyes.

"She's not." Leah snapped.

The sudden harshness to her voice shocked me. I stared at her, wondering where that came from. It was strange how quick she was in putting my fears to rest regarding Rose being dead. Call it paranoia if you want, but something was not right about that.

"What do you know?" I got straight to the point, watching her carefully. She knew something.

"Nothing," she spoke quickly.

If I was not convinced before, I definitely was now. As my eyes narrowed at her, she averted her gaze, and that told me everything. I walked over and stood in front of her with my arms crossed over my chest. She knew something, and I needed to know.

"What do you know?" I repeated, never taking my eyes off her for a second.

"I don't know anything."

"You're lying."

"No, I'm not."

"Tell me what you know!" My voice raised, unable to stop myself. "This is my friend's life we are talking about here! Your psychotic sister has taken her, so if you know something, then you better tell me right now because I need to know!"

Leah stood up so fast it made me dizzy, and I stumbled back. She took a step forward, a low rumbling coming from her—growling. Really?

"All I know is that she is alive." Leah snarled, taking a step towards me. Fear instantly took over, so I took another step backwards. Every time she took one step forward, I took another one back. Her words did comfort me, but the way she had reacted was strange. It did not make sense.

I did not reply to her though I was relieved that Rose was in fact alive. It filled me with hope, but there was a part of me that was not sure whether or not Leah was lying just to comfort me. It seemed like something she would do.

Before I had a chance to voice my thoughts, she started to speak.

"You don't get it, do you?" She spat, moving so quickly that I did not have time to get away. "It's my sister that has Rose. Don't you understand what that means? From your past, I would have thought you would at least understood me, but you don't, do you? Family is family, no matter how screwed up in the head they are."

"I know that." I defended myself, frowning a little. I was unsure of where she was going with this, but all I could do was just wait for her to finish her rant.

"Shadow will kill her. He will kill Raven the second he has the chance," she continued. The sight of her eyes darkening was making me nervous as she glared at me, flashing her fangs. I trembled, afraid of what she would do. If she noticed this, she did not mention it. She was too busy talking. "Of all the people to understand that I can't let that happen, I'd have thought it would have been you. Why do you think he made me stay behind to watch you? It's because he is going to kill her. He also knows I would try to stop him. That's why I'm stuck babysitting you while I could be out there saving my sister. So, for once, quit with the million questions because I have better things to worry about than your crush on Shadow, okay?"

I was not sure what shocked me more: the fact that she thought I was worried because of my crush on Shadow or because of her rant in general. Either way, her words instilled more fear in me than ever before. I did not ever expect her to be so angry at me, but it just reminded me that I really could not trust her not to hurt me. With the way she was looking at me, I could never be sure.

So when she suddenly disappeared in the blink of an eye—literally—I remained where I was, frozen to the spot.

***

Leah did not return. I assumed she had gone after Shadow so she could try to save her sister. I was not sure how to feel about that. I did understand where she was coming from. Of course, I did, but it did not change the fact that the only way to stop a vampire as crazy as Raven would be to kill her. It was the only way, and deep down, I think Leah knew that too. Perhaps that was why she was acting the way she was because from what I had gathered, the two sisters were not exactly on friendly terms.

Whatever Leah's reason was for leaving so suddenly, the fact that I was now left alone in a house where vampires strolled in and out whenever they pleased did not exactly fill me with comfort. The whole point of having a 'babysitter,' as Leah so eloquently put it, was because I was not safe, right? Well, surely I was in more danger now that I was alone.

What if Raven had somebody watching the house? What if they saw Leah leave? What if they knew I was now alone and were coming to get me? I took a deep breath, terrified.

Rushing up the two flights of stairs, I burst into my bedroom. After reading more of that vampire book I had bought and looking things up online, I knew if I were going to have to defend myself then I would need a stake. Which is why, when everybody thought I just needed time to myself, I had made a bunch of them.

I was not the best when it came to making them as the six I made were each a different length and were jagged in some places with bits of wood sticking out. I got more splinters than it was worth when making them, but at least now I had some weapon to use. At least I had something.

Whether or not it was because I was so tense and afraid, I heard the front door open. Knowing that there was a high chance it was not anybody on my side, I grabbed a stake that I had hidden under my bed and shut my bedroom door.

I stood just next to it so that when the door opened, I would be shielded from view. It would give me an advantage against my opponent in any case. I would be able to creep up behind them and try to stake them.

The mere thought of staking a vampire was enough to have my hands shaking, but it was my only chance to live. Why Leah had thought Raven would not have somebody watching the house, I was not sure; maybe she thought Raven would not do something like that now that she had leverage. I had not had defence lessons yet, but I had been given a little advice. Shadow had told me that staking a vampire was the only way, so I knew I had no choice but to do that if I had to.

Straight through the heart, he had told me.

I just hoped that I didn't miss.

Chapter Twenty-Nine

If you are ever attacked, you are supposed to make as much noise as possible. You are supposed to scream and shout because it is more likely that someone will hear and call the police. It is even likely that your attacker will be too afraid of being caught and will run before doing anything.

In this situation, however, screaming my lungs out probably would not help at all. A vampire against a human was not exactly a fair fight as it was obvious who would win. However, knowing my chances of making it out alive were slim did not stop me from wanting to try. If I was going to die, I was going to make damn sure I went down fighting.

Maybe it was me finally being brave and standing up for myself. Maybe it was just pure stupidity.

I probably should have grabbed all six stakes and shoved them under the waistband of my jeans. One might not last as long as I hoped it would. What if he managed to take it off me and snapped it?

I was just about to go grab the rest when I heard footsteps coming up the stairs. My breathing hitched, and my whole body tensed. They were making so much noise, it was obvious they were walking up the second flight of stairs. In a matter of minutes, I would be fighting for my life.

That sent a thrill through me, one I could not explain. I was more determined now. If I was going to go down, then so was he—or she. I had no idea who was in the house after all.

Confidence was not something that came easy to me. After living with an abusive man that had stripped me of any self-esteem and confidence I had, it was no wonder I found it hard to pick myself up and stand up for myself. Listening intently for the vampire, though, I felt a surge of confidence coursing through my body. I was more determined than ever that I could do this; I could fight against a vampire.

Suddenly, the door handle turned, and I clamped a hand over my mouth as my breathing picked up a little. I did not want to give away my position just yet, not until they were in the room and their back was facing me.

Until I remembered vampires could hear heartbeats.

The door flung open harshly. It would have hit me in the face if it was not for the fact I raised my hand at the last moment. A man walked in and immediately, he turned to look at me. With a start, I realised that I had seen that face before. I knew who he was.

Adam…

The very same vampire that had been there when Raven attacked me.

That only fuelled the fire burning within me, and I charged forward, ready to stake him. He had a smirk on his face, watching me with amusement. That amusement soon disappeared, however, when he spotted the stake in my hand, but by then, it was too late. I had thrust my hand forward, lodging the stake deep in his stomach. It was not high enough to kill him, but at least it gave me the chance to run away. If I got outside, then I would be safe; he could not attack me if there were people around. If he tried coming near me once I was outside, I was going to scream.

Racing out of the room, my heart thumping painfully in my chest, I almost fell down the stairs in my haste to get away. All the times I had sat watching a horror film with Rose, complaining about how someone would trip over while running away from whatever chased them, started to make sense to me then. It really is easy to trip over your own feet when you are running from danger because you are not focused on where you are going as much as you are on trying to stay alive. All you could focus on was getting the fuck out of dodge.

Or maybe that was just me.

I heard Adam's footsteps chasing after me just as I reached the bottom of the stairs. So when he appeared in front of me, I found myself cursing vampires and their speed all over again. It was so not fair. It was like cheating, in a way.

Raising the stake, I got ready to strike again, but Adam had grabbed me by the throat before I could do anything, starting to squeeze. My feet were no longer touching the floor, and the stake slipped from my grasp, clattering on the floor as I clawed at his hands. He was applying too much pressure, and I could not breathe. My eyelids started to flicker as my body started to shut down from the lack of oxygen.

My legs were flailing about as I continued to claw at his hands, and when my foot made contact with the part of his body no man wants to be kicked, I was immediately released. Collapsing to the floor, I struggled to get my breath back, choking. I rubbed my throat in a desperate attempt to relieve them, but it did not work.

"You fucking bitch!" Adam wheezed, clutching himself as he groaned in pain, doubling over at the waist.

My eyes darted around the floor for my stake, but just as I made a run for it, I was suddenly being picked up. I tried to scream, but it came out hoarse, a result of almost being choked to death.

Before I knew it, I was flying through the air. Adam watched on with a huge grin on his face as I was sent crashing into the stairs. I let out a cry of pain when my body landed painfully on the stairs, my head hitting the edge of one. I crumpled at the bottom in a heap as pain shot up my spine, and I lay there, breathing heavily.

What was it with vampires throwing people into things?

"You're going to pay for that," Adam said, stalking towards me. I moved at the last possible second just as he was reaching out to grab me again. Not wanting to be thrown around again, I crawled over to the stake as fast as possible and had just managed to get a good enough grip on it when Adam grabbed a handful of my hair and yanked me back.

I cried out in pain, thrashing about and trying to hit him with the stake, but it was no use. He was able to dodge any attempt I made and grabbed my wrist, rendering my hand that held the stake useless.

Adrenaline was still flowing through my body, but it was rapidly dissolving. I knew it would only be a matter of time before he decided to just end my life right here in the hallway. Maybe it was that thought that had me sending my head crashing backwards, hoping to hit some part of his body. Maybe it also had something to do with the fact that I never fought back against my dad, and I wanted to fight back more than ever before.

I was done with people throwing me around and treating me like a rag doll. I was done being their personal punching bag. I was done with it. It was time I stood up for myself. It was time I fought back for a change. I was so sick of people hurting me and me being too afraid to anything about it.

That only spurred me on, twisting my arm back and grabbing him. Before my mum left, she would always tell me that as much as I did not want to, if I was being attacked, the best places to hurt my attacker—if male—was to hurt them in the balls or punch them in the throat. Since I could not actually reach his throat, I settled for grabbing him in the same place I had kicked him moments before. It would have been more effective if I used the stake, but he was determined not to let that touch his body again.

I squeezed as hard as I could, and a twisted satisfaction brewed within me when he once again released his hold and I was able to get away.

"Why do you have to keep going for the balls?" he cried out, this time sinking to his knees with both hands covering his groin.

"I'd say sorry, but you really did ask for that," I retorted, not even thinking about what I was saying as I turned around, readying the stake.

I lunged forward, and his eyes landed on the stake. He knew what I was going to do. It was clear by the expression on my face. He went to snatch the stake from me, but with my other hand, I quickly punched him in the throat.

It did not even look as though that had any effect on him at all... though I could not say I was too surprised. Being hit between the legs would surely be more painful.

There was a pain in my back that made it difficult to move too quickly, but I pushed it to the back of my mind. I had to concentrate on what was happening. I could dwell on the pain later.

Yet when I went to stand up, I winced, and the momentary distraction was more than enough for him. Adam had me by the throat again, moving us both so quickly, everything blurred.

Now sprawled on the floor with him straddling me, he removed his hand from my neck, placing them on my shoulders. Realisation dawned on me with a start, and it had my heart racing even faster than before.

He was going to bite me. He was going to drain my body of the blood it needed. I could not let that happen again, I just could not. *Come on, Violet, fight for fuck sake!* I yelled internally as he started leaning down.

I squirmed beneath him, placing my hands on his chest in a desperate attempt to shove him off me. It was only then that I realised the stake laid on the floor just beside us. I was about to reach out for it when Adam's fist came down on my jaw so hard that it stunned me. The pain was enough to keep me laying still, unmoving.

Ow.

I tried, but it was like I was frozen in place. I was paralysed by fear. I could not move, and I was all too aware that the pain I was currently in was about to get a thousand times worse. I would rather have a hundred knives plunged into my body at the same time than go through the excruciating pain of being bitten again.

I had almost resigned myself to the fact that there was no way I could get out of this, no way I could win this fight, but then I reached out again for the stake. This time, my fingers brushed against it, and I was able to move it slightly closer to me. Thankfully, Adam had not noticed this as his head was now buried in the crook of my neck and his lips were on my skin. I was close to hyperventilating, and he had not even sunk his fangs into my neck yet.

Do something, Violet! My inner self screamed.

Summoning all the strength I had left in me, I managed to get my hand on the stake, and without pausing to think about it, sent it straight towards him. It did not hit his heart—not even close—but at least I had distracted him from draining me.

It was when he leaned backwards that he had made his mistake because he allowed me to attack again.

This time, I did not miss.

His jaw dropped, and he inhaled sharply as his gaze fixed on me. Then, he glanced down at the stake that was now lodged in his chest. It had struck his heart. That, I was sure of because it was not long before he collapsed, falling to the side with the stake still stuck into his body.

I had done it. I had fought a vampire and won.

Shuffling away, keeping my eyes on him just in case he was not actually dead, I did not stop moving until I was at a safe distance. Though I felt like I could not put enough space between us, I was not going to risk letting him out of my sight.

With my back against the wall, I brought my knees to my chest and rested my chin on my knees. I simply stared at Adam, the vampire, the man I had just killed.

This time, I really was a murderer. I had actually taken someone's life. Defending myself or not, I had just ended someone's life. A killer, a murderer, that was what I was now.

I could not take my eyes off his still body, knowing I was the cause of it. I should have been happy knowing that I had survived—a part of me was—but I could not stop thinking that I had just killed someone.

I was still sitting there an hour later when everybody else came back.

Chapter Thirty

"What the fuck happened here?" Were Shadow's first words when his eyes landed on me and the dead body of Adam. I had thought that it was obvious what had happened but apparently, he needed some sort of clarification.

"After Leah left—" I started to speak but was automatically cut off by Shadow, who looked shocked, as well as a little angry.

"What do you mean she left?" Shadow asked.

So Leah had not gotten there in time, I thought to myself, biting my lip. What would happen now? Leah was not going to be happy, and judging by the angry expression on Shadow's face, he would have some few choice words for her when she returned.

"She... erm..." I trailed off, getting to my feet shakily. I did not want her to get in trouble with him. I knew what he was like when he was angry, so I did not want that anger directed at Leah even though she really should not have left me alone.

"The last fucking thing I said to her was to stay here and keep you safe, and she can't even do that!" Shadow spat as he, Alec, and

Ric walked over to inspect Adam's body. That was when I noticed something, something that I could not believe I did not notice before.

Rose was not there.

"W-where's Rose?" I stuttered, taking a deep breath as I waited for them to explain. I watched as they all glanced at one another as if deciding who would be the one to break the news. Just seeing that interaction made me even more nervous and scared than I already was.

The more the silence was prolonged, the more it was becoming increasingly obvious that they had not gotten to her in time. My knees buckled, and my legs gave way underneath me, unable to stand the weight of my body, and I crashed to the floor. I did not even bother getting back up, feeling sick all of a sudden.

"Please... no," I choked out, shaking my head vehemently. "She can't be... No, no, please!"

They all turned to look at me, wearing similar expressions on their faces. I was trying my hardest not to break down because they had not said anything yet but somehow, their silence was just making it that much harder for me to cope. Silence speaks volumes. Silence can sometimes tell you more than words ever could. It was clear they had something to say, and I knew. I just knew that it was not good news.

Shadow approached me slowly and bent down. When he pulled me into him, wrapping his arms around me tightly, my worst fears were confirmed. Rose was dead. My best friend was dead and gone. I was never going to see her again.

That was when I broke down, sobbing into Shadow's chest, surprising myself at the fact I still had any tears left to cry. There was no stopping them. They did not even have to say the words. I knew. I just knew. I did not want to believe it. I wished it was just some sick prank they decided to pull on the emotional human that I am, but it was not. I wanted more than anything in the world for them to start laughing at me, telling me Rose was fine and that they just wanted to have some fun, but it was not going to happen.

I would take a sick prank any day over this. In just one minute, my life had come crashing down around me, caving in at the seams. I could not stop crying, and all Shadow could do was rub my back as though it would help anything. If I was crying about anything else, it probably would have, but this? This was just too much. It was too much for a person to bare. Nobody should have to lose a loved one especially so young. And I knew it was my fault. Raven only found out about Rose because of me.

"I know this is probably a bad time, but well done on killing this son of a bitch," Alec spoke suddenly, glancing at me as I raised my head to look at him. I had become a murderer and lost my best friend in just one day. It was too much; I could not cope with this at all.

I was never going to see my best friend. I was never going to see her smile again. I would never see her laughing at me when I tripped over thin air again. I would never hear her complaining about the male population ever again. I would never be able to talk to her about my problems ever again. I would never be able to go shopping with her, trying on multiple different outfits only to decide that we did not like any of them enough to actually buy them.

It was funny how it was the little things I would miss the most, but nothing could have prepared me for the reality of losing her. To have it confirmed, even if not by words, brought an overwhelming sadness over me. One that was not likely to go away anytime soon. I doubted it would disappear at all.

It felt like my tears would never end. Endless supply of tears or not, I never wanted to feel this much pain. The emotional pain had taken over the physical pain, and that spoke volumes. It just proved just how much I was hurting when the physical pain was no longer as bad as the emotional.

I was not sure how I managed it but eventually, my tears dried up. I still did not move, though. All the hope I once held of Rose coming back alive had quickly evaporated upon seeing the looks on their faces.

I felt everything and nothing all at the same time.

"Alec," Shadow spoke up, keeping his arms wrapped around me and running his one hand through my hair as the other rested gently on my back. "Help Ric move the body and then call Leah. Tell her to get back here."

"What are you going to do?" Alec asked him, sounding worried.

Shadow chuckled darkly and detached himself from me so he could stand up, pulling me up beside him immediately after and placing an arm around me to keep me upright. Whether he knew how weak I was or not, I was grateful for his help.

"Relax, I'm not going to kill her. I do have some things to say to her, though."

"There was no possible way she could have known he was waiting for her to leave." Alec tried to defend his girlfriend, but even he knew it was no use. He was standing right beside Leah when Shadow warned her that Raven would have somebody watching the house. There was no way he could get Leah off the hook.

To be honest, I did not even have it in me to be angry with her. It may have been her fault for leaving that resulted in me being attacked and almost killed, but the loss of my best friend was more important. Everything else paled in comparison.

"Violet," Shadow called my name softly, glancing down at me. I looked back at him, and he continued to speak. "What happened here? Did he hurt you?"

I quickly explained everything that happened from the moment that Leah had left, not leaving out any details. There was no point in doing that. It was useless trying to hide anything from them, especially Shadow as he seemed to know when somebody was lying to him.

When I got to the part where Adam had strangled me and thrown me into the stairs, I saw his jaw clench, and he pinched the bridge of his nose. He did that quite a lot when he was trying to control himself.

"Stupid fucker." Alec spat, glaring down at Adam's lifeless body and the stake still lodged into his chest. "Nobody lays a finger on people I care about. I'm so glad he's dead, but I would have loved to do it myself."

"You'd have had to get in line," Shadow replied.

Apparently, vampires did have some sort of morals. Who knew?

"Come on," Ric said to Alec, speaking for the first time. "Let's get this body moved. Shadow, you might want to take Violet upstairs. She looks a little pale."

Just as we were about to, my shaky legs feeling like jelly, the front door opened. In stepped Leah, who had a guilty expression plastered all over her face the second she saw us all turn to face her. She slipped inside and shut the door, locking it.

"Hey..." she spoke meekly, raising a hand to wave. I just stared at her, not really knowing what to say. I was not in the mood to talk. I did not want to do anything but mourn the loss of Rose. I missed her already.

People say that as the years pass, you start to get back to normal until you are able to get through the day without breaking down but to be honest, it did not seem like that would be possible for me. People say that time does heal all wounds, no matter how deep and scarring they may be. I found that hard to believe. It did not feel as though I would ever be able to get past losing my best friend the way I did—at the hands of a vampire who wanted to kill me.

Indirectly, it was my fault Rose was thrown into the firing lane of Raven's psychotic tendencies. That would haunt me forever.

Shadow moved too quickly for my human eyes to see, but suddenly, he was pinning Leah against the door, snarling in her face as she struggled to push him away from her.

"What the fuck did I say to you!" He snarled, getting right into her face. Alec and Ric were by his side fast enough, but even they could not get him away from her. It seemed to me like Shadow was a lot stronger than them. Or maybe they just did not want to annoy him any further. It could have been either, but I was leaning more towards the former. It seemed impossible that Shadow could get anymore angry.

"Not to leave Violet alone." Leah squeaked out, clearly afraid of Shadow. I did not blame her; I would be frightened too if I was in her position. I had been there often enough, so I knew what she was feeling though, again, I could not bring myself to care.

"So why did you?" Shadow asked, cocking his head to one side, waiting for her to reply.

"Because I knew you were going to kill Raven!" Leah yelled in his face. "I'm not stupid! I knew that's what you were going to do, so I went to try and stop you!"

"That's exactly what Raven was counting on, you idiot!" Shadow yelled as the loudness of his voice made me jump and take an automatic step backwards. "She knew you would try and stop her. That's what she was waiting for! She was counting on it! Why do you think Adam is now on our floor dead? He was sent to kill Violet!"

It seemed that Leah had not noticed the body laying on the floor when she entered the house as she glanced over Shadow's shoulder. Her eyes widened, and her jaw dropped.

"Oh, my God! I'm so sorry. I didn't know!" Leah said, shaking her head. "I thought Raven would've wanted to kill Violet herself, not send someone else to do her dirty work."

"Since when do you know the inner workings of Raven's mind?" Shadow asked. His voice was taking a sinister turn.

Leah was silent for a while. *Silence.* Again, it was louder than words could ever be. It was a girl's loudest cry; isn't that what people say? In this case, Leah's silence was deafening.

"Well?" Shadow asked, clearly not in the mood for messing around.

"I don't, okay?" Leah spoke, and when she did, her voice cracked a little. "I don't know who she is anymore. I couldn't let you kill her, though, so I went to find her... Why didn't you kill her?"

I was shocked by that revelation. Leah was so certain Shadow would not let Raven live. Even I thought the same thing, so why didn't he? He had sworn to often enough.

"Because you told me not to," he simply replied.

"I thought as much." Leah sighed. "So I killed her myself."

Another bombshell. I was relieved Raven was dead, but I felt sick. Everything I was feeling was just piling on top of one another until I could not cope a second longer.

I felt myself falling and the room spinning. That was when I fainted, and the darkness consumed me.

Chapter Thirty-One

When I was suffering at the hands of my dad, I knew what to expect, but at the same time, I didn't. That may not make sense, but to me, it makes perfect sense. I knew that he would hurt me, and I could always tell when it was going to happen, I just did not know how. I did not know whether he would use his fists or his feet, or whether he would use an object he found around the house. It could have been a lamp, a bat, or a bottle. It could have been a vase, a plate, or a knife. So while I had no idea what form the abuse would take, I just knew it would happen.

So obviously, I was filled with fear. I knew what to expect, but I also had no idea. That scared me for the simple reason being that I could not defend myself. Try, and it would only make things worse. Try, and I was only going to hurt myself more than I hurt him. Which was why I never did. I stopped trying after the first few months because I just knew there was no use in trying when it was absolutely pointless to do so.

It was kind of similar to how I had been feeling lately.

Now that Raven was dead, I did not know what that would mean for me, and yet I had an idea. I assumed they would let me go now that I was not in any danger. They had no reason to keep me around anymore, and it was never supposed to be a permanent place for me to stay. The only reason I had been here for a couple of months was purely because I had been in danger. I still think the only reason Shadow had been so determined to protect me was because he felt responsible—which he was. I could not deny that.

Though I was sure they were not going to turn on me, I would not even care if they did. I just did not care anymore. I did not care whether I lived or died anymore.

Rose's absence had been weighing heavily on my mind since I had been told yesterday. All I could think about was the fact I would never see her again. It reduced me to tears every time. In fact, I had barely been able to stop crying.

So when my phone buzzed in my pocket and the picture of Rose and I came up seeing as it was my lock screen, I had to cover my mouth, choking back the sobs that threatened to bubble over.

Then, I saw the message.

Saw your friend today. I thought I told you not to speak to anybody. I'm trying here, Violet.

P.S. The polite thing to do when you receive a text message would be to reply.

I read over the message once, twice, and a third time just to make sure I was not seeing things. The most shocking part of the message was obviously the first four words. Saw my friend? No. That was not possible.

Crawling out from the bed, I quickly got changed. I tried to put the message to the back of my mind, but I could not. Of all the people to spark some hope within me, I could hardly believe it was my dad. I never expected that.

It was not until I read the message again after having got changed into a pair of black skinny jeans and a loose grey top that I knew it was not the type of message I could ignore. If my dad knew Rose was dead, he would have rubbed it in my face; I knew that. So for him to tell me he had seen her, implying he had spoken to her... Well, it was safe to say that confusion was the understatement of the century.

I ran out of the room, down the stairs, and into the lounge. I had to speak to Shadow. He was not in there, though. Neither was he in the kitchen. In fact, as I searched the house, I found that I was the only one there.

Where had they gone? I asked myself, plopping down on the sofa with a frown. The threat might have been eliminated, but Shadow would not have left me alone, would he? Unless he was going to kill me now, he did not have to keep me around.

I bit my lip, waiting for them to come back. Maybe they were out buying bin bags and a shovel. That was what murderers seem to do in the movies though I could not see why vampires would need those sorts of things. They could kill with a snap of their finger and probably leave my body in one of the spare rooms. Perhaps they would keep my body in the same room Shadow killed Rolan.

It was impossible to forget I was living in the same house as murderers despite the fact they had been trying to keep me safe.

"We're back!" I heard a voice call, and I jumped out of my seat, immediately rushing out into the hall to see Shadow, Leah, Alec, and Ric walking through the front door, each one holding carrier bags.

"What's going on?" I asked, glancing at the bags. Had I been right? Had they actually been buying things they could use to dispose of my body?

I took a step back, eyeing them warily. I had killed one vampire, maybe I could kill another.

Maybe.

"I don't know." Leah shrugged. "Shadow just roped us all into buying loads of food and things."

"Food? Why?" That was not what I was expecting.

Shadow looked uncomfortable. "Comfort food. Besides, we were getting low."

Comfort food? He's gone out of his way to buy food... for me? My frown deepened. His caring side confused me, but I had more pressing matters.

"My dad text me again." I announced.

Their reactions were just as I expected they would be. Shock and anger ran across each of their faces.

"Again? What do you mean again?" Shadow raised an eyebrow. His grip on the carrier bag visibly tightened, and his knuckles turned white.

"Maybe we should take this conversation into the lounge?" Leah suggested.

I nodded. I would definitely need to be sitting for this conversation because the more I thought of everything that has transpired yesterday, the more clear it became that nothing was adding up.

They all took the bags into the kitchen, leaving them on the counter before piling into the lounge where I sat down in the same place I was before.

Leah and Alec sat on the other sofa while Ric sat beside me. Only Shadow remained standing, crossing his arms over his chest as he looked down at me. He looked so intimidating standing there that I actually had to glance down at my lap.

"Explain," Shadow said. It was clear it was meant more as a demand than anything else, so I quickly started talking.

"He messaged me before... before..." I could not even say the words aloud, yet in my mind, it was all that I could think. *Before Rose was taken and killed.* I hurried on anyway, digging my nails into my knees as I did so. "He just asked how I was, but obviously, I ignored it. Then today, he sent me another message... I don't understand it."

"What did it say?" Ric asked, taking my hand in his to prevent me from hurting myself.

"H-he..." I took a deep breath. "H-he... I can't."

I felt like an idiot for not being able to speak, so I just took my phone out and handed it to Shadow. The message was still up on the screen so while he read it, I watched the expression on his face.

He looked just as confused as I felt. His brows furrowed, and he bit his lip. That told me all I needed to know; whatever was going on, Shadow was just as in the dark about it as I was.

"That's not possible," he stated, raising his eyes to meet mine. "We saw the body. It was her."

"What? What are you talking about?" Leah asked, sitting up straighter.

"Her father says he saw Rose," Shadow said as his eyes locked on Leah. Something was running through his mind, but I could not be sure what that was.

Leah remained quiet. She seemed to like doing that, but unfortunately for her, I was observant. She always seemed to go quiet when she knew more than she was letting on.

"Is she dead or not?" I asked, keeping my eyes locked on Leah. An unsettling feeling was brewing in my stomach.

Leah's eyes widened by a fraction. Eventually, she sighed. "No, she's not."

I breathed in deeply, shutting my eyes tightly as the tears threatened to well up again. I was sick of crying so damn much.

"What the fuck are you talking about?" Alec asked Leah, taken aback by her confession. "We saw the body. Granted, there was no head, but it was the same clothes she'd left in."

I had to take another deep breath upon hearing that. I did not know the details of her death. I did not want to. It was something that I did not need to know.

"I got to Raven just after you'd left," Leah explained. "The body you saw wasn't Rose. It was someone else that looked like her. She changed the clothes, so you'd believe you were too late. I only realised what she'd done when I heard Rose screaming from upstairs while me and Raven... We got into a fight, and I had to kill her."

"Where the fuck is Rose now?" Shadow seethed, pinching the bridge of his nose. "And why the fuck has she let Violet believe she was dead?"

"She's back home," Leah said. "She begged me not to tell anyone that she was leaving. She was scared, Shadow, and she was trusting me to help her. So I let her leave because she doesn't want to speak to Violet."

"What?" I asked, finally finding my voice and gaping at her in shock.

"She doesn't know you think she's dead, I swear," Leah said, staring me straight in the eyes.

"Why doesn't she want to speak to me?"

"She blames you. She's angry she was put in danger because Raven was after you. So she left."

"So she trusts you but not me?" I was bewildered. Rose had shown her obvious distaste and hatred for all vampires, so it was hard to believe she has put her trust on one.

Leah laughed. "Are you kidding? She didn't want to be anywhere near me. The only reason she let me help her was because I'd just saved her ass. She'll speak to you, eventually. She just needs space to think, I assume."

"Thanks." I rolled my eyes. "That comforts me a lot."

"Well, at least she's alive. I mean, that's the main thing, right?"

Yeah, I thought to myself. At least she was alive. I would rather her hate me forever so long as she was alive. Better that than dead.

***

Turns out that the comfort food was needed more than I thought, but I quickly realised my appetite was long gone. Recent events saw to that.

I could not wrap my head around the fact my best friend did not want to speak to me. I had spent a day thinking that she was dead. That had been the longest and most painful day of my life, and yet Rose was not dead at all.

I sent her a message, overcome by the need to apologise.

Leah just told me... I'm so sorry about what happened, I really am. When I got the text from my dad this morning saying he'd seen you, I thought I was seeing things. I thought you were dead, Rose. I spent the night crying over the death of my best friend when it turns out you're alive. So I'm sorry that you had to go through that. I'll give you some space. I know you'll probably need it. xx

I did not get a reply until much later on in the night when we had all settled down in the lounge with a bunch of junk food. The plan was to just watch whatever crap came on TV as we had nothing else to do.

When Rose replied, I read the message quickly.

You thought I was dead?!?!?! I'm sorry! I assumed Leah would tell you I left... I'm sorry Vi, I am. I did see your dad, and I did kinda... maybe... punch him. I just lashed out. Everything was just too much. I just need time to think. Can you send my stuff back, please? I kinda forgot about it when I was leaving. I'm trying not to blame you, though. It's just hard. x

I typed out a response.

Well, she didn't. It's okay. I'm just glad you're alive. I'd never have forgiven myself otherwise. I'll send it off tomorrow or something. X

That was the end of our conversation, but relief spread throughout my body. I knew that she was struggling as anyone in her position would be. To hear that she had punched my dad did bring a small smile to my face, though. She had been wanting to do that since she found out about what he was really like.

"Are you okay?" Shadow asked. He was sitting beside me on the sofa with an arm casually slung around the back of it.

I turned to face him and sighed. "I have to be."

He frowned. "Why?"

"Because if I let everything get to me the way it has been, then I'll start crying. If I start crying, I'm afraid I'll never stop," I admitted, smiling sadly.

Shadow shook his head and stood up, holding out his hand for me to take. I did so, confused, but I let him pull me up and lead me out of the room, ignoring the curious gazes shot our way from the other three.

He took us outside, sitting on the step after he had closed to the front door so the others would not eavesdrop.

"Why did you bring me out here?" I asked him.

"Because you keep everything bottled up," he said. "It's not right."

"I'm sick of crying."

"I didn't say you had to cry." He pointed out.

"That's all I seem to be doing lately," I said, laughing sadly.

"You've been through a lot." Shadow shrugged. "Quite frankly, It would be amazing if you didn't cry."

"But it's all over now," I said, staring up at sky and the birds that flew by. It must be so peaceful to be a bird, to just be able to fly away whenever you wanted to. If you wanted to escape, you could.

"It's all over now." Shadow agreed.

"What happens now?" I asked, biting my lip.

"What do you mean?"

"Are you going to kill me or let me go?"

Shadow shot me a dark look, one that I recognised very well by now. It was a sign that he was not happy. Then again, he rarely ever seemed to be happy. I often wondered if he was even capable of being happy at all.

"Can't you see it yet?" he finally asked with a grim expression. "Everything that I have done has been to protect you. I brought you here because you were about to be attacked and you had nowhere to go. I saved your ass countless times. I healed your injuries time and time again. I protected you from Raven when I could have just let her take you.."

"Why didn't you? I've been nothing but a hassle since the second you brought me here."

Shadow sighed. "I couldn't. I'm not a monster. Not anymore."

That comment put everything into perspective for me. The way that his attitude has changed so quickly, the determination to protect me from Raven... It was all to prove himself, to prove that he was not the monster he believed he was. Maybe he just wanted someone else to see that too.

And I did.

How could I not after everything he had done for me? It dawned on me—finally—that if he wanted to kill me, he would not have gone to such lengths to make sure I was safe. He would have saved himself the trouble. Yet he didn't. I had been so blinded by fear that I could not see it before, but now I could. My eyes were wide open, and I could finally see that he truly was not that bad. Sure, he was messed up, but what person wasn't these days? Everyone has a past whether they liked to admit it or not. Shadow's was just a little darker than most.

I placed my hand over his own, and upon feeling this, he turned his head to stare at me.

"You're not a monster. You never have been."

Shadow smiled, one that I ever so rarely saw. It was a true smile, his grey eyes shining. It just proved that I was right; all he wanted was for someone to believe he was not a heartless monster.

"And you're not broken," he replied, squeezing my hand though he did not let go. If anything, he held on tighter.

I snorted. "If not broken, then what?"

"Lost," he answered, without a second's hesitation.

"Lost and broken." I corrected, sighing. "See those birds up there? I wish I could just flap my wings and leave. Wouldn't that be good? To just go wherever you want, and nobody knows a damn thing about you. You can start again, a fresh start, but I can't. My wings are broken and can never be fixed.

"My mother used to tell me even broken wings can fly once more," Shadow murmured. "Things can be mended. People can be fixed. You're not broken, you never were. You've just been a little lost."

"I'm afraid I'll never be happy again," I whispered, not caring whether he heard or not. I just wanted to be happy, but it seemed impossible.

"You will be. I'll make sure of it."

Chapter Thirty-Two

"Why are you doing this?" I asked Shadow, confused.

"I explained last night," he told me in response.

Granted, he had told me he would make sure that I was happy again though I never expected him to take that so literally. I just assumed he meant letting me go, so I could go where I wanted or something like that. I did not expect him to come into my room the very next morning and wake me up, claiming that he was taking me out and no, I did not need to bring any money.

I was not even sure I had any money left, to be honest, so I did not argue with that. Besides, it was not like I knew what we would be doing as he had refused to tell me. The only way I had figured out was when we actually arrived at our destination: Madame Tussauds.

The second I had seen the building, my excitement grew. I had never been here before, so I had definitely been looking forward to it. It was just as great as I thought it would be, too. Shadow and I walked around all the different wax figures and took poses with as many as we could. I must have been close to running out of memory on my phone with all the photos I took. Even Shadow posed next to some of them.

That did shock me. When he went and stood by the waxwork of Kim Kardashian, he just had to grope her breasts and smirk at me as I captured the moment on my phone. I was not expecting him to join in, particularly because he clearly meant this day to prove what he had said to me. It was good to see him enjoying the experience just as much as I was.

I knew that he was trying to make me forget about everything. I could tell by the way he avoided certain topics, swiftly changing the subject whenever it was heading into dangerous waters. I appreciated it. I really did. I did not want to think about everything. For just one day, I wanted to forget, and that was exactly what Shadow was trying to do.

Honestly, his nice side was showing, and it was shocking the hell out of me. I had grown used to seeing him snappy and arrogant, rude even, so it definitely came as a shock to see him letting loose and having fun. I rarely ever saw him like that.

"You didn't have to, though." I pointed out as we walked over to the wax work of Benedict Cumberbatch so I could take a picture beside it.

"I wanted to." He shrugged, stuffing his hands into the pockets of his jeans. "You've gone through a lot. It's about time someone treated you the way you deserve to be treated."

"And you decided that you should be that person?"

"Exactly." He looked at me with a grin on his face. "After all, I'm the one that brought you into all this. I should be the one to give you the day you deserve."

I smiled. I could not help it. He seemed to know exactly what I needed and when I needed it. At first, I found it weird, but I was actually grateful for it now. I appreciated it all.

It was safe to say that the pair of us were having a good time. Shadow seemed just as interested in the wax works as I was, even cracking a few jokes here and there. He had me laughing to the point where my stomach started to ache, and it was not because the jokes were that funny. It was because they were that stupid. Some did not even make sense to me. Still, I could not stop laughing. I'm sure I was attracting too much attention, but I just could not help myself. He was actually making me happy just as he wanted all along.

So when a hand was suddenly placed on my shoulder, I automatically flinched, jumping out of the way and closer to Shadow. That was something I suppose I would have to accept was never going to change. My past had scarred me too deeply; there was no getting away from that. Shadow seemed to realise this at the same time I had as he wrapped his arm around my waist and pulled me closer to him, spinning us both around so we could face whoever had tried to get my attention.

To my surprise, it was Jane and William that stood in front of us, smiling at Shadow and me.

"I thought it was you!" Jane said, still smiling. "I told Will that it was you, but he told me I was imagining things! Says you'd be long gone by now! But I was right, wasn't I?"

I saw William roll his eyes, but Jane did not spot that. I was sure she would have said something otherwise.

"I only thought she'd have been back home by now," William replied.

"Oh, I've decided to stay here," I told them, hoping they would not say anything about what I had told them. They did not deserve to die, but that was exactly what Shadow would make sure of if he knew just how much I had told them. "I'm living with my friends now."

That was when they both glanced at Shadow who immediately tightened his grip on me. I was not sure why I was not in any danger from Jane and William. All they had done was try to help me. Not that Shadow could ever know that, however.

"That's great news!" Jane said, gleefully. "Is everything okay now?"

I nodded, casting a quick glance at Shadow and hoping, just hoping that he would not catch on.

"So you're safe?" William asked, raising an eyebrow. I saw the look he gave to Shadow and tensed. *Please, don't say anything, please don't say anything*, I begged internally.

"Yeah, my friends have been looking out for me," I told them.

"Can I just say that you both look like a lovely couple? You're so cute together!" Jane's words were totally unexpected. Neither myself nor Shadow had been expecting something like that. The second she said that the two of us glanced at each other with bewildered expressions. Saying that we were cute together was strange though it did make me smile. Damn feelings.

Neither of us actually said anything to that, we did not know how to. It was unexpected, and so, I had no idea how to respond.

"Oh, I'm sorry! Are you not together?" Jane quickly backtracked, seeming to realise that she had made the both of us uncomfortable.

I shook my head. "No. We're just friends."

Jane and William made their excuses to leave after that. I was not sure they knew what to say either after that awkwardness. They just wanted to make sure I was safe, and now that they knew, they did not need to hang around any longer. It was lovely to see them both again, so after I hugged them both, they left to go and look at the other waxworks.

"You told them." It was not a question, merely a statement but his words made me tense, nonetheless. I was scared that he would hurt them, so I did not reply, knowing that nothing I said would make the slightest difference.

Too bad he was not having any of that. He moved, dropping his hand from my waist as he stepped directly in front of me, eyebrows raised. I took a deep breath, afraid of what he would say. He would not kill them in a crowded place, but that did not mean he was just going to let it go.

Imagine my surprise when he did exactly that.

"I'm not happy about that. Hell, I'm angry that you went blabbing to someone." He started, sighing as he ran a hand through his hair. "But I'm not going to hurt you or them, so don't look so worried."

"Y-you're n-not?"

"Don't look so surprised." He rolled his eyes.

"But I am... I mean, you never... you threatened me... why?" I stumbled over my words, a flood of emotions running through my body in waves.

"I'm not the monster you think I am."

I sighed, shaking his head. "You're not a monster, Shadow. I know you're not."

"Yet you seem surprised I'm not going to kill you or that old couple, despite the fact you deliberately went against my orders and told them things you shouldn't?" he asked, raising an eyebrow.

When he put it like that, I was even more surprised he had not threatened me yet.

"Well..." I trailed off.

"Relax, I'm not going to kill you. I seem to be saying that a lot lately." He mused, shaking his head in amusement.

"Sorry... You threaten me a lot so... you're not going to hurt them, are you?"

"No." He shook his head.

I let out a breath. "Thank God for that."

Shadow suddenly sighed, rolling his eyes as he once again wrapped an arm around my waist. Bringing me in closer, he leant down to whisper in my ear.

"I'm not going to kill them because it would upset you. Now, can you let it go, or I may just change my mind."

What the hell did that mean? Since when did Shadow care that much about my feelings?

For the rest of the day, his words stuck in my head like a broken record, repeating the same line over and over again. I just could not work out why he cared that much what I thought of him. He never had before, so what had changed?

Little did I know I was about to find out exactly why.

***

It was not until around four PM that I found out why he seemed to care so much. We were sitting on a bench while I had something to eat—Shadow insisted I eat something—so we were not talking much. People talking with their mouth filled with food wasn't exactly attractive, so I wanted to avoid doing it myself.

"You know, I never thought I had a heart," Shadow spoke up, just as I had finished eating.

I quickly swallowed the rest of my food before replying, furrowing my eyebrows. "Why would you think that?"

Shadow chuckled bitterly. "Isn't it obvious?"

"Not to me." I shrugged, wondering where he was going with this. He was not one to open up about anything, really. So rather than shut down his attempts to do just that, I waited patiently for him to explain.

"When Viktor turned me, I was so angry that I couldn't control it. He didn't help with that anger. He fuelled it. So all these years, I have lived with that same anger in me despite preferring this life to my human one. I accepted that I didn't have a heart because how could I have one when I had gone along with Viktor's wishes? Nobody that killed as many innocent people as I did could possibly have a heart... or a shred of humanity in them for that matter. I thought it would get better after Viktor was dead, but it didn't."

When he paused, staring straight in front of him almost as if he was afraid to see my reaction, I frowned. I was not sure why he was telling me all of this, but I wanted to be there for him. In the two months I had known him, it was clear he regretted the way he used to be. The important thing was that he was not that person any longer. He had changed, and despite what he thought about himself, a heart was something he did have. If he were as cold-hearted as he thought he was, then he would not feel so bad at all.

"Shadow, you can't think that way." I started, choosing my words carefully. "You're not that person anymore... You're not. I can see it. Leah can see it. Alec and Ric can see it. You're not cold-hearted at all. I don't get why you think you are."

"Because I am," he stated.

"You're not. If you didn't have a heart, you would not have put so much effort to keep my safe, would you?" I countered, raising my eyebrows as I stared at him. He still was not looking at me, though.

"I don't know."

"Why are you telling me this?" I questioned, trying to change the subject. It was clear that he was not going to see things the way I saw them. It would be next to impossible to make him change the way he thought of himself.

"Like I said, I didn't think I had a heart."

"So?"

"Now I'm starting to think I do."

I blinked, unsure of what to say. His words had hit me hard though I could not pinpoint why exactly that was. Perhaps it was the fact he had finally turned to meet my gaze as he spoke, and I could see the sincerity within their depths.

"When I changed and stopped killing everybody I saw, I vowed not to let anyone close enough to make me self-destruct again. Viktor had given me this new life, and I killed him. What does that say about me? I know the guy wasn't the best, but he did have his rare moments. Of course, Leah, Alec, and Ric are my friends, and I do care about them, but at the same time, if I wanted to, I could leave and never turn back, not giving them a second thought."

"That's..." I trailed off, not knowing what to say. What could I say to that? I hated that he was finally opening up and yet I had no advice to give him. I wanted to help, but I was not sure how to. All I could do was listen.

"Cruel? Harsh? Twisted?" He offered.

"Sad," I admitted, smiling sadly. "You have friends that do anything you ask, and yet you could still leave? That's got to be a sad and lonely existence if your friends aren't enough to make you want to stay."

"I've been alone since I killed Viktor." He pointed out. "I've really gotten used to it. I'm not used to people sticking around for so long, especially when I'm not exactly nice to them."

"Then be nice to them." Why couldn't it just be that easy?

"Which brings me back to me not having a heart. I don't like being nice to people because being nice gets you nowhere. But there is one person, only one person that has got me wanting to be nice to them," he said, lowering his voice slightly.

I frowned. "Who?"

"You."

Nothing at all could have prepared me for that. I gaped at him, jaw dropped in shock because I just could not understand why he would want to be nice to me of all people. All I had caused him was trouble. It would have been so much easier for him to be horrible to me twenty-four seven. He used to be horrible, but then he gradually started being kinder... At least now I knew why. I still could not make any sense out of it.

"Me?"

Shadow nodded. "Yes. You. Of all the people I have come across in my life, it's you that I want to be nicer to. I didn't understand it at first. I just put it down to your dad being an abusive asshole, so I was concerned about you. I didn't realise what it truly meant until after Raven attacked you."

If Shadow noticed that my heart had suddenly started beating faster than normal, he did not show it. Hands gripping his knees, he lowered his head, staring down at the floor while I was trying to figure out what he was trying to say. I was never that good at guessing games, though, especially when it came to feelings.

"So you figured it out?" I asked. My voice suddenly got a lot higher. I was trying to appear calm though there was an emotional roller coaster going on inside. I waited for him to speak, but when he did not, I bit my lip. What was he trying to say? I did not want to wait any longer. I just wanted him to tell me.

"You're in my head, all the time," he finally spoke, stunning me with his words. "Not just because of what's been going on. I've never had a girlfriend before, so I don't know what to compare this to. But when I think of you and that kiss, I feel something I can't explain. I sound like such a fucking pussy right now."

"You don't sound like a pussy," I whispered, mentally cursing myself. He was trying to tell me how he feels, and that was all I could say? I truly was a pathetic excuse of a human being. There was plenty that I could say, but the words seemed to be stuck in my throat, permanently lodged there.

"I even fucking talked to Alec about it." Shadow shook his head in amusement as he glanced back at me. "He told me I like you. I didn't even know what the fuck he was talking about, and I actually laughed in his face, but then it started to dawn on me... I do. I fucking like you, Violet. I like you, and I don't even know your last name for fuck's sake."

Again, out of all the things I could have said, the one thing that did come out was the one thing that really was not that important. All I could think about was the fact he liked me. He liked *me*. Of all people, and it was me he liked. I could hardly believe it.

"Winters," I blurted out, watching the confusion on his face. "My last name... it's Winters."

"Violet Winters," Shadow spoke, cocking his head to one side. "Well, Violet Winters, I fucking like you."

This time, I did not say something that could have potentially ruined the mood Shadow had created. He had confessed to something he had not felt before, and if that was not enough to make me realise he was not lying, then I was not sure what would.

So, I took a deep breath and said the first thing that came to mind.

"I fucking like you too."

***

Shadow's POV

Taking Violet out for the day was only supposed to be because I wanted her to be in a good mood when I finally told her how I felt. It had taken me long enough to realise how I was feeling and what that meant, but with the help of Alec—who did laugh for five minutes straight after I had asked him what it meant—I now knew how I felt about Violet.

I like her.

I could not deny it now. I had tried my hardest to push it to the back of mind and pretend it was never there at all, nothing but a nuisance thought that needed to be dismissed as soon as possible, but the more I tried to deny it, the more I realised how screwed I was.

I could not remember that last time I had feelings like this for a girl. It was back when I was human, so it had definitely been a while since I had to confess how I felt. I usually fucked and chucked because that was all I wanted. I could not get close to a human girl anyway without them running for the hills when they realised that instead of drinking alcohol like the rest of the human population, I chose to drink blood. Yeah, that really would not have gone down well.

All I knew was that girls like sweet, romantic, and thoughtful confessions. Didn't they? Or was that just some of them? I wasn't even sure. I was definitely going to fuck this up. I was not even sure how Violet would react to it. Girls like her would want a family of her own one day, but if she stayed with me, she would have to give that up because I could not give her a child. I'm not Edward Cullen. I can't have a child since, you know, I'm technically dead.

Woah, I thought to myself, *getting a bit ahead of myself there.*

Shaking my head of all thoughts, I concentrated on taking Violet out and showing her that I was not a monster all the time. I should have been more annoyed that she kept accusing me of being a monster, but it did not annoy me at all—she was right. I was a monster, and I knew it. Denying it would have been pointless and ridiculous.

Madame Tussauds had been the most fun though I wasn't sure why I had enjoyed that most. It could have something to do with the fact I got to grope Kim K's wax figure because it was the closest any guy other than Kanye was going to get to the real thing.

I fully blame Leah for the fact I knew who the fuck Kanye was.

Seeing that old couple gave me a weird feeling. I had been so tempted to just lure them away from the building so I could kill them. They knew too much about why Violet was here, and they were potentially a risk none of us could afford to have, but after seeing the look on Violet's face, I knew I could not do it. I wanted to. Fuck, I really wanted to. I would have drained the blood from their bodies without a care in the world because they meant nothing to me, but Violet did, and that was all that mattered.

I really was turning into a pussy.

I finally decided to man up and get it the fuck over with as we sat down on a bench. Resting my elbows on my knees, I spoke.

"You know, I never thought I had a heart," I said, keeping my gaze fixated on the pigeons in front of me. I did not want to look at her now, or I may end up backing out and just kissing her instead. She was far too tempting for her own good.

"Why would you think that?" she asked.

I chuckled bitterly and rolled my eyes. Was she acting stupid on purpose or was today just a special occasion? She had been accusing me of being a monster this whole time. "Isn't it obvious?"

"Not to me," she said. I rolled my eyes again, knowing she was lying. It did make me smile a little to know that she was lying to make me feel better, though.

I explained what I meant about my words, talking about Viktor and the anger I held inside. Even now, to this very day, I still held that same anger. I was just able to control it better. Viktor really did what he had wanted. He would be singing with the devil in hell if he had not already taken over it.

Violet once again tried to make me see that I was not a monster, but who was she kidding? It was what she thought of me, and it was who I knew I was. I had been a monster my whole vampire life, and that would not change anytime soon. Just because I now had feelings for a human girl did not mean that the anger inside me would disappear. I wished it would be that easy. It could get exhausting being so angry all the time.

"Why are you telling me this?" Violet asked, clearly trying to change the subject, but I let her. I did not particularly want to keep talking about it as this was supposed to be a confession.

"Like I said, I didn't think I had a heart." I shrugged.

"So?"

"Now I'm starting to think I do," I spoke, shaking my head and waiting for her to speak. She did not, though. She remained silent. I continued, "When I changed and stopped killing everybody I saw, I vowed not to let anyone close enough to make me self-destruct again. Viktor had given me this new life, and I killed him. What does that say about me? I know the guy wasn't the best, but he did have his rare moments. Of course, Leah, Alec, and Ric are my friends, and I do care about them, but at the same time, if I wanted to, I could leave and never turn back, not giving them a second thought."

"That's..." She trailed off, clearly unsure on what word to use.

"Cruel? Harsh? Twisted?" I offered, knowing that whichever word she chose would be the truth. I had accepted that long ago.

"Sad." She smiled, "You have friends that do anything you ask, and yet you could still leave? That's got to be a sad and lonely existence if your friends aren't enough to make you want to stay."

"I've been alone since I killed Viktor." I pointed out with a grim look on my face. I hated the bastard, but he had helped me come to terms with being a vampire. "I've really gotten used to it. I'm not used to people sticking around for so long especially when I'm not exactly nice to them."

"Then be nice to them."

"Which brings me back to me not having a heart. I don't like being nice to people because being nice gets you nowhere. But there is one person, only one person that has got me wanting to be nice to them," I spoke slowly, hoping she would understand what I was trying to tell her.

She didn't.

"Who?" she asked. She really was oblivious.

"You," I told her, glancing at her just in time to see how shocked she was. She clearly had not been expecting that, and that amused me a little.

"Me?" she asked, after a few minutes of silence. I let her come to terms with what I was saying before I explained further. I knew she had trust issues, and I didn't want her to suddenly stand up and scream that I was a monster again. I mean, I may agree, but that didn't mean I liked to be reminded of it every five seconds. That shit just got annoying.

"Yes. You. Of all the people I have come across in my life, it's you that I want to be nicer to. I didn't understand it at first. I just put it down to your dad being an abusive asshole so I was concerned about you. I didn't realise what it truly meant until after Raven attacked you."

I instantly heard the way her heart started beating faster, and I had to resist the urge to smirk, so I lowered my head so that she wouldn't see. She wouldn't have a reaction like that if she didn't like what she was hearing.

"So you figured it out?" she asked.

"You're in my head, all the time." I was feeling a whole lot more confident about this now that I knew the truth. "Not just because of what's been going on. I've never had a girlfriend before, so I don't know what to compare this to. But when I think of you and that kiss, I feel something I can't explain. I sound like such a fucking pussy right now."

"You don't sound like a pussy," she whispered.

I just gave her a huge fucking speech, and that was all she can say? There really was something wrong with this girl, and yet I liked her, anyway. It added to her charm and overall beauty because, fuck, she was definitely beautiful. It was no wonder I had a hard time keeping my hands to myself.

"I even fucking talked to Alec about it," I said, looking back at her. "He told me I like you. I didn't even know what the fuck he was talking about, and I actually laughed in his face, but then it started to dawn on me... I do. I fucking like you, Violet. I like you, and I don't even know your last name for fuck's sake."

"Winters." She suddenly blurted out, making me frown in confusion. What the fuck was she talking about now? "My last name... it's Winters."

Okay, that made sense.

"Violet Winters," I spoke her name, cocking my head to one side. It suited her. "Well, Violet Winters, I fucking like you."

I smirked, unable to help myself. Screw the sweet, romantic, and thoughtful confession.

"I fucking like you too," she said, turning my smirk into a smile.

Finally.

Epilogue

Throughout my life, I realised that sometimes, ghosts were not always the supernatural beings everybody believed them to be. Sometimes they were more personal—someone that, while still alive, was no longer in our lives, but we still thought about them, haunting us when all we wanted was to forget.

That was what my dad was to me, as well as my mother. He was a ghost that would continue to haunt my thoughts whenever something triggered me. So while I had his number blocked so I would not ever have to see his name come up again, even going as far as to delete his number from my phone, I would still be haunted by him. I doubted that would ever leave.

The more days went by, the more it became clearer that Rose would turn out to be another ghost to me too. She had not replied to my messages or answered my calls. I knew she needed time to figure things out, but I was worried about her. We had never gone so many days without speaking even if it was just to say hello. I did tell her about Shadow and me, but she had not replied. I wasn't sure whether I was expecting her to, to be honest.

It was strange to think that just two months ago, I was being used as a punching bag. Just two months ago, I was being beaten daily, trying not to move too fast in case I made my injuries worse. Now, I was sitting outside watching the world go by with my boyfriend by my side. I could not believe I could actually call Shadow that now.

Shadow had helped me realise a lot of things, the main thing being that I could not allow toxic people to be a priority in my life. My dad had taken over everything; he had ruined my confidence and self-esteem, making me just a shell of the girl I used to be. It was because of Shadow that I had the courage to delete my dad's number. It was because of Shadow that I was able to try to put the past behind me. I owed him a lot.

As we sat there, staring out at the world with my head resting on his shoulder and his arm wrapped around me, it started to grow colder, but neither of us wanted to move just yet, so I settled for snuggling up closer to him, draping my legs over his as he held me close.

"You know, this past couple of months have taught me something," I spoke up, breaking the comfortable silence between us. "I used to be terrified that everybody would turn out like my dad, so I pushed people away. I'm finally starting to understand, though, that the people that are meant to be in my life wouldn't let me do that. They'd stick around through the good and the bad times."

"It's taken you this long to figure that out?" Shadow seemed surprised. "I could have told you that."

I shrugged. "For me to move on with my life, there are some things I have to figure out myself."

"Do you feel like you can move on with your life now?"

"I've never been surer of anything before," I admitted.

"I'll help you every step of the way."

That was all I needed to hear. I knew he would be there for me. He had proved time and time again that he only wanted to look out for me. Now, I could finally believe him without a doubt in my mind. It was funny how things worked out in the end. Never for a second did I think I could be free of my dad, and yet I had done exactly that. He no longer had a hold over me.

I was finally free.

I had friends, I had a boyfriend, I had a place to live, but more importantly?

I'm happy.

THE END

Can't get enough of Violet and Shadow? Make sure you sign up for the author's blog to find out more about them!

Get these two bonus chapters and more freebies when you sign up at danielle-ogier.awesomeauthors.org!

Here is a sample from another story you may enjoy:

The Sweetest Kill

Amber Kalkes

Chapter One

DYSPHORIA

I want to die.

It's not an overdramatic exclamation of embarrassment or anything of the like. It's a real desire that has the strength to overwhelm, drown, and eventually fester into something darker and more twisted. It's also something that a lot of people will not understand.

They will not understand the need to no longer be on this earth. They will not empathize with the wish to make all the pain just go away, along with whatever it is that keeps somebody going. After years of feeling this way, I want to bail out. No matter how much I want to please those who want me to stay, I'm not sure how much I have left in me.

The bell above the door rings, and I snap out of my thoughts and get back to reality. My confusion as to why I feel this way is only matched by my confusion as to why I still work here. I'm not a people person and, as much as I try not to, I suck at my job. So why do I continue to linger in this place? Aside from the stability that this job offers and Dr. Reynolds' insistence that this will help me, I really can't think of any other reason.

"Can I help you?" My co-worker's cheerful voice catches my attention.

I peek over at Melanie, my co-worker for the day, and study her. She's the kind of person who fits in here and seemingly enjoys her job. She has a bubbly and charming personality, which is why everyone likes her. At least, I assume everyone likes her. I'm not much for gossiping around the water cooler—on that front, I'm pretty uninformed—but it seems that my other co-workers are on good terms with her. And, I'm sure she loves this job. In fact, she probably has a great life.

In a fantasy world I created for her in my head, Melanie is surrounded by friends and family. She has a boyfriend who is handsome, caring, and with whom she always has a good time. Her apartment is probably well decorated, often filled with generous laughter and fun times. She laughs genuinely and smiles so wide, that her cheeks often hurt from the joys of her life.

I avert my gaze from Melanie and frown. I wipe down the counter, envying this fantasy life I've given her. I wish I could be like that. Hell, I've tried to be like that. I used to have a few friends, ones that didn't look at me with pity or treat me like glass. But after my last release from the hospital four months ago, they too have faded away and have left me in my own misery. I guess I must admit that even before I left for the hospital, I didn't have anything close to Melanie's life.

My doctor thinks the new pills he gave me might help keep these kinds of thoughts out of my head. They taste like shit and make me feel even worse, but he says I have to give the anti-depressants another try. They aren't the same kind that sent me over the edge last time. They're from a new brand, and I'm not sure if that's a good or a bad thing. Being crazy seemed to suit me much better than whatever kind of false reality I'm making for myself now. But I'm not a medical professional, so what do I know?

"Hello?" An annoyed voice calls and pulls me out of my thoughts. I turn around to see a middle-aged man in a business suit and a long overcoat with an iPhone in his hand. I look around to see that I am alone and assume that Melanie has gone on a break, sending me into an acute panic. "Are you going to help me or what?"

I gulped and nod, as I hesitantly make a move towards the front counter. I don't really have much of a choice on this one, do I? I can't exactly pull Melanie out of her break to do a job I've been trained to do, right? But God, I wish I could. Willing myself not to run in the opposite direction, I place my shaking hand on the counter and try to stay calm.

"C-c-can I help you?" I ask quietly.

He sighs, still annoyed, "Yeah, a coffee. Black, to go, and a… cherry strudel. Make it fast, would you? I'm in a hurry."

I nod quickly and type the prices in slowly, so I don't screw it up. Clearing my voice, I try to speak a little louder, "T-t-that'll be s-s-seven dollars and s-s-seventy five cents."

"Here," he grunts while handing me a crisp twenty-dollar bill.

The cash register slides out suddenly, making me flinch before I start to retrieve his change for him. Apparently, I'm not fast enough because as soon as the money is in my hand, he practically rips the wrinkled bills from me. The three quarters sitting on top fall onto the counter, but I manage to save them before they land on the floor.

When I shakily hand them back to him, his hand brushes mine. I quickly pull my hand back, feeling like I'm going to cry any minute. I don't like the way he's glaring or his tone of voice. His reaction to me is overwhelming, and the skin contact is pushing me over the edge.

I don't like to be touched.

"You know, you should be friendlier," he says in a patronizing way that has me staring at him blankly. "I mean, you are in the food service industry."

I could see the frustration in his light brown eyes, so I look away and slowly nod my head. I really don't have much to say to that. He's probably right. But hell, I'm not going to tell him that. Instead, I move away from him and head to the display case, just in time for Melanie to come back.

She pauses and looks from me to the aggravated customer. Then, she places a wide smile on her lips and approaches him, "Can I help you, sir?"

"Yes, I'm in a hurry and she's taking forever."

"Oh," Melanie says in a surprised tone. But she recovers quickly and turns to the computer. "Right! Well, let me see here. A black coffee and a strudel. Am I right, sir?"

"Yeah, that's right and can you hurry it up? I wasn't saying I was in a rush just to be fashionable here."

"I totally understand," Melanie agrees before adding, "Shoshanna is a bit new here so you'll have to excuse her."

I can feel his eyes on me. My palms begin to sweat as I pull out the strudel from the display case. Wrapping it in one of those wax paper napkins, I head back to the counter and hand it to him. He stares into my eyes as if challenging me, and I immediately look down. I really don't like this guy.

"Yeah, you'll go places," he mutters as he turns to Melanie, who hands him his coffee.

"There you go sir," she chirps happily, "Have a good day."

He just snorts and gives me one last disgusted glance, before making his way to the door. My eyes follow him as he walks out and passes by one of the large windows at the front of the café. I watch, seemingly spellbound by his tie as it blows in the wind. It's a rather nice tie, dark navy blue accented by red stripes and lined with silver. If only the man were as nice as his tie.

"Did you give him the right change this time?"

I jump at the sound of Melanie's voice so close to me, but I still nod. "I-I-I think so."

"I don't know why Lawrence keeps putting you on the floor. It's clear that you're not right for it," she says as nicely as possible.

I just shrug, unwilling to dwell on the reasons why Lawrence—one of the two alternating managers of the café—insists on putting me where I obviously don't want to be. To me, he's just a sadistic pervert who doesn't know the meaning of the word "no". Talking to him makes my skin crawl but he controls the scheduling, so I have no choice but to deal with him.

That should probably be another thing I need to add to the list of reasons why I should quit this job. I'm saving as many reasons as I can, so I'll have something valid to present to my parents and my doctor when the time comes. I think they just like telling me what to do. They don't actually want to help me. Not that they can, though. But I think a part of me just likes to watch them try.

"Any plans tonight?" Melanie prods.

I shake my head, but again, I don't elaborate.

"I'm going to this new restaurant downtown called Sticky Icky. It's a Chinese place, but with a more hip vibe and a really cool atmosphere. You know what I mean?" she asks but doesn't wait for me to reply. "Anyway, my boyfriend Trevor is taking me. It should be fun."

I just nod, while silently marveling at how much she can talk about nothing.

"Do you want to come?"

I shake my head and give her a small smile. "I have plans."

"Like what?" she asks, beaming. "Come on, join us. It'll be fun. I have lots of single guy friends. Maybe you'll like one of them."

"Thank you, Melanie. But I just can't tonight."

She purses her glossy pink lips at me. "Okay. Maybe next time then?"

"Maybe," I lie timidly.

Another customer comes in, and thankfully, Melanie's attention shifts from me. I know that in reality, I probably am lying to myself. I have opportunities to try to be normal, to be like Melanie. She asks me to come do things with her and her friends from time to time, but I always say no. I think sometimes, I like to be this miserable. It's harder for me to be happy than to be a depressing mess. I've been the latter for longer than I can remember. What's that saying again? You can't teach an old dog new tricks? Well, you can't teach a manic-depressive to suddenly be well-adjusted.

About three hours later, my shift is over and I'm headed back home. It's the beginning of winter in this part of the country, and when it starts, it sets in fast. Clutching my second-hand coat close to my body, I walk home as I do on most evenings. I can't really afford to ride a cab or the subway so walking, even in this weather, just seems more economically responsible. Besides, I kind of like the bite of the cold and the feel of the city air weighing heavily in my lungs.

The best part about living in the city is that it's the polar opposite of where I grew up. I never liked it there in the suburbs. The mere thought of it makes me shudder. My dad is an ex-naval officer and currently an insurance salesman, while my mom is a teacher, who is now retired. They met when Dad was stationed in Japan and Mom was the one teaching him the native language. They got married, popped out two kids, and settled down in a nice plastic house, in a nice plastic neighborhood.

Things were pretty good for them until their younger daughter became terminally ill and their elder daughter turned out to be mentally unstable. I'm pretty sure that we were not what they had in mind when they decided to have kids. My sister Charlotte didn't make it past her ninth birthday, and I tried not to make it past my sixteenth. My parents really had a lot to handle. In retrospection, I have to admit, they've done the best they can. I can't even imagine how hard it is being cursed with so much bad luck.

After walking for about half an hour, I spot my apartment building and dig in the pocket of my jacket for the keys. It's a shitty place. Anyone looking at it can tell you that. But it's a roof over my head and one that my parents aren't paying for. It's probably the first thing in the twenty-two years of my existence that I actually ever owned. Well, that and my cat.

As I make my way to the fifth floor of the building, I feel my body begin to relax with every step I take. Every morning, I have to talk to myself into leaving my apartment, which has become my sanctuary. There are some days when I'd win and some days when I'd lose. Either way, that doesn't change the fact that I'm talking to myself.

When I reach my apartment, I get inside and quickly close the door behind me. I made sure to lock the deadbolt before placing my head against the door. I sigh and feel my body completely relax. But before I can savor my relief, I am distracted by something rubbing against my pant leg. Looking down, I see the black and white body of my cat Florence.

I found her one day in an alley while I was on my way home from work. She was abandoned and starving when I stumbled upon her, so I decided to take her home. I was wondering what to name her one night, then I spotted a biography of Florence Nightingale among my book stack. I decided to name her Florence not only because of my lack of creativity, but also because of her ability to consistently cheer me up. She puts a smile on my face more than anyone has during these past months. Although, I'm not sure if that is sweet or plainly pathetic.

I crouch down and pick her up, smiling slightly when her purrs intensify. Then, she begins rubbing her head against my jaw. I hold her for a little while but she starts to squirm, so regretfully, I let her jump out of my arms. I watch her crawl on top of my bed to groom herself and I smile a bit more. She always cleans herself on my bed and I have no idea why.

My apartment isn't much. Even for a studio apartment, it would certainly be considered a shit hole. I've been living in it for about a month. And so far, I haven't gotten around to do much decorating. I don't have much flair for indoor décor, to be honest. But I do try my best.

Since it is a studio, it mostly consists of one large room that I have filled with minimal furniture. There's a mattress on the floor with a box spring underneath and a small desk on the opposite side of the room with a terribly uncomfortable wooden chair, which I found on the side of the road. At the foot of my mattress, a medium sized box TV sits on top of a small cabinet that has a missing door. My clothes hang on a metal rack that stands near the only widow in the whole apartment. A small plastic container full of my bras and other underwear sit at the foot of the rack.

My bathroom is separate from the main room, but it's still too small. You can't stand at the sink without the back of your legs hitting the tub. You can also easily hit your knees on the tub when you're sitting on the toilet. My kitchen is a whole mess of its own and is hidden behind folding closet doors. All it really consists of is a sink and about four feet of counter space, which I've managed to balance with both a hot plate and a toaster. Above the sink are two cupboards: one is filled with my minimal flatware, while the other is filled with as much ramen and soup as it can hold.

The entire place isn't much, but it's something I call my own.

I start stripping off my winter gear and place it in a pile on top of the nearby desk. Then I begin removing my work clothes. My black skinny jeans are stained and are in need of a good washing, but my dark purple Roast Rage Café work shirt could still be worn for a few more days. Dropping them on the floor as I walk, I head for the bathroom in just my white long sleeve thermal top and a pair of underwear.

As I wait for the water to warm up for my shower, I stare at my reflection in the mirror. I reach up and pull my hair from its ponytail, letting my chin length bob fall around my face. I tilt my head as I take in the oval-shaped face in front of me with apathy. Dull, almond shaped hazel eyes stare back at me. There are dark circles underneath them, proof of the many sleepless nights I've been having lately. My lips are full but pale, and chapped from all my nervous lip chewing. My skin, though naturally pale, looks washed out and even a bit waxy.

Of course, my face isn't really the only problem I have with my physical appearance. There's also my body. I don't eat much, due to either my preference or lack of interest. I can't be sure anymore. What I do know is that my irregular eating habits have made me so thin that some would say I look unhealthy. But then again, that isn't even the worst part. My skin is the main attraction in this freak show.

Over the years, I've developed a habit that both my parents and my psychiatrist don't approve of—self-harming. I've mainly focused this new hobby on my arms. The advantage of this is that I can easily hide the scars under my sleeves so no one will notice and ask prying questions. I decide to remove my shirt and admire my handiwork. The scars would probably look monstrous to anyone who saw them. My dad cried when he first saw the thick lines that formed on my arms as a result of the cutting and the circular marks that were from the time I experimented on burning myself. Mom, on the other hand, didn't say anything. But then again, I didn't really expect her to.

I slip off my bra and underwear before getting into the shower. Once inside, I let the water cascade down my scarred body and wash away the grime of the outside world. Right there in my tiny bathroom, I know I'm safe. I know I'm in a place where no one can see me and touch me, so I let it all out. Everything I've been holding in comes out in sobs, as I lower myself into the tub.

I don't like crying in front of others. I never have, and most likely, never will. But when I'm in my sanctuary, I can let all my inhibitions go and just do whatever I want. I curl into a ball and I rock myself back and forth, until I literally can't cry anymore. With the little hot water left, I wash myself before turning off the shower. I let all the emotion drain away with the excess water. I don't need it anymore.

When I exit the bathroom, I hear my phone ringing. As a lifelong hater of cell phones, I only have a landline, and only four people ever call me on it. Glancing at the alarm clock on the windowsill by my bed, I deduce the caller is either my mother or someone who dialed my number by mistake.

I pick up the pale yellow phone and press it to my ear, as water droplets trickle down the stained carpet below. "Hello?"

"Annie?" my mother says in her heavily accented voice. "Are you there?"

"Yeah, Mom, I'm here."

"How are you feeling?"

I roll my eyes at the question and place the receiver against my shoulder. I sit down on my bed, wearing only a towel. "I'm fine, Mom. How are you?"

"I've been well. Your father wanted me to call you to invite you to Sunday dinner."

"Why?" I ask with a frown at the reminder. "Is it at a different time or something?"

"No."

"Then why are you calling me when we have Sunday dinner every week?"

She's silent on the other end of the phone and this confirms the real reason why she's calling. She just wanted to make sure I haven't killed or seriously injured myself. She does this out of worry, I know. But hell, I doubt if the woman herself will admit it. Her concern is always dressed up in some half-assed and barely reasonable excuses.

"So, are you coming?" she eventually asks.

I sigh as I dig my nails into my damp scalp. "Yes, I'll be there."

"How was work today? Anything good happen?"

"I was able to leave," I quip before I can stop myself.

"You have to be positive, Annie. You know what the doctor says. A positive mind and a positive outlook makes a positive life."

"Yeah. Well, Dr. Reynolds is full of shit."

"Shoshanna!" she gasps through the phone. "What did I say about swearing? It makes you ugly."

"Right. Sorry."

She's quiet for a minute before speaking again, and I know she's digging for a topic to keep me on the phone. "Have you been taking your pills?"

I glance at the twin brown bottles on the windowsill and chew on my lower lip. "Yes, every morning."

"Have they been helping?"

I could tell her the truth. I could say that I feel like I'm living in a haze. I could tell her that, more often than not, I cry myself to sleep. I could tell her that, after I take the anti-depressants, I have to bargain with myself so I don't throw them up. I could tell her that the pills didn't help or stop me from mutilating myself. I could tell her, but that will not do either of us any good. So what's the point?

"Yeah, Mom. They've been helping."

"You'll get better this time. I'm sure of it."

I know she can't see me, but I give the phone a small reassuring smile. "Of course I will, Mom."

"Well, I have to go. Your father wants to go out for dinner."

"Okay, Mom. Tell him I said 'hi', okay?"

"I will. You'll call tomorrow?"

No. It'll only worry you more than you already are. That's what I want to say but instead, I decide to lie. It will make hanging up easier for both of us.

"Yeah, I'll call."

"Okay. Bye."

"Bye."

I hear the line disconnect as I'm holding the phone against my shoulder and staring blankly at an odd stain on my carpet. I don't know how long I sat like that, but Florence's meow snaps me out of my thoughts. I turn to her and figured she wants me to put more cat food in her bowl. I replace the receiver and decide to feed both my cat and myself.

I get off the bed and make my way to the pseudo-kitchen with Florence on my heels, meowing incessantly for more food. As I grab the only pot I own off its place on the hot plate and begin filling it up with water, I feel my patience begin to wane. Suddenly, my phone begins to ring again but my hands are full, so I just leave it be. When Florence begins stretching up to dig her nails into the fabric of my towel, I lose my cool.

The sounds of the ripping fabric under her claws, the meowing, the ringing phone, and the running water become all too much. I feel my heart beat faster in my chest, and I swear, I can hear the deafening thump in my ears. A sweat breaks over my forehead. I throw the pot into the sink, feeling my body go into hyper drive.

It's stupid. I know it's stupid, you know it's stupid, and I'm pretty sure even Florence knows it's stupid… but it's happening. I am having a damn anxiety attack over a hungry cat and a ringing phone. I don't know how to stop it or why it's happening. Leaning on the sink, I try to calm my breathing and collect the shreds of my sanity to drum up something close to patience. My heart eventually calms down and the urge to vomit subsides, as Florence leaves me alone to sit on the bed.

The phone stops ringing and I exhale, trying to gain some equilibrium. Once I'm a bit more stable, I calmly grab the handle of the pot and place it on the hotplate before switching it on. I continue to tell myself to stay calm as I grab Florence's bag of food from the large cabinet drawer. I pour her food into her bowl and watch as she cautiously comes towards it, before beginning to eat.

Then the phone starts ringing again. I place the bag of cat food beside Florence's bowl and stomp over to the phone. Yanking the receiver off the cradle, I say in an annoyed voice, "Yes?"

"Uh, is Jessica there?"

I scowl at the phone. "Wrong number."

"Oh, sorry."

The line goes dead and I hang up. Sitting on the edge of my bed again, I run my fingers through my hair and pull at some strands. When a chill goes through my body, I realize I'm still in my towel. *I should probably get dressed now.* I slip on a pair of underwear and an oversized t-shirt, which I got from the Goodwill store down the road, and decide to watch a little TV while waiting for the water to boil. Using my towel to dry my hair, I sit on the edge of my bed and watch the news as it comes on with a special report about a traffic accident

Two dead and three injured. The cars are mangled clumps of metal behind the reporter while he talks about the details. They were about to release the names when I hear the water boil on the hot plate and I reluctantly get up to turn down the heat and add the noodles. When I come back to my original spot on the bed, the report is no longer about the car accident. Instead, it's about something much more gruesome.

"Here's Christina Collins with more," the overly tanned male news anchor says, before the camera switches to a grim looking young brunette.

"Thank you, Tim. This is a case that has shortly become a riddle to not only the police department, but also the citizens of this fair city. The discovery of twenty-year-old university student, Kimberly Moss, has been met with devastation and shock this morning. Her death is the third similarly executed murder in the city in recent weeks, leading some to believe that this may be the work of a serial killer."

My attention is immediately grabbed by the term "serial killer." This city has had its fair share of crime, but a serial killer? It seems too Law & Order. It's seems too reminiscent of movie and television series plots to actually be happening here. When I realize my Ramen is done, I stand and get it while keeping my eyes on the TV.

"The first confirmed victim, discovered just a month ago, was Karen Hyland, a single mother on her way home from work. She was found two days after being reported missing by her boyfriend. Her remains were found in a dumpster."

A picture of a cheery looking brunette with a toddler in her lap comes on the screen. She looks happy in the picture and I wonder why she had to die. When the news reporter speaks again, the picture changes to another brunette. This woman looks less clean cut as the first one. Instead, she is pouting flirtatiously at the camera in the same way I've seen girls do at the café.

"The second confirmed victim was identified as Julie Schaffer, another young university student who was found in the bathroom of a nightclub downtown. Both women's throats were slit, but with no evidence of a sexual assault. The police have yet to find a motive for these crimes."

"Thrill killer?" I think out loud. "That would explain the lack of sexual assault and quick deaths."

"As the body count continues to rise, the police are urging young women to stay in groups when going out at night. All three women were seen walking with a white male, sometime before their disappearance. There are no suspects at this time." Christina Collins says gravely before her image on the screen is replaced with the picture of a bright-eyed blonde with a huge smile. The caption, *"In memory of Kimberly Moss"*, flashes below the photo. Christina comes back on the screen and says, "Please stay safe on the streets. Back to you, Tim."

I tune out the rest of the report as they change the subject back to something less troubling. I switch the channel to reruns of The Simpsons and pick at the ramen in my bow, thinking that those women didn't want to die. They were just in the wrong place at the wrong time. Then my thoughts go a bit south.

What if it were me? What if I was the woman this guy went after? All those women had so much to live for, so wouldn't it mean that the next victim would as well? What if instead of her, it was me he took interest in? What if a person with nothing to live for was the one who had their picture on the news? What if that person was, in fact, me?

The idea seems insane, but it also seems like the perfect way out for me. After my last attempt at ending my life, I made a promise to my parents. I told them I wouldn't try again. It was a promise I quickly regretted making, but one I made all the same. Now, there's this perfect loophole placed right in front of me on a silver platter. I could end all this and not hurt anyone with the knowledge that it was, in fact, my desire to die like this.

Emptying the other uneaten half of my ramen into the small trashcan in the kitchen, I place the dirty bowl in the sink. Could I actually do that? Even if I was able to track down this killer and put myself in his way, what are the chances he would take me? I glance down at myself and feel my stomach drop. My chances aren't good if his previous victims are any clue. He apparently has a liking for prettier women, and I am nowhere near desirable.

After turning off my TV, I set my alarm and get into bed. I stare at the darkened ceiling above me and try to think of some way that my plan could work. It's a fucked up idea, but one that I can't help but let my mind linger on. What if I could do it? What if I could find him and let him put me out of my misery? I let out a heavy sigh and turn onto my side as I push the ridiculous idea aside. It would never work and even if it did, it probably wouldn't stop him from killing again. Psychos like that never stop.

Florence crawls up on the bed and curls up against my stomach. Her purring vibrates through my body, as I slowly run my fingers through her soft dark fur. She kneads the blanket draped around me while unknowingly lulling me to sleep. I don't think much more about the serial killer as my eyes begin to close.

Meanwhile, across town, the very man I want to be the scapegoat for my death is probably doing something that would give me another reason to seek him out.

If you enjoyed this sample then look for **The Sweetest Kill** on Amazon.

Other books you might enjoy:

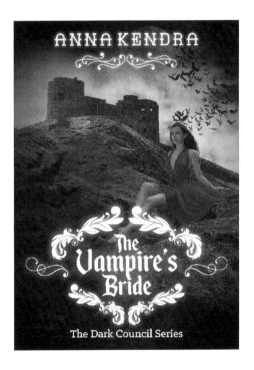

The Vampire's Bride
Anna Kendra

Alina Deluca is arranged to marry the vampire prince and gets embroiled in an ages old feud and a struggle for power of mind-boggling proportions. Is Eric the heartless monster Alina makes him out to be? Will a prophecy made eons ago be the undoing of the whole vampire race?

Other books you might enjoy:

My Beloved
T. M Mendes

Lore about a vampire buried alive with the old townspeople's silver piques the interest of Wendy. With the intention of using them for her brother's surgery, she sets out and somehow finds the mound of silver. However, things become more complicated than it should be when she indeed finds not just the riches but also the corpse of the vampire.

Introducing the Characters Magazine App

Download the app to get the free issues of interviews from famous fiction characters and find your next favorite book!

iTunes: bit.ly/CharactersApple
Google Play: bit.ly/CharactersAndroid

Acknowledgements

There are many people that I would like to thank for their continued support—whether it be from an online reader to my family—but there are a few that stick in my mind most.

I would like to thank my best friend, Carrie, who continued to support me no matter how many times I went to her for advice.

I would like to thank BLVNP for enabling me to achieve my dream of publishing my book. I wouldn't have been able to do this without them.

I'd also like to thank my grandad, who this book is dedicated to. He always tried to help me with my writing, and I will never forget that.

Author's Note

Hey there!

Thank you so much for reading Broken Wings! I can't express how grateful I am for reading something that was once just a thought inside my head.

I'd love to hear from you! Please feel free to email me at danielle_ogier@awesomeauthors.org and sign up at danielle-ogier.awesomeauthors.org for freebies!

One last thing: I'd love to hear your thoughts on the book. Please leave a review on Amazon or Goodreads because I just love reading your comments and getting to know YOU!

Whether that review is good or bad, I'd still love to hear it!

Can't wait to hear from you!

DANIELLE OGIER

About the Author

Living in Scarborough, North Yorkshire, I am the complete opposite to my twin brother; I am the more creative one with an overactive imagination. I have been writing since I was 14 years old and haven't stopped since, preferring to create a whole new world that people can use as an escape for a little while. I didn't start posting my stories online until I found out about Wattpad, a free website for writers. When I'm not writing, I'm either reading, listening to music or binge watching Supernatural.

Printed in Great Britain
by Amazon

61074748R00187